THE GREAT COOL RANCH DORITO IN THE SKY

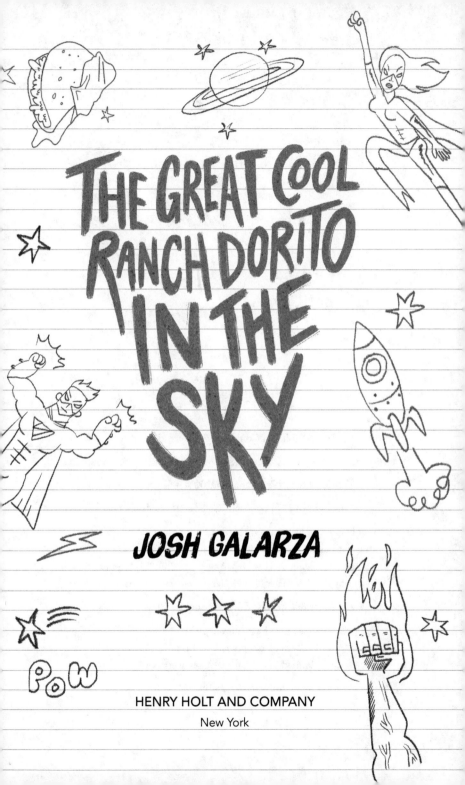

THE GREAT COOL RANCH DORITO IN THE SKY

JOSH GALARZA

HENRY HOLT AND COMPANY

New York

Henry Holt and Company, *Publishers since 1866*

Henry Holt® is a registered trademark of Macmillan Publishing Group, LLC

120 Broadway, New York, NY 10271 • fiercereads.com

Our books may be purchased in bulk for promotional, educational,
or business use. Please contact your local bookseller or the Macmillan
Corporate and Premium Sales Department at (800) 221-7945 ext. 5442
or by email at MacmillanSpecialMarkets@macmillan.com.

Library of Congress Control Number: 2023948928

First edition, 2024
Book design by Julia Bianchi
Printed in the United States of America

ISBN 978-1-250-90771-4
1   3   5   7   9   10   8   6   4   2

For Marilee Swirczek:

This book exists because you loved me.

AUTHOR'S NOTE

Dear readers,

It was during a spell of unbearable grief in my own life that *The Great Cool Ranch Dorito in the Sky* was born. Night after night of that painful summer, I'd lie on the trampoline in my backyard, one of the few places I could be alone with my feelings. I'd stare up at the stars and wonder if I was capable of overcoming the circumstances that had left my life in ruins. In my pain and confusion, the art of writing didn't seem to matter anymore. My career and my future didn't seem to matter, either. I wondered if I'd ever tell stories again, and I wondered if I'd even be healthy enough to do so. I could no longer lie to myself about the destructive behaviors I was using to cope. I'd come to suspect that there was something terribly wrong with my relationship with food—that there had been for many years, in fact—and I recognized that the mistakes I was starting to make with alcohol were indefensible.

But I was not without hope. I didn't *want* to be sick. I didn't *want* to cause harm. On these nights of quiet contemplation, I'd look to the stars for comfort, understanding, and even forgiveness. It was during one of these nights that a new voice arrived unbidden in my mind, the voice of a sixteen-year-old boy who was feeling all the grief and shame I was feeling. At first, I pushed this annoying kid away. I swatted at his voice like you might a mosquito at your ear. But the boy was nothing if not persistent and, I realized reluctantly, charming. He became as real to me as any character I'd ever crafted. And while I struggled to show myself an ounce of compassion, I felt nothing *but* compassion for him.

For the first time in a long time, I wanted to write. I wanted to tell this kid's story. Most of all, I wanted to see him through his pain. Even then, some part of me understood that doing so might contribute to my own healing. *If* I were brave enough to seek help.

I chose to be brave.

This boy, whom I eventually named Brett, is now the protagonist of the book you hold in your hands. His is a story of hope and love, but it is also a story that honestly and authentically illustrates one person's experience with grief and disordered eating. The fight against an eating disorder is a fight for one's life. There's no way around the gravity of that truth. So while I have taken as much care as I can to avoid triggering language, if you are struggling in your relationship with food and your body—or in other aspects of your mental health, including suicidal ideation or substance abuse—you may find some scenes and passages too affecting. If that happens, please prioritize your well-being. Reach out to a friend or mental health professional, and consider flipping to the back of this book for resources that can help you find the support you need.

You are valuable. Your body is valuable. Your life is valuable. It is my sincere hope that this book underscores those truths on every page, even, and maybe especially, on the pages that ask the most bravery of you, for it is those pages that best illustrate my profound faith in you and all you're capable of.

With gratitude,
Josh

CHAPTER ONE

The tiny car icon in my Uber app twists around in circles, its location three blocks from where I stand outside Evelyn's house in the Catalina Foothills. Like all houses in the neighborhood, Evelyn's modest three-bedroom sprouts unobtrusively from the Sonoran Desert. Each residence up here is a different take on ancient Pueblo architecture— stucco exteriors in various shades of sand and dirt, perpendicular lines that disappear like a mirage in the right light. I take in the expanse of Tucson stretching endlessly to the south—by most standards, a truly killer view. But I know better. The *most* killer view of the city can be found on its west side—at the top of Tumamoc Hill—and it's this view I'm chasing this evening. If my driver ever finds me, that is.

My driver, Reynold (red Toyota Camry, 3.8 stars), turns around, idles, turns again. My driver's test can't come soon enough. Two more weeks.

The car on my phone reminds me of those plastic cars Evelyn and I used to fill with blue and pink peg children in the Game of Life. He's two minutes away—no, now it's three. I think about running inside for one more swig from the massive Costco-sized bottle of vodka I've hidden beneath the heating vent in my old bedroom.

Maybe Reynold is as buzzed as I am. But of course that's not it. I'm used to waiting twice as long for an Uber as I should. The streets in the foothills are mazelike, and when I lived here with Evelyn, I'd often have to walk halfway to River Road to meet up with my buddies, their parents apt to give up and drop them off just north of the Zinburger near Campbell.

I wipe a bead of sweat from my temple—feeling moisture in way too many other places—and grin as the flash of red comes around the corner. I wave. Wish I'd stored some extra deodorant at Evelyn's house—summer in the Old Pueblo means short shelf lives for showers. I pop open the passenger-side door and hop in, energized by the blast of air-conditioning. My head feels light from the alcohol, and the friendly-dad look on Reynold's face makes me sure he's about to become my new best buddy.

Reynold says, "I thought my phone was going to have an aneurysm trying to find you. These foothills. Pretty up here, but . . ." He flips a U-turn on the lane—more an asphalt driveway. A single zombie apocalypse is all it would take for the cacti and desert brush to reclaim the road for nature.

"Yeah, man. My friends' parents have gotten lost a thousand times. Thanks for persevering, though. This is a nuggs emergency of epic proportions."

"Why don't you just DoorDash?"

Some sober part of my brain thinks I shouldn't be so forthcoming with this stranger, that I should get a new Uber from Wendy's—and another new one, and another new one after that. That I should only talk about what I'm doing right now with Ms. Finch at school because she's the only one I ever talk with about what I'm doing right now, and even then just barely. But Reynold is a cool dude. I can tell.

"Actually," I say, "I'm going drunk drive-thru'ing. It's no fun if you don't go through the drive-thrus."

2

"Drive-thrus? Plural?" Reynold gives me parent eyebrows. I don't like those eyebrows. "Aren't we a bit young to be drinking?"

Can Uber drivers snitch? Is there such a thing as driver-rider confidentiality? I recover quickly just in case. "Not too young if you're just drunk on life and a six-pack of Monster, bro!" I've brought shame upon seven generations of my offspring, but my committed performance was probably worth it. My backward cap, flip-flops, and the neon-green Wayfarers hanging from the neck of my tank top should win the costume department an Emmy.

Reynold's sidelong glance suggests he's not convinced, but he doesn't press. He navigates out of the foothills and zooms down Campbell Avenue. I love how the streetlights strobe when I try to concentrate on them. I love the warm feeling in my cheeks, the part of me the air-conditioning can't cool off. I poke at my belly, not caring that it's softer than those of my buddies. My favorite part of drinking is not caring about stuff. I whisper, "You ready for some nuggs, bruh?" My laugh comes out more like the giggle a little kid would make, which makes me laugh some more.

I say, "Okay, Reynold. Let's go over the itinerary so we don't make any mistakes. First stop, Wendy's." I'm ticking off our agenda on my fingers. "Then we'll punch through McDonald's even though they're painfully pedestrian. All those delicious chemicals, though, am I right?"

Reynold opens his mouth but I'm talking too fast.

"Then we'll hit Taco Bell. Actually, no." I'm shaking my head. Evelyn would be bummed if she knew I was eating an Anglo facsimile of Mexican food. Mexican is kind of *our* thing, a cooking-as-a-family thing, and we do it up right because Evelyn wants me to be proud of my heritage. I revise on the fly. "Screw that no-nuggs noise. Third stop: *Jack*. We're getting chicken for days. You can even get some if you want. My treat.

Then you can drop me off in the medical center parking lot across from Tumamoc. You know where everyone parks illegally?"

"No clue, kid. You'll have to program each stop into the app. You know that, right?"

"Hell yeah, buddy. I've got my Uber game down. You've never done Tumamoc? Put it at the top of your list. The U of A has an observatory up there or something, but you can hike up the hill whenever you want. It's the closest I've ever been to the Great Cool Ranch Dorito in the Sky."

Reynold gives me the type of face Evelyn would call *quizzical* or *flummoxed*. Before she became my mom—which happened when I was six years old—Evelyn had a whole career as an English professor at the University of Arizona. She's forever telling me to employ mature diction. *Never use just any word, Brett. Not when only the* right *word will do.*

I explain. "The Great Cool Ranch Dorito . . ." I crane my neck to find it through the windshield. Here in the city proper, dusk's hold is still acting like a gray blanket over the stars. "That big-ass triangle constellation? That's Captain Condor's headquarters in the cosmos. He chills up there with Kid Condor, and they save the universe from the evil Archer von Adonis and whatnot. I mean . . ." I lean in like I'm about to tell Reynold a secret. "I'm pretty much Kid Condor." I shrug like it's no big thing. "You know what I mean?"

"Uh-huh. Kid Condor, got it."

Wendy's is fast approaching on our right. Reynold gestures toward the familiar freckled girl on the signage. "All this is a little pricey for a kid your age, isn't it?"

Damn it, Reynold. Don't be such a buzzkill. Reynold's question reminds me why I have enough money to do stuff like drunk drive-thru'ing, and suddenly the storm clouds are gathering inside. Not cool, Reynold. Not cool. It's weird how drinking can make you the happiest guy in the world in one minute but make you want to cry your eyes out in the next. I wish I'd thought to put some booze in a water bottle. I'm only just learning the ways of the drunkard. It appears I have a long way to go.

I blink away the feelings I don't want to have, put a fat smile back on my face, shrug, and say, "Big allowance," which is true enough.

Reynold pulls into the Wendy's, the one in the Safeway shopping center on Prince, where I get a ten-piece nuggs meal with Dr Pepper. Next, we're across the street at McDonald's. I get another ten-piece— *ba-da-ba-ba-baaah, I'm nuggin' it.* And then we're heading to the Jack in the Box on Grant. Reynold pulls up to the menu and turns to me, my Wendy's and McDonald's bags warming my feet. "Nuggets?"

I shake my head. "No, no, no, no, no. You want the chicken *tendies* here. Jack is basically the Ritz-Carlton of all the fast-food places, and you want to order the filet mignon of processed chicken products." When the speaker crackles to life, I lean over Reynold's lap and say, "I'll take a number twelve, please—with curly fries and an Oreo shake." I'm thinking I might mix all the nuggs together in one bag and surprise my mouth when I eat them in the pitch-black atop Tumamoc. "Oh, and lots of ranch. And some ketchup. Please. Oh! And give me another Oreo shake for my buddy Reynold here. He's a stand-up guy, and don't let anyone tell you otherwise."

"That'll be $21.48 at the window."

I turn to Reynold, nod at the Dr Peppers I'm holding in each hand. "The shake is a bit of an extravagance, I know, but I'm trying to limit my soda intake because diabetes and all."

At the window, I pass my debit card to the nugg slinger, who takes it with a hand bedazzled in glitter nail polish. Her wrist is heavily accessorized in plastic rainbow jelly bracelets. I recognize her—she's in my earth science class and is hard to forget because you have to scoot your chair in whenever she needs to walk behind you to get to the door. She has this purple-and-blue hair—mermaid hair, I once heard it called. What's her name? Something you'd name your grandma. Marjory? Mildred? She recognizes me, too. She tenses, as if losing her anonymity as a faceless, nugg-slinging corporate drone—even for the span of a fast-food transaction—is painful. "Hey, Brett."

From somewhere in my memory come the taunting voices of the jerks at school. *Mallory, Mallory, Miss Ten Thousand Calorie.* "Hey, Mallory." Sometimes when I'm at school, I try not to look at Mallory. I especially try not to make eye contact. I don't know why. I'm not one of the jerks, I swear, but something about her, maybe everything about her—the redness of her face on sweltering days, the way her clothes strain to hold her inside, the tiny scabs on her arms from where she picks at her skin when she thinks no one is looking—makes me uncomfortable. I know my avoidance is uncool. Evelyn would give me a lecture on being the kind of guy she expects me to be. I take a breath and try for some small talk. "You got your dirt report done yet?"

She makes a sour face, passes my debit card through the reader. "It's going to be an all-nighter. You?"

"Yeah, I'm done, so I'm treating myself to a hike up Tumamoc. Ever been?"

Mallory hands Reynold our shakes, no longer bothering to wear her Jack-approved smile. "Why would I want to do that?"

Reynold takes a sip of his shake, kindly ignoring that I'm basically lying in his lap.

I say, "It's hella rad. You can see a three-sixty view of the city, plus you feel almost close enough to outer space to touch the Great Cool Ranch Dorito in the Sky."

Mallory rolls her eyes. I grin anyway because her recognition means she's at least stumbled upon my comic book, *Kid Condor: Cadet First Class of the Constellation Corps*, several dozen copies of which I hid throughout the school library last semester in a stealth operation. Forgive the bragging, but Kid Condor is kind of going to be a big deal someday.

Mallory delivers my food.

I use my sweet voice. "Extra ranch?"

She grabs a handful of ranch cups, drops them into the open bag, which I'm still holding extended from the car. Reynold lifts his foot from the brake. I cry out, "Wait!" The car lurches.

Mallory glances to my feet, to the bags from Wendy's and McDonald's. She raises her brow. "Something else?"

I can't say why exactly, but I was about to ask Mallory if she wanted to go to Tumamoc with me sometime. Something in that look on her face, though, something in her tone, makes me self-conscious.

My buzz has worn off, hasn't it?

I feel that quick cramp in the gut that comes when the teacher calls on you but you have no idea what he's asking because you've been daydreaming. I look to the bags on the floor, the one in my lap. Suddenly, I'm hyperaware that I'm double-fisting a Dr Pepper and an Oreo shake. Another Dr Pepper sweats in the cupholder beside me. Heat builds in my cheeks.

"Nothing. I'll . . . I'll see you at school."

"I'll count the minutes."

Reynold steps on it. Mallory's face disappears before I've registered what I saw on it. Now I don't know if I want to go to Tumamoc. I wish I hadn't gone to Jack.

I take a sip of my milkshake. Another.

Reynold and I don't chat as we drive the ten minutes to our final stop. All the feelings I wasn't feeling an hour ago are filling up my insides and I kind of want to start crying. I don't think Reynold would be cool with that, so I just pull harder on my milkshake, wishing it were full of vodka.

As Reynold eases into the lot across from the poorly paved driveway that winds up Tumamoc, I gather my nuggs and my remaining cup of Dr Pepper. "Thanks, Reynold. You've been a real champ and I'll never forget you."

I'm closing the car door when Reynold catches me. "Hey, kid?"

I blurt the first thing that comes to mind before he can say what I'm afraid he's going to say. "Don't worry, bud. Your tip is going to be the envy of all the other drivers at your annual Uber Christmas party this year. We good?"

Reynold gives me those parent eyebrows he's quickly becoming famous for, and I'm wondering if my face and voice are doing what I think they're doing.

It turns out they're not. Reynold says, "Are you all right?"

I fight to speak through the tightening in my chest. "I'm bomb as hell, bro! Better than ever, too, thanks to your next-level driving—you should go into stunt driving, for real."

Reynold opens his mouth, but I plow forward. "Well, gotta get these nuggs in my belly while they're warm." I pat my stomach. "He's growling. Later, buddy!"

I slam the door and set off in a jog across the street, desperate to get as far as possible from the face Reynold was making, the face Ms. Finch always makes when she pulls me from journalism to talk about my feelings, the very face Mallory made when she saw the bags I'm carting to the top of Tumamoc Hill.

This face chases me, and I hike a little faster than usual.

CHAPTER TWO

Reed affects a wizened and measured tone. "Wax on . . . wax off." He glances over the hood of his battered Chevy pickup to be sure he has my attention. He repeats the words, louder this time, as he mimes jerking off to the sacred text from my favorite movie of all time, *The Karate Kid*, a kick-ass film from the 1980s in which a teen boy, Daniel LaRusso, is mentored by a Japanese karate master, the lovable Mr. Miyagi, and must defeat the school bullies in a karate championship. Basically, a save-the-world-get-the-girl sort of thing.

Reed's fist bobs over the crotch of his swim trunks. "Wax on, wax off . . ." This time the words sound painful. He tilts his head back and his eyelids flutter. He's widely known as a harmless scamp, but this performance is pure sacrilege. "Oh God, brohhhhhhh! Wax *off*!"

I dunk my sponge in our bucket of sudsy water, sloshing my feet and flip-flops, and hurl the water bomb. I nail him in the face. Reed drops to the ground, releases a death rattle sure to echo through the courtyards of his apartment complex. *My* apartment complex, too, I remind myself. I've been living with Reed for seven months—which still doesn't feel real—bunking above him in the cramped two-bedroom he shares with his dad.

Reed has been my best bud since second grade, when we were the only seven-year-olds sorted into the kindergarten reading group. I guess I should be happy to be living with him, but even after all these months I catch myself longing to go home—my real home—at the end of the day. Evelyn's words from the day I moved out spring to mind unwelcome, particularly because I hear them in her new voice, her hospital voice, which rakes across her vocal cords in a way that sounds painful. *What ineffable fun. It'll be a true boys' club, a bachelor pad.* She could see I was trying not to cry, so she pulled me close and roughed my hair. *Just promise you'll pull your dirty socks out from under the bed once a week to wash them.*

In a fluid, Daniel LaRusso–like move, Reed rocks onto his shoulder blades and performs a kip-up, landing lightly on his feet. "You could bake a cake on that asphalt!"

We're enjoying what little shade is provided by a gnarled mesquite whose roots have left this corner of the lot looking like an excavation site. Reed retrieves my sponge, dunks it and squeezes it over the back of his neck. He gives his headlights some attention, flicking mosquito carcasses off the plastic. Reed's tank top—featuring a rendering of Andre the Giant in his famed caveman singlet—clings to his chest, which has become markedly swole in the past year since he decided to join the wrestling team. Reed's body couldn't look more different than Andre's— trim and well-defined.

A familiar feeling of discomfort washes over me, and I avert my eyes before Reed notices me looking. This awkward moment happening inside me—this awkward moment known only to me—it isn't a gay thing, even if being gay would be hella dope because you'd get to buy a fixer-upper and build furniture and remodel a master bath with your best-buddy-slash-husband, all of which seems way less scary and loads less confusing than navigating the world of women, an endeavor Reed is super excited about. He can't shut up about girls all of a sudden, and his new five-month plan—getting laid by winter break—has me feeling like I'm falling behind in the race of adolescence.

The attention I pay to Reed's body isn't the same as the kind I pay to, say, Thandie Gellar's body. Thandie Gellar enjoyed an incredible glow-up over the summer, and whenever she rolls the waist of her gym shorts to expose more of her thighs—why do girls do this? *why?*—I have to look away before I embarrass myself.

Reed and I have always been as comfortable as brothers around each other, but lately I get this pit of dread in my stomach whenever he changes his clothes around me or even just takes off his shirt, whenever I notice the type of guy he's turning into. This feeling is not unlike the discomfort I feel when I eat in front of him, which kind of blows because for obvious reasons I eat in front of him a lot. I guess Reed has glowed up, too, and girls like Thandie Gellar notice when guys like Reed notice *them*. I, on the other hand, might as well be the Invisible Kid.

Reed lifts our bucket of suds and effortlessly transports it a parking space over, sets it beside the wheel of my nondescript Toyota sedan, which I only get to drive with Reed's dad in the passenger seat (a total buzzkill, for sure, even if Marcus is a pretty chill dad-bot). Reed says, "Speaking of whacking—I mean waxing—off, you want to watch *Karate Kid* tonight?"

I recharge my sponge and begin my now-expert rendition of Mr. Miyagi's signature move. The paint job on my car, a gift from Evelyn when she could no longer drive, is so sun fried that washing does nothing to improve its exhausted appearance. It's the principle that matters, though, so I clean with loving care. Saturdays may be for the boys, but Sundays are for the toys.

I say, "Maybe we should watch *Scarface* instead. It's been hella days since we watched your favorite. We don't always have to watch mine."

"No, dude, it's chill. I love *Karate Kid*."

I know what Reed is up to; it's this annoying thing he always does, trying to make me feel better about having to move in with him, even when I'm not acting sad, even when we're doing stuff that's fun. It's been seven months of him favoring me like a sprained ankle. I'm not injured. I don't want to be pitied. I realize I'm scribbling on the pad of my thumb with my index finger, this nervous thing I do sometimes, spelling out invisible words I can't bring myself to say aloud. *I'm not pathetic*, I write. *I'm not fragile. Stop treating me like a baby.* I douse my fist in the bucket to wash the words away, as if Reed could see them. I determine I'll force the issue, but our negotiations are interrupted by Marcus, who calls from the tiny balcony of the second-floor apartment. "Pizza, guys?"

Reed says, "Is that even a question?"

"Brooklyn or Rocco's?"

We respond in unison. "Brooklyn."

"Want to eat there? Afterward we could shoot hoops at Himmel."

Before I can respond in the affirmative, a habit of mine with Marcus—don't be a pest, don't be a burden—Reed declares we want delivery because we're going to chill at home and watch *The Karate Kid*.

I suppress a groan. Marcus won't like this idea—he wants so badly to be the involved dad and spend time with us on the one night a week he's freed from the labors of machining at the metalworks factory. I'd like to give him this because he really tries and I think Reed might take him for granted. Reed, on the other hand, never looks too deeply into his dynamic with his dad. He just wants autonomy—and pizza.

As expected, Marcus deflates. "*The Karate Kid*? Again? What is it with that movie?"

I open my mouth to correct Reed, to say that we're actually watching *Scarface* (which should go over better because it only became Reed's favorite movie because it was Marcus's favorite), but Reed steamrolls me, his enthusiasm characteristically infectious, even when the subject matter produces eye rolls. "Dad, show some respect. According to our resident aficionado"—he gestures to me—"*The Karate Kid* is the greatest superhero movie of all time. Apologies to *The Dark Knight*."

Marcus raises his hands. "Spare me the dissertation, son. I've heard it all before."

What Marcus would pay money to never hear again is my well-thought-out TED Talk positing that Daniel LaRusso is actually a superhero and *The Karate Kid* is his origin story. Think about it. Daniel is just your average kid like any one of us, but he loses his father (glaring hero trope); journeys to a new, challenging land where he's faced with a seemingly insurmountable force of evil (the Cobra Kai); has to save a girl from the clutches of a cliché eighties supervillain (Elisabeth Shue as Ali, am I right?); is mentored by a great and powerful sage-slash-mage-slash-healer with supernatural abilities (that's Mr. Miyagi, obviously); and acquires preternatural fighting skills, complete with a unique costume and signature move that countless fanboys have been mimicking on beaches since before I was born. All of this cements Daniel LaRusso's place as a textbook martial artist superhero.

While one might argue that the above is merely circumstantial evidence, no one can deny that just like all superheroes, Daniel never gives up, no matter how insurmountable the odds, no matter how injured he is, no matter how much pain he's in. His heroism is grounded in real life, and his story gives me hope that something special might lie within even me. The fact that my protagonist, Kid Condor, has no supernatural abilities and instead must rely on his kick-ass fighting skills and alien tech is my nod to Daniel. No matter how fantastical my world-building, I wanted my hero to be a real kid, too.

Ever the pushover, Marcus agrees to Reed's plan. "Fine. You guys can watch *Karate Kid* if you must, but then I'm going to kick both your punk asses in *Mario Kart*. Have fun with the scrap characters. I've got dibs on *my* hero, Princess Peach."

CHAPTER THREE

Ms. Finch doesn't like to be called a guidance counselor. She says school counselors abandoned that title a couple decades ago because their most important job isn't helping sophomores escape the barbarism of gym by spiriting us into marching band; it's helping guys like me feel better about the bad things that happen to us.

I'm sitting at Ms. Finch's desk on her bouncy-ball chair, which she says she wrote into her budget last year because it's good for her posture and productivity. She sits on the edge of the threadbare sofa usually reserved for students. I think Ms. Finch lets me sit on her chair during our check-ins because she feels sorry for me. I go ahead and let her.

Ms. Finch drapes one leg over the other. I admire her new Chuck Taylors—low-tops, bright red—with more than a little envy. Ms. Finch is one of the coolest adults at Tucson City High. Even though I don't like talking about my feelings, even though I hate talking about why I'm here, my mood always brightens when she asks if she can steal me for a chat.

Today, Ms. Finch wants to talk about food. She always wants to talk about food (even rad adults have their flaws). She says, "Why do you think you felt bad when Mallory noticed you were eating food from three restaurants?"

I look to the disturbing stains in the ceiling tiles, pulsating nebulas and swirling black holes. Why *did* I feel bad in the drive-thru? Why do I feel so bad right now? It's not like Mallory is anyone to judge, right? She's like the fattest kid in school. Evelyn's voice springs to mind. *Physical characteristics describe a body, Brett, not a character. Look deeper.* Thinking of Mallory as the fattest kid in school feels mean, even if she is. The biggest kid in school? Is that kinder?

Ms. Finch says, "Brett? You know our talks are more productive when you express your inner narrative aloud."

I know I'm starting to get kind of chubby—I can feel the bite of my belt buckle when I sit down (I don't want to tell Ms. Finch this). I know three fast-food meals is a lot for one person—I'm not completely oblivious (I *do* want to tell Ms. Finch this). But teen guys scarf down everything in sight all the time. When I still lived with Evelyn, she would buy all sorts of snacks when my buddies showed up for sleepovers, even giving me money to order pizza for everyone. There was never a speck of Dorito dust left when the sun rose.

I don't know how to answer Ms. Finch's question because saying what I'm thinking would feel like defending myself. So I take the coward's way out. "I don't know."

Ms. Finch makes a note on her legal pad and regards me, her head cocked like she's examining my face for the answers my voice won't give her. "I think you're ready."

Ready for what?

Ms. Finch steps to the bookcase behind her desk. "I have a present for you. I thought of giving it to you sooner, but I wanted it to be special, so I had the cover doctored."

16

A present? Sounds like the sort of gesture a friend would make. Ms. Finch doesn't like the word *friend*—the other f-word, she calls it—because it undermines her authority, but I know her protestations are merely for show. One time, she let Reed and me hide in the bank of cabinets lining one wall of her office. We'd been released for a bathroom break from in-school suspension, serving a day's sentence for violating dress code for the third time, and instead of heading straight to the boys' room, we ran in here and crawled into the cabinets while Ms. Finch pretended not to look. When Dean Ricamora asked if she'd seen us, she feigned ignorance like a pro. Once her office door latched closed, Reed and I busted up. Ms. Finch finally spoke. "You'll have to go back to prison now. As much as I enjoy being an accomplice, I enjoy my paycheck more."

Now she slides a squat spiral-bound journal from between several dusty copies of psychology and sociology books no one would ever want to read. She passes the notebook my way.

I suck in a breath. "Holy shit." Kid Condor stares up at me, his masked expression determined, his bright-purple-and-yellow fly suit sleek, the lines of his body svelte, feet disappearing in a streak of jet flame, his form stretched to show the intense speed at which his propulsion pack sends him zooming through the cosmos. The journal's cover is a laminated copy of the cover of the flagship issue of *Kid Condor: Cadet First Class of the Constellation Corps.* "Where did you get this?" I leaf through the pages, ruled but all blank.

Ms. Finch gives me her best disapproving look—she sucks at disapproving looks. "I'm friends with the librarian, you know. She's still finding issues tucked into the encyclopedias. I found this one in a copy of *Red Rising*."

I lift my arm for a high five. "Good taste, Finch."

We slap palms and Ms. Finch settles once more on the couch.

I say, "So what did you think of the issue? I assume you read it before dismantling it."

"I found it . . . illuminating."

"Plot? Characters? Don't leave me hanging. I'm especially curious if the condor thing made sense since Captain is partially based—obviously loosely, I mean, because don't even get me started on the Dorito-dust thing—but, like, he's *inspired*, anyway, by this Inca sun god named Inti, and Kid is obviously mestizo—or whatever the Monosian equivalent of mestizo is, which I guess is whatever I want it to be since Monos isn't Earth, but its displaced peoples *are* basically the same as humans, though kind of more highly evolved—totally *La raza cósmica*, you know?—but only in the good, modern sense, not in the original sense from like a hundred years ago, which was *definitely* still kind of racist. But I have to bring all this up because most people associate the *eagle* with Mexico, not the condor, and, sure, I get that. I mean, why wouldn't they? But they're not aware of the whole South American thing, the important connection between the condor and the eagle, and of course they're only thinking about the Mexico they *know*. I've been reading up about this. This whole part of the world was all colonized to hell and ransacked and turned into Disneyland and whatever—and of course none of that was cool at all, and oh my *God*, I mean, I myself am a *product* of all this horrible stuff that happened centuries ago and I don't really know how I feel about that yet, but what I'm driving at is that where the condor is concerned, even the indigenous people as far north as—"

Ms. Finch raises her palm. "*Whoa* there, my friend. Let's slow that roll for a second."

I give Ms. Finch a sheepish grin and shrug. "It's canon."

"I very much appreciated Kid's mythology, and am particularly intrigued by your own. I'd like to hear more about both, but those are topics for another day. Today, I want to talk about the journal."

Oof. My whole body deflates. "Okay. No *Dear Diary* crap, please."

She raises her hands in defense. "I'm going out on a limb because you seem to be struggling to talk about something that might be worth talking about. This is a food journal."

My stomach fills with a team of rugby-playing butterflies. I don't think I want this present anymore.

Call her Jean Grey, because Ms. Finch is forever sensing stuff I don't mean for her to know. "This is going to feel like homework, but tracking your food intake might help you learn some things that could really improve your life in the long run."

"I don't know . . ."

"Could I convince you if it meant I'd ask fewer questions about what you're eating? If recording such information in the book could answer those questions for me?"

I'm not convinced. Not even a little. But Ms. Finch has never steered me wrong. I mean, maybe even *I* dislike the word *friend* because Ms. Finch is something more than a friend. After all, look at what she did for my food journal. You ever try to buy a journal at a store? They're all girly and florid. That's the word Evelyn would use: *florid*. Evelyn's voice comes to mind—her old voice, before all the oxygen tanks and tubes, the voice she used when I still lived with her. *Imprecise diction is the currency of the misunderstood, Brett.* Ms. Finch is really more of a *bro*, right? Come to think of it, Ms. Finch is an even bro-ier bro than my bros because I can say stuff to her I wouldn't even tell Reed. I make a mental note to tell Evelyn about my new nomenclature for Ms. Finch the moment I visit her. Evelyn adores words, but she hates the word *bro*.

I say, "What would I have to do exactly?"

"You'd start by recording what you eat and at what time. Not too tough, right?"

I'm staring at Kid Condor; he could perform this task in his sleep. I should tell Ms. Finch that sounds easy, but I think it might be hard—really hard.

"That sounds easy."

"Good. Excellent. Now for the trickier part. When you eat a lot at once, when you eat past the point of fullness, I want you to jot some notes about how you felt before or during the eating—what you were thinking about at the time—and I want you to write about how you felt afterward. You can write as little or as much as you like."

It's not lost on me that Ms. Finch didn't use the word *binge* when she described what I do. I know that *she* knows that *I* know that word, but I also know that she knows that I don't *like* that word. I don't like its specificity, and I hate that it feels like something you'd write in Sharpie on one of those stickers you wear on your chest where nobody knows your name. *Hello, my name is Binge.* Evelyn would be such a mom if she were here right now, disappointed in both of us for skating around the just-right word.

"Brett?" Ms. Finch leans forward. "You know I feel more respected when you make eye contact."

Evelyn is on one shoulder, and she's telling me to be brave. Kid Condor is on the other, and he's telling me Evelyn is always right. "All right, I'll do it. I'll try, I mean."

Ms. Finch slaps her hands on her knees. "That's what I'm talking about!" She jumps from her perch to shake my hand. "Deal?"

I can't help but catch Ms. Finch's enthusiasm. I hop from her bouncy-ball chair and grab her hand. "Deal!" I toss my head back and crow, pounding my chest with a fist. To anyone else, I'd look like a total weirdo, but making noise is something Ms. Finch taught me to do when I'm so filled up with feelings I might burst if I don't get them out of me—joyful, miserable, it doesn't matter. Ms. Finch just wants me to express authentically, and I'm allowed to come here to do so whenever I want. This is one of the reasons Ms. Finch is totally a bro.

When the dust of my enthusiasm settles, I slide my food journal into my backpack and slip my arms through the straps. At the threshold, I turn. Ms. Finch is seated again, recording a few more notes to save for all eternity in my psych file. I say, "Ms. Finch?"

"Yes, Brett?"

"Only you'll read what I write? No one else has to see it?"

"Just me."

"Cool."

And as I head back to journalism, I do feel pretty cool.

CHAPTER FOUR

The journalism classroom is set up to look like a segmented office where people slowly die from the inside out, skin turning translucent beneath fluorescent lights. We even have a break area with couches and a small conference room. A couple of my classmates are on the hunt for the perfect fax machine on eBay so we can re-create the iconic fax-machine-murder scene from *Office Space* on TikTok. There are only so many ways legends can be born in a dream graveyard.

It's from one of the break area's osteoporotic couches—cushions insulated by decades of freshman farts—that I steal glances at Thandie Gellar, my new food journal carefully positioned on my lap to keep my drawing out of view of the casual passerby. Ms. Finch's gift is standing in for my sketchbook—just this once—because I didn't want to miss the work-free window that presented itself after I turned in my write-up of the new season of *The Umbrella Academy* (five stars, stream it yesterday).

Thandie's cubicle is conveniently positioned to provide a perfect view of her backside, plus a tantalizing amount of thigh if she swivels just right. I'm glad I recently sprang for a new set of Prismacolor pencils, which includes the just-right shade for her rich brown skin (PC 947, a pencil that, considering the amount of skin showing in the character studies I'm drafting, will soon be as worn down as Kid Condor's PC 1031). The series' second volume is going to the presses this week, and I'm thinking volume three is the perfect time to introduce a new character into the Constellation Corps Universe: Therma, a brilliant and preternaturally beautiful humanoid capable of manipulating temperature, a superpower inspired by Thandie's real-life power to make me feverish with a single glance. She'll be a great ally to help Kid save the universe—and, you know, do other things with.

My pencil glides smoothly down the small of Therma's back—there's no logical reason for an exposed back in Therma's fly suit, but it would be irresponsible not to experiment with costuming variations, right? I'm lost in the perfect, athletic arch of her hip when a lanky body flops onto the couch beside me, nearly landing in my lap. I jolt in terror, my pencil making a mangled wreck of Therma's thigh, but then the scent of Old Spice and the sound of Ajay Mukherjee's outrageous laugh flood me with relief. Ajay is a senior who edits the school paper and even had a short story published on *Broken Pencil*. He's known for his incessant clowning, but he's actually kind of a big deal around here, a voice to be laughed with in person but respected on paper.

"Yoooooooo, little man!" He grabs the journal from my hands, examining the sketches with great interest. "Hellooooh, nurse. Who's the foxy femme fatale?"

It's far too late to hide my drawings, so I just stammer pointless syllables as Therma works her magic on my cheeks.

Ajay's gaze moves from my sketchbook to Thandie, back to my sketchbook. It seems impossible that Ajay's smile could broaden, but it does. "You little perv!"

His laugh reignites, and he grabs me by the scruff of the neck, pulling me from the couch. My food journal and pencils clatter to the floor. He mock punches me several times in the gut, an act we've been pulling on each other almost daily since I admitted I was the one who used up the last of the toner without replacing the cartridge last month.

I give my best performance yet, my face contorting in *oof*s and *argh*s, my entire body hopping from the ground with each punch, which Ajay delivers with well-practiced slow motion. Why we're not internet famous with this bit, I'll never know.

A quick glance to see that no teachers are watching, and Ajay thrusts his arm right under my crotch to pick me up—sort of. He's at least a foot taller than me but about as scrawny as a cardboard Halloween skeleton. He dumps me on the couch, feigns a powerslam on my chest. "Bow to my earth-shattering might, weakling!"

Apologies to Reed, but I actually think we're the better wrestlers.

It's here that Robyn Fletcher—a class-president nominee destined to make a long line of personal assistants experience complete mental and emotional breakdowns—exits the conference room. The disdain on her face could be documented by the crew of the International Space Station. "Save it for the gay-for-pay porn you shoot on the weekends. This is a *professional* environment." The election won't even happen until spring, but Robyn already coordinates her campaign buttons with her skirt—just long enough to avoid detention. My eyes hit the curve of her calves in those impractical high heels, and suddenly I remember that she was my first crush in fifth grade. Sometimes I appall me.

She looks to my pencils strewn across the stained carpet tiles. Fortunately, my journal fell with the open pages face down. The cover is visible, but nothing else. Robyn wrinkles her nose like she's just caught a whiff of dirty gym shorts. "Maybe put the crayons away while you're at it, toddler. This isn't art class. Besides, no one deserves to be tortured with more of your cringe-ass Captain Crotch Bulge stories."

Ajay's grin never falters as Robyn power walks away—I don't think she's capable of walking at a normal pace. He releases a low whistle. "Now, there's a character I want to see in your comics—lickably fresh but obviously evil. She'd get all the best lines."

"Naturally."

Ajay helps me replace my pencils in their trays. Before heading back to his work, he puts a hand on my shoulder. He nods toward Thandie. "You should talk to her. Ask her to hang out."

I give him an incredulous laugh. "I couldn't."

"Oh yeah?"

Ajay saunters up to the half wall of Thandie's cubicle, shoots me a nefarious grin as he leans over the edge.

Oh no.

"Yooooooo, my lady. You got a sec? Brett needs to gnaw your ear about something."

Gnaw your ear? The image would be more welcome if I were home. Alone. During my designated private time. (After a mentally scarring incident where I walked in on Reed, we posted a sign-up sheet, no joke.)

Thandie stands, shoots me a friendly smile that weakens my knees. I'm scribbling on my thumb: *No, no, no, no, no.* I have no way of knowing if the smile is genuine or the type you'd use to humor a child. I only realize my legs are frozen when Ajay motions me over. "Don't just stand there, my man. The lady's time is valuable."

With monumental effort, I silence my thumb scribbling and approach the cubicle. Ajay drapes an arm over my shoulder and gives it a rattling squeeze. His patronizing smile moves back and forth between Thandie and me. This will undoubtedly go down as his favorite moment of the day. His voice, for once, comes gently. "I'll leave you to it, then. Bye now." He's halfway across the office when he turns back, finger guns blazing. "I'll expect a full report on my desk by quittin' time come Friday, my man."

As the silence grows awkward, I hug my food journal to my chest to obscure the cover. Does Thandie think my comics are as stupid and childish as Robyn does? Thandie never carries herself with the icy sophistication of Robyn, and she's known for kindness, not cruelty, but she's still several rungs above me in the social hierarchy. Last semester she organized a wildly successful fashion show benefiting the local Black Lives Matter chapter where all the models were girls of color who wore their natural hair. The event got real news coverage. She's not just above me; she's top tier.

Thandie breaks the tension, her tone encouraging. "You . . . wanted to tell me something?"

"Oh, uh, yeah, I mean . . ." What the hell am I going to say? If I don't nut up and ask her to hang, Ajay will never let me live it down. Then a solution dawns on me, one that will fulfill the assignment but give me a bit of buffer room. "I mean, like, uh . . . it's my birthday next Friday—"

"Awesome! Happy birthday!" Thandie nearly gives me a heart attack by launching into a birthday dance, the curves of her body fluidly responding to the beat in her head, a hint of midriff showing with each grind of the hips.

It's entirely possible I've forgotten the English language, but I attempt to pronounce the words in my head anyway. "So on Saturday, a few of us—Reed and me, obviously, and a couple of his teammates—we're going to hike the Phoneline Trail in Sabino Canyon. It's like ten miles and I've never done the whole thing. Do you think . . . ? Um, I mean, if you'd like to join us . . ."

What am I thinking? Why would *she* want to join *us*?

Her expression brightens further. "I love that trail. I've done it half a dozen times." She extends an expectant palm. "Your phone."

"My . . ." I'm shaking my head. "Of course. My phone." I almost fumble the device slipping it from my pocket.

Thandie punches in her contact info—*she punches in her contact info!*—and passes my phone back. "Text me."

With that she sinks back into her chair and swivels back to her computer screen.

I'm just about to run for the nearest walk-in freezer when Thandie's silky voice catches me. "Oh, and Brett?"

Am I still breathing? Breathing is important.

"Reed's single, right? No one special?"

I saw this horror movie once where the killer used a scythe to open a gash so wide in his victim's stomach that the entirety of his intestines fell out. Instead of keeling over dead, the victim actually gathered his insides and shuffled out of the frame, as if he could put himself back together if he could just get far enough away from that merciless instrument.

"Uh . . . yeah," I rasp, guts steaming, cradled in my arms. "Fully on the market, that one."

"Cool." Thandie flashes a radiant smile. "Thanks, Brett. I owe you one."

CHAPTER FIVE

The awesome thing about getting in trouble every five minutes, Reed once explained, is it allows a guy plenty of chances to snoop through Dean Ricamora's office. Kids aren't supposed to be in there alone, of course, but once, last semester, Ricamora left Reed to contemplate his myriad faults while dealing with some irate parent who threatened to get physical with his secretary if Ricamora didn't get his "worthless ass out here right now." The prize? A keycard that gets us in wherever we want to go. Why would anyone want to get into school when he's not forced to be there? Reed and I have our reasons, the latest of which fills the duffel bag resting between us in the cab of his rusting Chevy.

"People care more about things when you shroud them in mystery," Reed says. He smooths his hair back and snugs his ski mask over his ears. He kills the engine, having just pulled into one of the parking spaces on Third Street, directly in front of the field at Tucson City High. "This is how J. J. Abrams builds suspense for upcoming projects."

We pull our ski masks over our faces. Even though we're decked in black from head to toe—no purple or yellow to catch the eye—donning my mask makes me feel like Kid Condor when he dons his fly suit, no longer just a punk-ass orphan from the wasteland Aoratos system but a motherfucking hero, motherfucker.

Reed says, "This is how you get people to lose their shit on Reddit. Believe me, man, everyone knows Anonymous's face for a reason." Reed is explaining for the millionth time why I'm not supposed to put my name on my comic book series, even if we both know that the author of *Kid Condor: Cadet First Class of the Constellation Corps* is the worst-kept secret on campus. My social status, which relied mostly on Reed's popularity anyway, has taken a hit since the release of my first edition. The general consensus seemed to mirror Robyn Fletcher's response: the work was immature and lacking nuance. *"Was he high when he wrote this? I mean, cosmic Dorito dust?"* *"Yeah, and were those* tater tots *the bad guy shot out of his helmet?"* (For the record, they were bionic pus pods.) Even the dialogue, which I thought was clever, was mocked mercilessly by class clown Ben Rivers in his now famous nasally impression, complete with Coke-bottle glasses and excited evil hand rubbing. *"Adonis will reward me handsomely when I deliver Kid Condor to him in chains because I'm what? Iiiin-telligent! Iiiiin-dustrious! And iiiiiiiin-defatigable!"*

But Ajay Mukherjee gave the work a C+ in his official review. He declared that one day my fans would look back on this early self-published artifact as a campy time capsule of "immeasurable promise." He praised the work's allusions to pre-Columbian civilizations and called me "a storyteller to watch," which gave me the balls to pen a sequel.

We glance around, making sure the street is deserted. It usually is this time of night, all the stragglers long since kicked out of the bars on Fourth after last call. Reed grabs our duffel bag and we exit the pickup. The back of my shirt is already damp—the low tonight was supposed to be seventy-eight degrees, but in my cat burglar getup, it feels like a hundred or more. Reed tosses the duffel over the fence and pulls himself smoothly over the bars. His new muscles make such stunts look easy. Getting over this fence is *not* easy.

I look to the Great Cool Ranch Dorito—the biggest constellation in the sky after Captain Condor. Its three points straddle the Milky Way. Here in the city, you can't see the Dorito dust—the dimmer stars that fill the space between the chip's three points—but I know it's there. Dorito dust is the heavily guarded source of Captain Condor's cosmic power. It's what fuels Kid Condor's propulsion pack and the propulsion packs of the other cadets in the Constellation Corps. Reed warned me that this aspect of Captain's mythology wasn't doing the work any favors. "Lean into the Latin American stuff instead. Food constellations take up way too much space in the narrative; besides, Frito-Lay is probably going to sue if you don't rename the Great Cool Ranch Dorito, preferably something that isn't a food at all."

I imagine licking the Dorito dust anyway, powering up on the spicy cosmic goodness. I know there's a certain immaturity to my comic book in its current iteration—that maybe I'm holding on too tightly to mythology I built before hitting double digits—but I don't think I'm ready to retool Captain's universe for a more mature edit quite yet. Cosmic Dorito dust comforts me, and I'm grateful for its power now.

Reed whispers, "Come on, bud. Get your ass over here." He's standing with the duffel slung over one shoulder—Jason Bourne, this kid. Of course this image leads to another, the image of the hot female the kick-ass action star gets to save. Thandie Gellar fits the role. I allowed myself to be miserable for a few days after what happened in journalism, but how can I blame her? She's a ten. Of course she'd want to be with a guy like Reed. I chastise myself for even thinking the next logical question, which might be too self-pitying, even for me: Who, then, would want to be with a guy like me?

I put Thandie and next week's hike out of my mind and leap for the horizontal support bar at the top of the fence. I give it my all but fail to swing myself over. "You gave me a boost last time."

"Ah, yeah. My bad." Reed goes full Spider-Man, landing beside me.

Even with his help, I barely clear the fence without ripping my pants. I land sharply on my butt.

Reed joins me and we jog toward the library building. The campus is well lit, almost bright as day along the walkways and covered ramadas. Our outfits are pretty pointless, obviously, but I insisted on them to protect our anonymity on the off chance we end up bumping into the night security guy, even if he is about a thousand years old and likely asleep in his office right now. Besides, the operation is more fun this way. Behind our masks, there's a *story*. I can still hear Evelyn's voice from when I was little, back before she adopted me, back when I still cried most days about things I don't remember anymore, before Captain Condor came into my life, before he ever discovered Kid Condor in the wreckage of the destroyed planet Monos. *As long as there's a story in your heart, you'll always have somewhere to escape to when things get hard, and as long as you're a storyteller, you'll always be able to build your own escape route.*

Tonight, our story might be a black-and-white espionage thriller. At any moment we'll be found out, the wail of an alarm freezing us in our tracks. Spotlit and surrounded, we'll be shot to death by rat-faced Nazis in their drab uniforms, attack dogs losing their minds, teeth dripping foam. Or maybe this is a balls-to-the-wall crime-spree romp, Reed and me pulling off one last heist before retiring to the Lesser Antilles or some jungle-choked country whose economy is built on mountains of cocaine and the kidnappings of wealthy tourists.

We stop short at the library's glass doors. Reed says, "Okay, dude. In and out in under five minutes, got it?"

I nod as Reed presses Ricamora's keycard to the sensor. Inside, pin-pricks of colored light from the computer desks and the soft whir of the ventilation system are all that register while my eyes and body acclimate. In the stillness, the soft thud of the door resonates like the airlock of a vault. No turning back now. The air carries the faint scent of glue, not quite sour but musty, and I remember why I avoid the library in the daylight.

Reed drops and unzips the duffel. He grabs a stack of issue two of *Kid Condor: Cadet First Class of the Constellation Corps*. He passes several copies my way. We've got a hundred copies fresh off Office Depot's presses. He fishes out two small flashlights, twists them on, and passes one to me.

"Kill it," he whispers. Then he's bounding past the study carrels and the hangout couches, toward the back of the library, where the periodicals are displayed. I head straight for the teen vampire and teen zombie and teen postapocalyptic warrior books, ignoring the dusty stacks loaded with biology or anatomy texts, the type of books that might include a detailed breakdown of the periodic table of the elements. I avoid anything that explores the motivating factors behind the Cold War or women's suffrage. There's an art to covert comic-booking. Judicious placement means a higher likelihood that the issues will be discovered. I hold my flashlight between my teeth and yank the new *Percy Jackson* adventure from the shelf. I slide an issue between its pages. I wander into the graphic novels and reach for a *Heartstopper* and an *Invincible*. I hide at least a couple issues in the encyclopedias to be discovered by some nerd thirty years from now, but for the most part, I plant in fertile soil.

I move on to the classics. I'm about to slide an issue between the pages of *Where the Red Fern Grows*—right at that messed-up part with the ax—when suddenly I'm sucking in a stunned breath, clamping my eyes shut against a blinding light. My heart pummels my ribs.

Shit, shit, shit.

"All right, fellas. Come out nice and slow." This is the graveled type of voice usually employed by the golden-age pro wrestlers Reed and I binge-watch on YouTube. Did they hire a new security guy?

I drop to the floor and crawl behind the end of the bookshelf. I hear a crash from Reed's corner of the library—a felled magazine rack?

Pounding footsteps.

The library goes black again.

Reed must have given the fuzz the slip and made it back to the light switches at the main entrance. I fumble with my flashlight, fingers trembling, finally twisting it until the bulb winks out. Back against the bookshelf, I work to slow my breathing. The mask isn't helping. I scribble on my thumb, random words, spelling-bee-winner words.

If the fuzz walks past the stacks, merely glancing down each aisle, he might miss me. How carefully will he make his circuit? If Reed and I play this right, we could still escape. We just have to find each other before the fuzz finds us.

"Boys . . ." A thick flashlight beam passes one bookshelf after another. I watch as it plays against the wall, disappears, reappears, disappears. I hold my breath and lean away from the beam as the guard passes my shelf. "Don't make your punishment any more severe than it has to be." What's worse than in-school suspension? Surely not the vacation of real suspension.

"Pssst."

I jolt. A beam of light hits me in the face. It's coming from . . . from above?

I crane my neck and go full Mr. Fantastic with relief. It's Reed, lying on his stomach on top of the shelf. He whispers, "You smell pork chops, bruh?" He extends an arm. "Let's ditch the piggy party."

I climb to join him. The shelves seem solid enough, but each is eight feet high. I'm overcome by a wave of dizziness. Times like this, I wish I were as fearless as Kid Condor when he first broke into the launch bay at Constellation Corps' headquarters to try out a propulsion pack before gaining fly-boy certification. Captain Condor was pissed, of course, but deep down he was impressed with Kid's massive stones—amused, too, having been similarly mischievous when he was a cocksure young demigod.

Reed stands, vaulted ceilings giving him plenty of room. He points toward the computer workstations that sprout between the stacks and the periodicals, the guard's beam of light bobbing here and there as he checks beneath each table. We've got the tactical advantage, much closer to the exit. I crouch, not quite ready to let go of the shelf.

Reed hops silently to the next row, maybe a distance of five feet, then the next, moving toward the lobby. He glances over his shoulder, gestures for me to follow.

God. Okay. All right, okay.

I stand and hop to the next shelf, certain this is going to end up like some tentpole movie where we narrowly escape a domino wave of crashing bookshelves in our quest to find Thomas Jefferson's magic Freemason pinkie ring.

We reach the final stack. Before us spread a dozen study carrels. Reed leans into my ear. "We jump to the tables, then the floor, and then we shoot straight for the doors. I'll grab the duffel. All we have to do is outrun Randy Savage back there."

I'm nodding, imagining what a botched jump could do to an ankle.

34

"We good?"

I'm not good at all, but there's no way I'm going to let Reed sense as much. "Hell yeah, we are." My words come out as a whisper, but they pack the punch of a howl. "Hardcore parkour as *fuck*."

"That's what I'm talking about, killer."

And we're jumping.

Reed's dismount is textbook. He's already running for the doors when I land on the edge of a carrel and fall into a rolling chair, smacking my head against a support beam. The monster plows toward us, light bobbing. "Don't run, kids! Don't make me call the police!"

Reed laughs. "Eat farts, pig!" He bursts through the doors. I'm right on his tail with desperate strides, head throbbing. A clattering and a curse behind us suggest Randy Savage has run into some obstacle in his pursuit.

We take off across the field, hit the fence. Reed crouches to give me a boost; I leap, but the run has taken the wind out of me. I jump, pull. Again. I'm out of breath and out of strength. I shake my head, panting.

Reed cries, "Move it, fat ass, come on!"

The words almost take my legs out from under me. I'm grateful Reed can't see my face, hope he can't hear the feelings all over my voice. "I'm sorry." I look behind us, frantic. The fuzz charges onto the field. "I'm sorry."

The fuzz is almost on us, shouting stuff about not moving a muscle, about giving up before our academic records are forever tarnished.

Reed's head whips around. I can almost see the smile forming in his body language. "This way. Plan B." We're off again, this time toward the back of the field. We're halfway there before I realize what Reed has in mind. There's a gap in the fence on the southeast corner of the property where we used to slip through when we wanted to ditch gym class.

The fuzz looks strong, but he's not a fast runner. Even I outpace him easily. Reed slides to a stop near the gap, shifts sideways, pulls himself free. The duffel follows. I shove my head and shoulders through, and here the worst thing in the world happens. I press my body forward—and lurch to a stop. Jesus, *no*. This is *not* happening. I suck in my stomach, only managing to wedge myself more tightly. I'm not this fat, right? When did I get this fat? I say, "Just go, dude! I won't snitch on you!"

Reed drops to his knees and grabs my arms. "Fuck that noise. No one gets left behind. Wiggle down. It's wider at the bottom."

I'm squirming; he's pulling.

This is when I feel the security guard's hands on my ankles. Oh God. He yanks. I slip backward.

Reed screams, "Get off him, Randy Savage!" (Much to Reed's amusement, the new night guard really does look like Randy Savage.)

The guard takes a sumo-wrestler stance. One more yank and I'll be a lost cause. A humiliating buck of my body, like a seal on a beach, is all I've got left. I give it my all. The guard loses his balance, falling violently on his ass. Reed doesn't waste the respite. He tugs at my wrists, sliding me across the dirt. The guard lunges but miscalculates. He faceplants into the fence with a nauseating *crack*. Blood bursts from his nose, nearly spraying my shoes. He paws at his face and screams a garbled word he should definitely *not* be saying at school.

Reed laughs like a maniacal supervillain. He grabs his crotch and thrusts his hips forward. "Snap into *this* Slim Jim, ohhhhhh yeeeaaahhhhhhh!"

Then we're running for the safety of his pickup, Reed laughing and fist-pumping all the way.

I join in the merriment. All the parts of me Reed can see suggest I'm feeling as bomb as he is, but while he yanks his mask off the moment he slides behind the wheel, I leave mine on for several blocks, afraid that if I remove it, Reed might see just how *not* bomb I really am.

CHAPTER SIX

I'm lying on the top bunk, staring at the popcorn ceiling, connecting the figures in the drywall into constellations by the light of the lamppost in the courtyard outside, its soft glow filtered through the Venetian blinds at sharp angles. The apartment is a second-story walkup in a moderately priced complex off Glenn, the type of place where you don't have to be afraid of getting shot but you might have to fistfight a feisty granny for the only working dryer in the shared laundry facility. I'm grateful Marcus was willing to take me in, but it's hard to sleep with so much light. At Evelyn's house, it's actually dark at night.

I wish I could take a Sharpie to the ceiling to map it properly. I imagine drawing several lines until PB & J Monster materializes. I draw some more lines and there's $5 Footlong. These fake constellations aren't as good as the real thing, and I wish I were lying on my trampoline in Evelyn's backyard, deep enough in the foothills to enjoy a killer view of the starscape. I miss Cheesy Gordita Crunch and Hot Dog Jesus and Uncle Panda's Fat Fortune Cookie—all the constellations I haven't seen since I visited Evelyn a few days ago. I miss Captain Condor, his wings spread so wide across the sky that you can barely see them all at once without turning your head. I miss Kid Condor, who flies safely beneath

Captain's wing. I even miss Archer von Adonis, the sadistic snot rocket. I don't want to be here, feeling these feelings that hurt too much to put into words. I want my house and I want my mom. I want my trampoline, where I can jump so high that I rocket into the cosmos, far away from my problems on Earth.

The trampoline was the first gift Evelyn ever bought me—and the first time anyone ever bought me a gift so extravagant. I was obsessed. That night, I refused to come in for my bath. I threw an epic tantrum right there on the trampoline while dodging Evelyn's attempts to nab me by the ankle. Her growling threats to dismantle the thing if I didn't calm my tits (my words, not hers) were pretty comical in hindsight. There she was, this little white woman—already in her early fifties by then—dressed in one of her signature flowy dresses, intricately patterned as always, her graying hair flying in her face, Birkenstocks falling off, anklet bells tinkling as if she were on her way to a meditation retreat instead of kicking up dust in a tragic attempt to wrangle the feral boy she'd foolishly welcomed into her home. The next night, Evelyn rolled out two sleeping bags on the trampoline and slept with me under the stars. I think I understood even then that no one had ever loved me that much before—that she'd do something like that for me. I was a hella lucky kid for an orphan.

I lift my arm and trace the outline of the faint burn scar that runs from my bicep to my elbow to the outside of my hand. This lengthy blob of discolored skin predates Evelyn—it predates even my concrete memories, so old and so faint that you can't even see it in such gentle light. I know the shape by heart, though.

Suddenly, I really want to visit Evelyn, just to feel close to her. I can see her in vivid relief, sleeping peacefully in bed. In my head, I run through every careful footfall down the hallway. I wouldn't wake her, only look in on her. Don't push the door open too wide or it will hit that spot where it creaks.

I already feel a tiny bit better. I should go to the house now, shouldn't I? Why not? Maybe hang out on the trampoline for a while. I'm the three-time reigning world champion of extreme trampoline air-drumming, a sport I invented myself, and drumming while my favorite rock music blasts in my headphones always clears my head. If I'm quick about it, I can be there and back before Reed's dad wakes up for Sunday pancakes, a tradition in the Sheldon household since Reed was a little kid. I don't like how tonight's covert comic-booking mission made me feel, and I just want the comfort of being at home—my real home—even if only for an hour or two.

Reed shifts beneath me. His voice comes hesitant. "Hey, Brett? You still awake?"

"Yeah."

"I'm sorry about the fence thing, what I said. It was a dick thing to say and I didn't mean it. I was just freaking out, afraid we were going to get expelled."

We might yet. I mean, Randy Savage might have bloodied his own nose, but I can't shake the feeling that his blood is all over our hands.

It's like trying to swallow one of those massive jawbreakers, but I tell Reed what I'm supposed to tell him. I tell him what I *want* to tell him, even if it's not how I really feel. "It's chill, man. I get it. Tense situation and all."

"It doesn't matter . . . how you look. You're my best bro and . . . you're my *brother*, so—"

My words spill out before I have a chance to edit them. "Ms. Finch gave me a food journal this week. She wants me to write down everything I eat because she thinks I might be eating wrong, like, um . . ." I can't say the next part. I can't say what Reed must be thinking.

My eyes fill. The jawbreaker lodges deeper in my throat. I let the silence lodge deeper, too, afraid if I try to speak, the words will get caught on the way out.

"Brett?"

I swallow hard.

"You don't have to talk about it. It's okay."

Despite my monumental efforts to hide my food problems from Reed, he knows anyway. Of course he knows. Does everyone know? An image of Thandie Gellar's pert body flashes in my mind. I haven't had the nerve to even look at her since our encounter on Monday. I'm so far beneath her—it didn't even occur to her that I invited her to Sabino Canyon because *I* was into her. She thought I was playing matchmaker. What would she think of me if she knew what I do with food? I manage a feeble "Okay. Thanks, dude." I wipe at my tingling nose and roll onto my side.

Reed says, "Red Hots in the pancakes tomorrow?"

I have to smile at this. Reed and I always get to choose what special ingredient goes into the batter. I say, "Hella Red Hots." Even as the words leave my mouth, I'm thinking about how it will feel to write them in my food journal. My smile fades.

In minutes, I hear the measured breath of sleep from Reed's bunk. He's predictable in this way, like a windup toy: all clatter and motion until his gears are spent.

I slide carefully from my bunk, slip into a pair of joggers, and pull a dirty T-shirt over my head. I step into my flip-flops, grab my keys and my phone. I've got the Uber app open even before I've hit the courtyard.

Later, I step lightly down the hallway at Evelyn's house. I stand in her open bedroom doorway. I blink several times until her form—just an outline, then a detail here and there, then a recognizable human being—emerges from the darkness. She's sound asleep, peaceful, and yet the tubes trailing from her nose to the oxygen tank beside her bed remind me that she hasn't actually been at peace for many months. I rub my eyes, blink a few more times. I squeeze my eyes tight and pop them open, determined to edit the offending apparatuses from my vision by sheer will. I want to see her as she was when I was small, her skin not blanched from illness and moonlight but ruddy from the sun, which she could never get enough of whenever she ventured barefoot onto the patio to water her potted plants or read student essays in her favorite deck chair.

I can't make the tubes and tanks go away, no matter how hard I tax my imagination. Her ragged breathing and the bandage over the hole in her throat remind me that her once-strong voice is little more than a drowned rasp. I loved her voice. I loved when she'd read my stories back to me. They always sounded better when she read them. Now she looks like she's been taken captive by Archer von Adonis, that demented dick hole. That's what's happened to her. I'm sure of it. He's experimenting on her in his space lab. Her ankles and wrists restrained, her neck stabbed open by the piercing punch of one of his light-year arrows, he's pumping her full of xyrinium-P complex, fortifying her limbs and erasing her memories of her life here on Earth. When she wakes, she'll be the perfect killing machine . . .

My phone vibrates, shaking me from my fantasies. Just a rando Instagram like. I note the time: four fifteen. I'd better get out back if I want any time on my trampoline. I backtrack to my old bedroom, kneel and pull the duct cover from the floor to retrieve my vodka. I take several swigs, savoring the heat in my chest. The night's events flood through me as if the vodka were laced with them: falling from the fence at school; the awful thing Reed said; getting stuck because I'm fat and horrible;

admitting to Reed that there's something wrong with me, something so awful I can't even say it out loud; Evelyn.

Evelyn. Evelyn. Evelyn.

I replace my contraband and head out the sliding glass door that opens to the back patio. I pass the imprint of my tiny palm in the concrete where Evelyn had new pavers installed when I was nine. I climb up on my trampoline mat, flop onto my back, one arm hooked beneath my neck. My head feels like it could roll away. The sky is straight-up brilliant, every star in the universe right here at my fingertips. I'm floating. I feel the hum in my bones as my propulsion pack powers up. Just have to make a fist to activate the burners and I'll be punching through the cosmos.

I lift my arm above my head, squeeze my hand into a fist.

I squeeze.

Squeeze again.

I let out a small noise of pain. *Please.*

I close my eyes.

Please.

I squeeze my fist once more, digging my nails into my palm.

But nothing happens. I'm still here in the yard that used to be mine, at the house that used to be mine. I'm still here thinking about how many pancakes I can eat before Reed wakes up so he won't actually know how many pancakes I've eaten. I'm still here thinking about the tubes Adonis shoved in my mom's nose and the fountains of blood that sprayed Kid Condor's face when Adonis ran her through the neck with his arrow. I'm thinking I'm scared. I'm thinking I'm scared, I'm scared, I'm scared, I'm scared.

I'm scared.

And this is when I finally start to cry.

CHAPTER SEVEN

I stare at my rapidly wilting pancakes through sandy eyes. The Red Hots leave bloody trails in my syrup. I know I have to take another bite, to finish my plate, to never waste an ounce of Marcus's kindness—but I'm not sure I can, not after what Marcus just said. *You trying to tell me you can't find a place to pack away a second helping?* Ever the cheerful goofball, Marcus grinned and gave his dad-bod stomach a squeeze as he said the words, as if he and I have something in common, like he knows a belly like mine must contain many empty hideaways and he's just the pancake peddler to fill them.

I didn't want to decline. I didn't mean to, I don't think, but just as the second round of pancakes and bacon were coming off the hissing griddle, Reed wandered out of our bedroom in a pair of boxer shorts, yawning and scratching at the back of his head, looking like one of those guys they'd cast in a teen drama where everyone has sex all over the high school—the type of show, I realized, that would certainly cast Thandie Gellar as a lead. My throat closed up, and I wasn't sure I could take another bite, let alone another plateful.

Now my second helping sits atop Reed's first. He's scarfing through the pile like an animal at a trough, as if it means nothing, as if eating is perfectly normal, and I'm wondering if I can make it through what's left on my plate without gagging. Would it kill the kid to put some clothes on once in a while? I take a small bite, push my roiling heartburn down, chew, swallow.

Just five more bites, maybe, and I can be done. I'll clear my plate and take up dish duty, a welcome activity that makes me feel more at home. I was the dedicated dishwasher at Evelyn's house, and the normalcy of the activity still calms me. I even miss the time-consuming work of cooking. Evelyn handled most of the meal prep, of course, but I'd join in at least once a week as we taught ourselves to prepare ever-more-ambitious Mexican and Mesoamerican dishes. Evelyn wanted my culture to be an integral part of our home, and food was the most practical route in for a gringa and a kid regularly *called* a gringo by dick-for-brains jerks who can't feel big unless they're putting down kids like me, kids who can't speak Spanish fluently, kids with Anglo blood, kids without family south of the border, kids who *look* like them but somehow *aren't* like them. Here, though, with Marcus at work most evenings, I don't get many opportunities to do the dishes—and no opportunities to cook. The refrigerator is like a cramped urban landscape of paper, every inch prime real estate for takeout menus.

Marcus reaches across the kitchen bar—there's a dining table in the apartment, but it's only ever used as a place to pile up homework, bills, and phone-charger cords. He roughs up his son's hair, which is already standing on end at cartoonish angles. "Today marks three Sunday pancakes in a row without a call from the dean. I'm proud of you, buddy. The discipline of being on the team is doing you good."

Reed stiffens and his eyes widen before he masters himself. Marcus doesn't notice Reed's alarm. He's already diving into his own breakfast. Reed catches my eye, activating our psychic bro link. We're thinking the same thing: A call from the dean, or worse, the police, could be imminent.

"That, or this one"—Marcus hooks a thumb in my direction, words mangled by the mouthful he's still chewing—"has been a good influence around here." He reaches for the syrup to give his pancakes an extra dousing. "Always so polite, straight As, an eager helper around the apartment. We're lucky to have you, Brett. I'll bet your mom never even learned the dean's name, right?"

Three more bites.

"No," I say, "I don't think so." I hope the embarrassment in my voice rings more sheepish than shameful. Marcus doesn't know how often I've been in trouble right alongside Reed over the years, how little interest I have in being a good influence on anyone. And if he knew about the things Ms. Finch and I talk about? I can't chew and entertain such thoughts at the same time. The syrup glues my teeth together.

Marcus gives me my least favorite kind of eyebrows. "You doing okay, kid? Your appetite is nonexistent and you look a bit—" He raises his arms in front of him and sways in his chair, moaning like the undead.

Stealing in at five thirty for a mere two hours of sleep will do that to a guy.

"You better not get sick right before your birthday. I'm looking forward to seeing you ace that driver's test. Your mom's ride must really be missing the open road."

I manage a feeble smile. "Just didn't sleep too great. I'll be fine."

Marcus isn't convinced, but he lets the vague explanation slide. This, I'm learning, is one of the benefits of living with Marcus. There's no way Evelyn would let me off the hook so easily. She'd be all over me, in fact, holding a hand to my brow, forcing one of her nasty hippie concoctions down my throat, something brewed from leaves that only grow in the

Jiangnan region of China, something smelling of armpits and black tar and . . . Suddenly, I'm holding back tears. *Not again.* Where did these tears even come from? And why do they always come at the most inopportune times? I keep my eyes on my plate, grateful that Marcus's attention is on stealing extra bacon from Reed.

One more bite and I can escape. I'll stand at the sink, my back to the others so they won't notice my reddening eyes, and once the dishes are done, I'll make up a lie about needing a walk to clear the sleep from my head. What I'll really mean is I need to visit the QuikTrip on First to grab some junk food because, despite what I said to Marcus, I'm still hungry. Painfully hungry.

I chew extra carefully, just to be sure my last bite makes it through the constricted canyon of my throat. I push my chair back and move to the goopy mixing bowls in the sink, let the water run hot, hotter, the pain in my hands drawing focus from my stirring emotions and the desperation in my gut. The lighthearted banter of the happy father and son sitting a few feet away barely registers.

At the QuikTrip, I ensure the clerk is distracted, then shove two Snickers bars into my pocket. Snack Snatching is a new game I've been playing lately, though I can't say why. I checked my bank account this morning. Like clockwork, there was the automated monthly deposit from a separate account Evelyn set up months ago. I can afford to buy whatever I want, but for some reason I just don't want to right now.

I move to the next aisle, feigning indecisiveness, pick up a bag of Cheez-Its, put it back, give the clerk a friendly nod as I slip a pack of Twinkies into my pocket. Besides having Nightcrawler's teleportation abilities, the best way to steal is to behave like the kind of guy Marcus thinks I am: friendly, polite, nothing at all to hide. At the register, I clinch my Oscar by paying for a bottle of vitaminwater and an apple. Just an upstanding kid who thinks better of gorging himself on sugary snacks, that's me. After what has felt like an epic quest worthy of the Constellation Corps, I walk out back to eat the rest of my breakfast in an alleyway, a private place where my usually annoying tears are finally welcome company.

CHAPTER EIGHT

The game? Chocolate Box Roulette. The stakes? Same as always: a week's worth of trash duty—which makes no real sense since I don't live here at Evelyn's anymore and she couldn't take the trash out even if she wanted to. Regardless, I'm still pretending I've got a lot riding on tonight's match. I don't want to sound overconfident in the benevolence of fate or anything, but I kind of think the universe owes me this win since it's my birthday. *My birthday.* I thought the day would never come. "My sweet boy is turning sweet sixteen." That's what Evelyn said the day she signed her car over to me, her ragged voice mournful as if every kid who ever turned sixteen got shipped straight off to adulthood never to call or write again. When Evelyn is mushy like this, I'll beat my chest or pump my fist in the air. I'll say something like "Savage sixteen, Evelyn. Your sweet boy is turning *savage* sixteen!" She'll press a sponge to the hole in her neck so the air won't get out and say something even more soppy like, "What happened to my darling little Brett in his Superman cape and Batman undies?" Evelyn's favorite way to deal with my impending adulthood is to embarrass me, her lamentations rarely ending until my hair has been mussed or my forehead has been kissed. Joke's on her, though; I *still* wear Batman undies. I can feel the heat from my brand-new driver's license burning a hole through them now. I can't believe I passed my test this morning; I lost hella points for changing lanes at an intersection, nearly dipping below the 80 percent needed to pass.

I reach into my pocket, pull the license out to stare at it for the millionth time. I look kind of chubby in my picture—which blows—but my hair is hella fly, my euro mullet swooped up in the front. I'm feeling pretty radical about it. Being sixteen is the coolest.

I drop my box of chocolates and my shopping bags full of birthday crap—paper and ribbon and tape and candles—on the floor of my old bedroom. Every time I visit, I miss living here all over again. I miss the view and the flowers blooming—especially the bright orange ones that grow on the portico; don't know what they're called, but they're pretty dope. I miss the desert trails where Evelyn would take me for walks when I was a kid and where I saw my first rattlesnake. More than anything, I miss my trampoline. *The perfect gift for a boy who's always got his head in the clouds.* That's what Evelyn said at the time.

I sit cross-legged on the carpet and carefully unroll the wrapping paper—Spider-Man, naturally. I identify with Peter Parker's plight. Sometimes fighting the guidance of Ms. Finch feels like fighting crime while going through puberty. Peter and I are basically twins. Suddenly I see Reed scaling the fence at school as if his fingertips could take him up a skyscraper. Is it Peter and *Reed* who are twins?

I push the comparison away before it can sour my mood. I cut thoughtlessly, wasting as much paper as I want. *Waste is a mark of the ungrateful, Brett*—that's what Evelyn would say. But I bought all my birthday stuff myself since Evelyn can't. I'll be as indulgent as I please. I wrap up my box of chocolates—a two-pounder because why not?—and wind a ridiculous amount of ribbon around it. I can't remember why, but I didn't like cake when I was little—I didn't like a lot of benign things that must have held upsetting associations with my life before I met Evelyn—so I haven't had a cake on my birthday in years. Chocolate Box Roulette is our tradition instead, but we can't start the game until I unwrap the box and pretend to be surprised.

I toss my scissors and tape into the closet. I gather the trash, shove it in as well, slam the door. Everything neat and tidy. I shake sixteen candles from their box and line them up beside my gift. It looks like a toddler wrapped it. I call out, "Ready, Evelyn!"

From the master bedroom comes the dragging sound of Evelyn's oxygen tank, wheels squeaking as she pulls it down the hall. She appears in the doorway. "We're doing this on the floor, are we?" Her voice comes wheezing, her words more air than consonant and vowel sounds. Her face is lined and drained of color. I try to imagine it without plastic tubes jutting out, but lately seeing the old her—the best her—has grown nearly impossible. I shake off my disorientation, which still comes every time I visit, and force a smile.

Evelyn joins me on the floor. "I wonder what your gift could be." She lifts it, weighing it in her hands. "Definitely a nose-hair trimmer."

We both laugh, but Evelyn doesn't press her sponge to her trachea hole in time and her laugh comes out sounding like a fart, the dangerous kind that makes you want to check your pants. This makes us laugh harder. Sometimes, Evelyn purposely leaves her neck hole uncovered because she knows it makes me smile.

Despite her age, Evelyn used to remind me of those little gymnastics women you see on TV during the Olympics, the type who could drop everything and complete a tumbling pass just to get rid of some pent-up energy. Now, with the oxygen tubes coming out of her nose and the frailty of her frame, she resembles those poor little alien guys being experimented on in the UFO Museum in Roswell, where she took me with my sketchbook when I was going through my alien-obsession phase. *If you're going to be a professional storyteller, Brett, you've got to conduct your research.*

I scoot a bit closer. I always feel better when I sit close enough to look into Evelyn's eyes. It's how I can tell she's still herself; even if her body is shrinking, her eyes remain bright.

Evelyn says, "Open it, champ."

I give her a grin and tear into the paper, wrestling with the ribbons in my best Hulk Hogan shirt-splitting impression. I kind of regret being so extra about it when I wrapped the box. I gasp. "How did you know? Why, it's just what I've always wanted! Thank you!"

I shred the shrink-wrap and lift the lid.

"No peeking at the chocolate map." Evelyn knows I'm a notorious cheater and doesn't want to take any chances. The point of the game is to take turns biting into one chocolate after another until one of us finds the best chocolate in the box: the caramel. You have to gag down whatever shitty chocolates you bite into in the pursuit of glory, though, so choose wisely. One time, I ended up having to eat *two* cherry cordials (cough syrup truffles, I call them), and I still lost the game. I'll often forfeit a turn by choosing a turtle or a toffee—obviously not a caramel—just for the break from the peanut-butter-nougat and coconut-cream nightmares if the game goes epically long.

I toss the lid aside. Evelyn carefully inserts a candle into each of sixteen chocolates on the top tier and tells me to light them. "A little space between the open flames and my oxygen is probably wise." She sings "Happy Birthday," her voice so ragged that I want to tell her to stop, that she doesn't have to. I don't need the song; I don't need it. But I know how much *she* needs it, so I try to be a man about it and I don't say anything.

As the final note limps out, I fill my lungs to capacity. I can't tell Evelyn, of course, because then it wouldn't come true, but all I wish for—all I want in the world—is for her neck to stop farting when she talks, for her energy to come back so I don't have to buy my birthday gifts for myself, so I can move back in and fall asleep knowing she's just on the other side of the wall, not a couple dozen city blocks away. I don't believe in any gods, not even the Inca or Maya ones I'm obsessed with, so this may be my only chance to call upon a force greater than myself to turn things around. I don't waste an ounce of air as I blow out my candles, making damn sure I don't miss even one.

Evelyn is clapping and laughing.

But wait.

The candles spark back to life.

Oh God. Oh no. I bought the *trick* ones. No, *no*.

Evelyn is happier than she's been in months. But something inside me crumbles as those little flames crackle. You have to blow them out on the first try or your wish won't come true. I suck in another breath, pretty sure I'm going to start crying. I blow with all my might. *Don't cry. Don't cry.* Maybe the universe won't notice that the candles relit. Maybe it'll give me another chance. The candles go out; they light again. *No.*

This is when Evelyn notices something is wrong. "Brett? You all right, honey? It's fun, right? Trick candles?"

I'm shaking my head. My shoulders slump. *Don't cry in front of her.* A pressure builds behind my eyes and I'm just so angry, and suddenly I'm slamming my arm into the box of chocolates, scattering them across the floor, one stubborn candle still flaming.

Evelyn gasps. "Brett!"

The carpet begins to smolder. "I'm sorry." I'm momentarily paralyzed, stunned by my outburst. "I'm sorry, I'm sorry." And then I'm leaping from the floor to stomp out the flame, grinding the chocolate into the carpet fibers, knowing that stain will never come out, knowing I've ruined the carpet, knowing I've ruined the night, knowing I've ruined everything.

Chocolate sticks to my sneaker—and something else. Caramel.

I turn from Evelyn so she can't see my face. I stare out the window, my breath heaving. The lights of Tucson blur as my eyes fill with the tears I'm rarely strong enough to hold inside anymore. I clamp a hand over my mouth to keep the sobs from escaping. *Not* in front of Evelyn.

"Brett?" This voice is even worse than her usual gravel-and-sand. The sound of it—the subtle things you can only hear if you're really listening for them—they say I've broken her heart. This is a voice that reminds me that Evelyn is sorry for what's happened to her, that she's sorry for me. How can she be sorry for *me*?

I breathe through my emotions. I blink carefully to test how wet my eyes are. No tears fall, so I turn and sink to my knees, gather the chocolates I haven't ruined yet. "Forty-five-second rule." I don't laugh. Evelyn's neck doesn't fart. I'm putting the chocolates back in their papers when I feel Evelyn's hand on mine. I'm ashamed to meet her eyes. There was a time I'd have been punished for such a tantrum. I might have been grounded or expected to work off the cost of repairs. *Punish me, Evelyn. Punish me, please.* But I know she won't, not now, not ever again. This isn't our relationship anymore, and for a terrifying instant, I hate her for it.

She says, "We don't have to play the game, Brett. It doesn't matter."

How can I tell her she's wrong? How can I call her a liar without hurting her even more than I already have?

I give her a stiff nod and go back to my task. Together, we arrange the chocolates back in the box and close the lid.

Evelyn says, "You want to watch a Marvel movie? I think there's popcorn in the pantry."

I don't want to say no. I don't want to let Evelyn down any more tonight, but I think I just want to be alone. I'm staring at the box of chocolates in front of me and I really just want to be alone. "Can I . . . ? Would it be okay if I was just alone for a little while?"

A pained look crosses Evelyn's face, but then she smiles. She presses her sponge to her neck. "Yes. Yes, of course, my sweet birthday boy. If you change your mind, I'll be lying down in my room. Just come get me, okay?"

I watch as she closes the door behind her.

This is when I pull the lid from my birthday present and shove a dark chocolate something in my mouth—raspberry truffle, maybe. It could be strawberry cream. It doesn't matter.

I chew. Chew and swallow. I lie down on the floor, the box cradled beside me. I suck the sugar from my teeth. And then I choose another.

I choose another. And another.

And then I choose another.

CHAPTER NINE

Reed strolls through Tucson Mall like there's a sale on *Scarface* merch at the Suncoast store. After hiking behind him and Thandie Gellar for ten *goddamn* miles, the two full-on sucking face by the time we piled back into our separate vehicles at the Sabino Canyon visitors' center, I'm about out of energy—and fully sapped of the desire—to chase him.

"Keep up, birthday bro! We gotta get to Suncoast before it closes."

Evidently, there really *is* a *Scarface* sale.

I'm not sure if I'm the best actor ever or if Reed is just too high on Thandie's pheromones to notice my ever-darkening mood. Either way, he thinks I'm having the best day ever. He thinks that he, my best bud, has *given* me the best day ever. What a hero. He can be such an ass sometimes.

We finally checked the Phoneline Trail off our hiking list—so maybe I should be riding high—but I couldn't help but want to throw myself down a cliff as I watched Reed's entire demeanor change around Thandie. Out of nowhere, the dork who meticulously dusts his vintage WWE action figures and regularly watches tutorials to make his house cuter in *Animal Crossing* morphed into the meathead jock, hanging on Thandie's every word, placing his fingertips on the small of her back at every bend as if at any moment she might forget how to walk and tumble down the trail. He even lowered his voice—like, he used a *new* voice. I watched the mating dance begin, and for the first time since I fell for her, I felt something less than utter devotion to Thandie Gellar. It doesn't help that she was every bit as engaged and kind and funny as I imagined she'd be.

I'd like this best day ever to be over.

We're passing the Hot Topic when we're lassoed in by the insistent voice of a smokin' woman at a kiosk marked *Benjamin Lerner Talent*. "Have you ever considered modeling?" The woman thrusts a business card in Reed's face.

Reed's disorientation evaporates as quickly as his boyish grin. He uses the same lower voice he used on Thandie. "You know, I've never thought myself a pretty boy"—he glances to the card—"Kath Purdue of Benjamin Lerner Talent, but I'm listening." He extends his hand. "Reed Sheldon."

"You've got *the look*, you know? California, the beach. A couple inches short, but . . ." The woman actually reaches out and plays with Reed's hair. "A dime a dozen, to be sure, but with the right grooming . . ."

Reed is clearly enjoying himself, and I wonder how long this is going to drag on before either realizes I'm standing here.

I'm saved by a gentle chime over the mall's loudspeakers. *Tucson Mall will be closing in fifteen minutes. Whether you're a fashionista or an outdoor adventurer, we thank you for shopping with us today.*

Reed touches the woman's arm. "I'll tell you what, Kath. I'm going to save this card and think carefully about what you've said. For now, though, I'm afraid I must run. Important birthday surprise for this guy." He hooks a thumb in my direction.

Reed's new bestie actually startles. She literally didn't realize I was standing here. "Oh! Happy birthday."

In no mood to let her off the hook, I give her my best one-word response. "Quite."

Oblivious to the sudden tension, Reed motions me forward and we're back on our trek. Something tells me he's already forgotten the entire exchange—it was a joke, a farce. That same something tells me I'm not going to forget it anytime soon, if ever.

Reed halts just before rounding the corner that will bring Suncoast into view. He presses his back to the wall and motions for me to join him. He lifts a fist as he peers carefully around the corner, the way a soldier might in some badass movie where everyone gets blown up and shot in the face. "All clear." He pulls a bandana from his pocket and reaches for me.

"What's going on?"

"Do I need to define the word *surprise* for you? No peeking." Reed secures the bandana over my eyes, tying it gently behind my head. He takes me by the shoulders. "Ten paces forward. Great. Yeah. Turn to your left. Uh-huh. Thirty paces. That's it. Almost there. Now turn to your left one more time. You ready to completely shit your pants in public?"

"That's exactly what I wanted this year. How did you know?"

Reed pulls the bandana from my eyes, and I have to admit, I'm glad for the youthful power of my sphincter. Behind a pane of plate glass stands a life-sized cardboard standee of one of the greatest comic book heroes of all time. His cape billows out behind him, powerful arms crossed over his swole chest. The look in his eye is one of paternal pride—at least that's what I was going for when I drew the character study. Captain Condor. He's looking at Kid—he's looking at me—and he's really freaking proud to be Kid's dad. I finally put my hanging jaw to work. "How did you . . . ?"

Reed affects his Scarface voice, his only fake voice I can really get behind. "That's what I'm talkin' about, you fuckin' cock-a-roach!" Fully himself again, no longer the suave Lothario on a quest to lose his V-card, Reed pumps his fists in the air, takes a victory lap around a gargantuan potted plant. When he returns, he drapes an arm around me, leans his head on my shoulder, and stares lovingly at Captain. "How'd I do, king?"

Whatever animosity I was carrying has vanished. No one knows me like Reed. No one's there for me like Reed. So what if girls make him stupid? It's not like I fare any better around them. "Absolutely crushed it."

"Hell yeah, I did. Now get your ass over to that window for a selfie."

We take a dozen pictures, posing like heroes, like damsels. In one shot Reed drops to his knees and opens his eyes as wide as they'll go in a look of shock and fear, his gaze directed at Captain's purple trunks.

When we've had our fill of absurdity, Reed pops into the store. He waves at the clerk, a kid I recognize from school. Reed snugs Captain Condor under his arm and walks out like he owns the place. "Shall we head home and find a spot for this big boy in our bedroom?"

I nod, letting myself fully embrace how good—how perfectly right with the universe—I feel right now. We pass the talent scout once again on our way out of the mall, an unfortunate reminder that this feeling can't last, that I'll be lucky if it carries me through the night. I have to take the meager scraps of joy where I find them, though, and this gift? This reminder of who Reed really is?

It's a whole meal.

CHAPTER TEN

Recently, Reed and I streamed this crappy sci-fi movie wherein Oscar Isaac and Natalie Portman get their DNA rearranged by some sparkly alien creature. The whole thing was pretty cringe. Trust me, skip it and watch *Moon Knight* for the eighth time instead (that starscape-rewind scene, am I right?). But at one decent point in the film, Isaac cuts open his buddy's stomach to reveal these fat snakelike creatures—like the guy's organs are rearranging into snakes or something—and these snakes are just writhing around making knots of his insides. It was gross but also the movie's most awesome moment.

This is what my insides feel like right now.

It's the middle of the night and I'm sitting on a boulder at the top of Tumamoc Hill, surrounded by the garbage from tonight's epic drunk drive-thru'ing adventure—well, drunk drive-*to*-ing adventure, seeing as how I went to places without drive-thrus tonight. In the sci-fi movie of my life, this scene is littered with product placements from Panda Express, Wetzel's Pretzels, and Cinnabon.

I turn from the dappled glow of Tucson—which is broken by a pair of saguaro cacti in my eyeline. I reach into my backpack and retrieve my food journal. My next check-in with Ms. Finch is tomorrow, and

I'm determined to have at least a few pages filled for her. Admittedly, I skipped recording several days this week. My birthday is only half recorded, everything up until I arrived at Evelyn's with my box of chocolates.

When I tried to write about my evening at Evelyn's, I didn't like how my pen would get stuck as it moved across the page, like it wanted nothing to do with my tantrum. The couple days I recorded properly didn't include any journaling, just food and times and quantities. Ms. Finch is a good bro, though, so I want to try to tell her the truth tonight. I want to write about the thoughts that flood my brain after I eat like this, the feelings that rarely go away except when I'm eating or drinking—or eating and drinking.

I activate my phone's flashlight and prop it on a makeshift rock easel, then flip past my sketches of Therma and my written entries to find the journal's first empty page. I balance the journal on my lap and record the six items I just downed, all bought with the twenty bucks Marcus left on the kitchen bar. Reed had wrestling practice and was planning to eat with his buddies afterward—all the more for me. My stomach aches a little more with each word. Seeing the act on paper kind of messes with my brain. I think of the concerned face Ms. Finch is always making—the face my Uber driver and Mallory made last time I went drunk drive-thru'ing, the face that the lady behind the register at Cinnabon made this very evening when she saw the other restaurant bags peeking out from my backpack. I reach up to touch my own face. I run my fingers over my brow, which is more ridged than I'd hoped. I can't be certain, but I think I'm making the face right now. It occurs to me that this is totally the face Evelyn would make if she knew what I was doing up here.

I write, *I'm thinking about.*

I write, *Um.*

I write, *FML*.

I look to the Great Cool Ranch Dorito in the Sky and mark the points of Captain Condor's wings. Captain isn't the type to run away when stuff gets hard. I hear his voice echoing across the cosmos. *That's right, Kid. They don't call me Captain Chicken, do they? I believe in you. The Constellation Corps doesn't accept cowards.*

I force my pen to move. The words come more easily than expected. I write about what happened when we were covert comic-booking. I write about how Reed might have been right to say what he did, about how I'm afraid I'll never have sex because what if girls don't like me the way they like Reed? I write about Sunday pancakes and about Kath Purdue of Benjamin Lerner Agency. I write about how girls never see me when I'm around Reed. I write about how I wish girls would see me. I don't write about all the drinking. I want to write the truth about what happened with Chocolate Box Roulette, but I've never been more ashamed of anything in my life, so instead I write about how I don't want to go to Evelyn's house anymore, but I also want to go to Evelyn's house every day. The contradiction confuses me.

Evelyn's house.

My house.

Here's where I get stuck. Usually when my thoughts wander to such dark territory, I just take another swig of vodka, but I never risk bringing my bottle out of my room. I kind of screwed myself by doing this up here above the world. I try to write some more, but I can't move my hand; it trembles in place.

I want to write, *I'm lonely even when my best bro is on the bunk beneath me.*

I want to write, *I don't know how I'm supposed to survive this.*

I want to write, *I don't want to be an orphan again.*

But despite what Captain Condor thinks, I *am* a coward. I can't write these things, just as I can't say them out loud. Saying them, writing them—it would make everything I'm going through with Evelyn real, and I don't want real, not if real feels like this. I'll take the snakes inside my belly any day over the pain throbbing in my chest right now. It feels like Archer von Adonis, that pube plucker, has strapped me into his cadet-constrictor apparatus. He's squeezing the air from my lungs like when he kidnapped Kid Condor and swaths of other cadets right from their dormitory. Only a handful made it back alive. I look to the southwest and count the stars of Adonis's belt. One, two, three. I hear his wicked cackle as my heart bursts.

My pen rips the page, slipping under the tension in my hand. I slap the journal closed, let it clatter to the gravel at my feet. I pound my fists into my rocky perch, savoring the pain that lances up my forearms. I imagine the entire boulder crumbling like it would if Kid Condor punched it with the brechenium gauntlet his birth father nestled beside him in the escape pod just before jettisoning his son into space during Monos's last moments.

I'm hungry.

I grab the Panda Express bag discarded in the dirt. A quick sweep produces the fortune cookie I'd abandoned. Just the weight of it in my hand makes me feel better. I push Evelyn from my mind, tear away the wrapper, and breathe in the scent of the little treat, which actually makes me smile. I break it open, carefully setting its pieces in my lap while I read my fortune—three simple words: *Ask your mom.*

A classic.

CHAPTER ELEVEN

Ms. Finch glances over the lists of food in my journal—one page, then the next. Though the central air is totally killing it in her office, my armpits go moist. My mouth compensates by going dry. I'm bouncing on Ms. Finch's posture-ball chair—bouncing, bouncing—examining her face for what Evelyn would call *telling expressions*. Because she's like thirty, Ms. Finch has had many years to perfect her poker face. Her brow tells me she's engaged with the material before her, but she doesn't seem alarmed. Walking into her office today felt different than usual in a bad way, more like walking into Dean Ricamora's office, but Ms. Finch's posture tells me maybe I'm not in such hot water after all.

She turns to the fifth page, where my feelings should be—the page I filled at the top of Tumamoc Hill. But all she sees is a blank sheet, skinny blue lines split by a pink line at the left-hand margin. She turns another page, another. Both blank. She closes the journal and sets it beside her on her shabby couch. She clasps her hands on her lap.

I'm bouncing, bouncing.

"Brett," she says. "Tell me what you think about your lists here. How was the activity for you?"

I gulp in an effort to wake my salivary glands. My mouth feels too parched to form words, and the missing page from my journal, which is folded tight in my pocket, seems to smolder, its molecules heating up as it fights the fabric of my jeans to escape. Keeping this page from Ms. Finch feels like lying to her. I imagine the page combusting, my pants burning right off as I streak wildly through the halls toward the water fountain. *Liar, liar, pants on fire.*

I say, "It was okay, I guess. I mean, like, I didn't really *like* it. It made me feel kind of bad. I know you've been concerned about my eating, but I was pretty chill about it until . . ." I'm hesitant to say more—this conversation already feels like waving a white flag. But if I'm not going to give Ms. Finch my journal page, I owe her at least this much honesty. "I guess, like, I wasn't really concerned about what I was eating or how I was eating, but lately . . . I don't know." My eyes dart from the framed photo of Toast, Ms. Finch's Queensland heeler, to the potted succulents in the windowsill. Anything to distract me from the words that come next. "Seeing what I ate written down like that, it felt the same as when I saw Mallory in the drive-thru. Eating is . . . Is there something wrong with me?"

Ms. Finch leans forward. "Sometimes our coping behaviors hurt us more than the things that cause them."

When I was new to Evelyn's care, I was obsessed with the Eric Carle version of the story of the little Dutch boy with his finger in the dike; I'd force Evelyn to read it to me every night until she begged to read the one about the cranky ladybug or the kid making pancakes instead. I feel like that Dutch boy now. For months I've been holding my finger in my dam, but the cracks are widening, fissures opening. I'm running out of fingers, so much water getting through. I'm about to start leaking again.

I grit my teeth, grab my mouth to hold it closed like on my birthday, but this time the sobs pummel through. I can't believe this is happening, not here. I turn my back to Ms. Finch, wipe frantically at my eyes. "Sorry."

I sense Ms. Finch behind me before I feel her hand on my shoulder. "Authenticity is never something to apologize for, Brett."

I'm the only kid I know who cries every day. Crying every day isn't normal; I know this. Ms. Finch doesn't want to tell me something is wrong with me because she's trying to be nice. But look at me. I'm a total freak.

Ms. Finch hands me a box of tissues. I wipe at my face and blow my nose. I don't think I've ever hated myself as much as I do right now. I don't want to be this guy anymore. I want to be like Kid Condor—strong and brave and ready to kick ass at a moment's notice even though he's a tragic orphan. When did I stray so far from the Kid Condor I've always been? I think of the Condor boys up there defending the universe every day without fail. I gather my courage.

Ms. Finch watches me from beside her bookcase as I walk around the desk.

I retrieve my journal and open it to where the missing page should be, lay it on Ms. Finch's desk, and fish the missing sheet from my pocket. I unfold and smooth my journal entry, pull a length of tape from Ms. Finch's dispenser, and affix the page to its rightful place. I close the notebook and hand it to Ms. Finch, then sink into the couch and stare at my sneakers. It's done now.

Ms. Finch sits beside me and turns to the crinkled page. After a few moments, she gives me a thoughtful glance. "You stopped writing when your mom came up."

"I don't want to write about her."

We sit in silence for several minutes, my breath still shuddering.

Finally, Ms. Finch says, "Brett, do you believe you might have a problem with food?"

I don't want to, but I nod.

"Will you tell me what you think the problem is, in your own words?"

I pull my brows together. Ms. Finch raises hers. We both know I'm not ignorant. My mind fills with that just-right word—*binge*—as big as a billboard. I realize I'm scribbling it on my thumb, over and over. Last year, at the last-day-of-school bash, I overheard some girls talking about Mallory when they saw her take a doughnut and disappear behind the math building. *That fat bitch. You know being a fat bitch is classified as an eating disorder now, right?* Laughs all around. *Binge eater, that's what she must be. You can't get that big without shoving it in your face twenty-four seven.*

I say, "I eat too much."

Ms. Finch just stares at me. This is her super-effective trick to make me keep talking.

"What I do . . . I think it might be an eating disorder. I don't know." This is the first time I've said the words out loud, and immediately my stomach monster wakes from his slumber. I don't even know what I'm feeling right now—sickness or hunger?

"Would you consider seeing a therapist? I can set you up with someone who can help you understand what you're doing and help you stop if you decide you should."

My queasiness is replaced by fear. "Can't you be my therapist? I'll talk about Evelyn if I have to. I don't want to talk to anyone else."

Ms. Finch angles toward me. "I don't mean to minimize what you're going through, Brett, but there are dozens of students in similarly difficult situations. School counselors can't provide therapy. We aren't qualified, and there aren't enough hours in the day to meet the needs of every student who's struggling."

"But what about our check-ins?"

"They're merely that—check-ins. I'll still be here. But a therapist can give you the kind of focused attention you need. They can help you get to the bottom of why you're eating as you are, and they'll have the expertise to help you. One of my jobs is to facilitate this sort of arrangement."

I'm thinking of Marcus. He's a real good dude, but what would he think of this? "Do you need an adult to sign papers?"

"Yes. You'd be treated on your guardian's insurance."

I can't involve Marcus, no way. I can't stand him thinking about my food problems, let alone paying for a shrink. I picture the pain in Evelyn's eyes if she were to find out about something like this. Her only son in treatment for an *eating* disorder?

I say, "Is there another way? I don't want to involve any adults. Reed's dad doesn't know about any of this, and—"

"I think a therapist would be best, but if you want to try an alternative, there's an Overeaters Anonymous group that meets every Wednesday night in the Methodist church off Fort Lowell. You know the one?"

Overeaters Anonymous. I want to rewind this conversation. I want to lie and deny. But this isn't what the Condor boys would do, even if they dared tinker with Professor Verist's Time Twister, which is kept under strict lock and key at Constellation Corps' headquarters.

"It's a chance to meet others like you and talk about what drives your behavior. You might gain some valuable insights from those who've been there. You can bring your journal with you if you want. You might feel brave enough to talk about some of the things you're writing about. Or you don't have to say anything at all. You can just listen. You can go alone or bring a friend along if that would make you feel more comfortable."

Reed and I haven't talked about my food problems since the night of our covert comic-booking mission, but he was cool with it. He's always been there for me. Any hero is braver with his trusty sidekick at his shoulder. I can do this, right?

"Okay," I say, shrugging like it's no big thing. "Why not?"

"This is a big step you're taking, Brett. Are you proud of you?"

This is one of Ms. Finch's favorite phrases, so much so that she had *R U Proud of U?* screen printed on T-shirts.

I give her a nod.

"You can do better than that."

I mumble, "I'm proud of me."

"Weak sauce."

I raise my voice and puff out my chest. "I'm proud of me."

"I don't think you mean it."

I leap from the couch and pump a fist in the air. "I'm proud of me! Did you hear that? I'm proud of me!"

Ms. Finch grins.

Much to my surprise, I do, too.

CHAPTER TWELVE

Marcus is more observant than he lets on. Sure, he plays the part of oblivious overworked dad pretty well, giving Reed and me a great deal of personal latitude to live our best lives, but his liberal approach is actually a well-thought-out choice, not a sign of neglect. I know this is true because one day I got curious and opened some of the dog-eared parenting books lined up on the top shelf of the bookcase in the living room. The underlined passages spoke to a parenting model that stresses minimal control and correction. It's not about letting your spawn run wild, exactly, but about giving your kid the freedom to make good choices and trusting him to do so. Not sure the approach has done Marcus any favors, what with Reed's history of troublemaking and my penchant for sneaking out in the middle of the night, but let no one accuse Marcus of not caring. He certainly exemplifies the single-dad clichés you see on TV by showing up to all of Reed's sports events and meeting with Dean Ricamora whenever Reed finds himself knee-deep in detention swamp.

Reed is lucky, I often think, and maybe I am, too. Evelyn would never have let me live here if she felt Marcus wasn't up to the task. This is why I know Reed is in for a fresh lecture on expectations—and that he'll be signing one of Marcus's "responsibility contracts," a non-legally-binding and therefore essentially meaningless document—when Marcus walks into the kitchen and hits the play button on the answering machine. He's just woken from day-sleeping, his hair plastered up on one side like a wave, his stubble as long as he ever lets it grow. In an hour he'll be on his way to his late shift at the factory.

Reed stiffens, almost drops his Switch Pro controller. Reed and I have just sold our turnips for hella bells on *Animal Crossing*, basically getting rich as fuck, but the voice of Ricamora's secretary knocks the wind out of our revelry. Can Marcus please give the school a call at his earliest convenience?

Reed checks the machine daily in an effort to delay Marcus finding out about his myriad acts of delinquency—a pointless endeavor because after failing to reach Marcus on the landline, the school invariably calls his cell—but Reed must have been too distracted this afternoon. He literally pulled me from the pool when he got home from practice, dragged me into the apartment still dripping. Hadn't I checked Discord? If the price for turnips hadn't been so good (590 bells!) as to drown out all other thought or good sense, this unfortunate turn of events might not be happening.

I whisper, "Covert comic-booking?"

Reed grimaces. "Security camera. My license plate was on file."

Marcus pours himself a bowl of Fruity Pebbles and drops two slices of bread into the toaster. He doesn't speak, but when Reed finally risks glancing over the peninsula, Marcus gives him a look that says *I hope you're already composing your apology letter*. Another disciplinary activity Marcus is famous for. The worst punishment a parent like Marcus doles out is an exhaustive series of exercises in personal growth and self-reflection.

When his toast pops, Marcus scrapes it with a layer of Nutella, a product Reed finds disgusting but I'd happily eat from the jar. Marcus brings his breakfast into the living room, props his bare feet on the battered coffee table. He eats slowly. Very slowly. He keeps his eyes on Reed the whole time. (I guess making Reed squirm is another punishment, harmless in the long run but nerve-racking in the moment.)

When the three of us are together, the apartment is never this quiet. Sure, Marcus acts like a grown man when he has to, but he's still as obsessed with video games and WWE as we are, so these little windows of time are usually raucous, spent packing in quality dad time before Marcus has to leave for work.

Reed quietly navigates our island, his avatar decked in full competitive wrestling gear, fishing aimlessly. He reels in a sea bass, a tin can. I casually pick up my Earth sciences textbook from the coffee table and begin reading about geothermal power. (Don't quiz me on geothermal power; none of the words are sinking in.) I'm not the one in trouble, I know, but that's what worries me. If Reed was called into Ricamora's office, or worse, dragged there by security, why wasn't I? Why am I not sharing the blame?

Finally, Marcus stands and reenters the kitchen. He washes his dishes, with far more care than they need, and retreats to his room for his shower.

The moment we hear the water running, I say, "What the hell happened?"

Reed breathes deeply, deflating more than usual with the release. "They tried to make me give you up, but of course I wasn't going to do that. They know it was you who was with me—who else would it be?—but without the proof, you're scot-free."

"What about you, though?" I can't let Reed take the blame for what we did together, plus whatever extra punishment he might receive for refusing to rat me out.

"It's not that big a deal. You know Ricamora and I go way back. He thought the whole thing was kind of amusing, actually. I've got lunch detention for two weeks, which is nothing, and I had to surrender the keycard. Turns out keycard usage is logged by the evil Skynet, so he knew that's how we got in."

That much is probably for the best. But how is it possible that Reed's punishment is so light? Stealing a keycard, breaking in. Everyone knows Reed is a charmer, but he must have given the performance of his life to come out so intact.

I say, "I'll talk to Ricamora tomorrow. I don't want you to do all the time if we were partners in the crime."

Reed looks at me like I just drop-kicked a kitten. "You sure as fuck won't. I didn't go to all the trouble to work my magic so you can get your ass in lunch prison, too. Besides, I'll need someone on the outside to do my bidding—move the drugs, carry out the hits and whatnot, keep an eye on my lady."

I wince at the reference to the lady I've scarcely turned my gaze from all semester, but of course Reed doesn't notice.

"Trust me," he says. "It's fine."

I shake my head, resigned. "All right, I'll keep my trap shut, but is your dad going to be pissed? This is kind of bigger than your usual fare."

"Nah, Dad's easy. He's always been Good Cop, and since Bad Cop is guilty for being out of the picture, the worst she'll do is visit to make sure I'm not a career criminal yet—win-win." Reed groans as his avatar pulls another tin can from the ocean.

While I'm stoked Reed will get to see his mom, I'm worried that if she flies in right away, I might miss my chance to ask him to come with me to Overeaters Anonymous on Wednesday. Whenever she's in town, he stays with her at her hotel, enjoying room service and pay-per-view, whatever he can squeeze out of her guilty conscience. I'm mortified to ask, but I better not waste any time. Even if Reed's mom comes tomorrow, maybe he'll still go with me if we've set a plan.

"Not to change the subject," I say, "but to change the subject."

Reed laughs. "Back to you?"

"Exactly. I was talking with Ms. Finch today, you know, about my food journal, and she thought . . . she figured it might be good if I . . . I guess I'm going to try—"

"Use your words, bruh."

"She thinks maybe Overeaters Anonymous could help me, so I'm going to give it a try. This week. On Wednesday."

Reed lets out a whoop, slaps me on the back. "I'm proud of you, man. Handling your shit. I'm coming along, right?"

I grin, my anxiety lifting. I was so afraid to ask, but of course I didn't have to ask. This is Reed we're talking about. "Thanks, buddy."

"No thanks necessary. This, my man, is a job for your best bro, and I've got my eye on a corner office."

CHAPTER THIRTEEN

Imagine the beigest church you've ever seen and you'll have an idea of what we're dealing with here. The church rises from beds of low cacti, dirt, and gravel—a practical landscape in a desert city, so nondescript that I wonder if Reed and I are even in the right place. Isn't this the latest abandoned strip mall in town? But I guess the church *should* be nondescript. I watch movies. Anonymous meetings are all about making yourself known to unknown people who will never actually know you. Anonymous. That's what they call it when you show up to a support group in a Methodist church and talk about your most shameful secret to people who swear to keep it a secret. We hear you but we don't. We understand you but we've never met. Who aren't you, again? I'm afraid of what's to come, so I cling to this word. Anonymous, anonymous, anonymous. Anonymous means I can edit these panels out of the comic book of my life if they suck.

Leaving the fatiguing heat and frenzied rush hour noises of Fort Lowell behind, I enter the church, Reed at my heels. The hallway before us is eerily dim and quiet, cold in the way air-conditioned spaces always are without warm bodies around to counter the refrigeration. I immediately regret forgetting my hoodie. I hope no one notices such a mistake; I might get my Tucsonan card revoked.

We stride forward. The walls are littered with children's drawings of Jesus, die-cut crosses, and lilies in colors straight out of a Crayola box. These bulletin boards make me feel smaller than I am. They make me wish I believed in a god, someone—anyone—who could make everything go back to the way it was before Evelyn started going in and out of the hospital, before it was decided I was better off with Reed's dad, before Evelyn said things like *You need to be able to concentrate on your schooling*, before she said things like *I can't have you always taking care of me; you're the one who's supposed to be taken care of.*

I walk until I find a set of stairs—these sorts of meetings always happen in basements on the big screen. I glance over my shoulder to make sure Reed hasn't disappeared. I wouldn't have made it this far if not for him. I flash back to the parking lot: My hand was on the door handle of his pickup. I wasn't sure if I had it in me to open it. He'd already killed the engine. We were sweating, probably minutes from death if we stayed in that cab. I wanted to say maybe we should call the whole thing off and go home. Reed said, "I'm not getting out if you're not. I can turn this key and we can go home right now, but you have to say it if that's what you really want."

I didn't say anything.

We descend the stairs.

The light shining from below is too white to be natural. This is bunker lighting, limited-escape-route lighting. After a few steps, my nose registers the lacy scent you'd expect to find deep in your great-aunt's closet—a sickening mix of spice and flower petals only someone who lived through the Great Depression could find alluring. I rub my sweaty hands on my pants.

We emerge from the stairwell into a room of painted brick, an eclectic space characterized by hand-me-down furnishings that might once have resided in rooms aboveground. A couch the color of baby diarrhea sags against one wall. The few pieces of artwork—posters of impressionistic rowboats abandoned by the tide—are hung in silver plastic frames, the kind that pull apart into four separate pieces. The images are bleached from hanging in direct sunlight in a former life.

The assembled population is even more distressing. I'd give anything to blast through the ceiling like Kid Condor with his gauntlet. This room? It's full of middle-aged *women*. There's not a man in sight. Not a single teenager. These women strain inside stretchy pants; they smile beneath hairstyles you'd see in old-school sitcoms or behind bank counters, the type of women you'd find throwing cordless phones at Tony Soprano. I take a step back and bump into Reed. These women definitely own cats.

Reed says, "You okay, bud?"

I whisper, "We need to go."

But it's too late. A frizzy-haired woman wearing a denim jumpsuit has already made eye contact. She's much thinner than the others, yet the planes of her face still hang heavily, as if she knows personally the weight the other women carry. Her smile is too kind, eager, like a nursery school teacher trying to coax you off your mom's leg. This is the type of woman who will follow me up the stairs if I try to bolt, so instead I take a breath.

Reed nudges me forward.

The frizzy-haired lady stands before a buffet table covered in colorful pamphlets and books. More pamphlets line the wall in a plastic rack.

A Commitment to Abstinence.

Before You Take That First Compulsive Bite.

Where are the cookies? I imagined there'd be cookies.

Is Food a Problem for You?

Of course there are no cookies.

The frizzy-haired lady takes my hand. Can she feel the trembling in my fingers? She wouldn't tell anyone if she did—anonymous, anonymous, anonymous.

She says, "Welcome, boys. I'm Tina."

My tongue feels like chalk. "Brett. I'm looking for . . . Is this . . . ?"

"Overeaters Anonymous."

I'd hoped I'd wandered into a Christian ladies' knitting circle, even if the pamphlets proved I was in the right place. The women gather around a rectangular conference table in the center of the room, some already settled in a mix of metal folding chairs and wheeled office chairs. Engrossed in their various conversations, most ignore us, but two—one well acquainted with hairspray and the other with Pepto-pink makeup—glance our way, their expressions curious.

Tina is still shaking my hand. Shaking, shaking.

I bring my gaze back to the table. It's not as scary to examine the literature—it can't look back.

Maintaining a Healthy Weight.

Members in Relapse.

I don't belong here.

Now Tina holds me with both hands, the way you would some dying person. Her eyes are kind but sunken. I wonder if she's ever allowed out of this dungeon to feel the sun on her face.

Reed steps forward to save me. He points a thumb to his chest. "The best buddy."

Tina gives his arm a good rattle, then addresses me again. "It's your first time. I can always tell, especially with men. You get so nervous."

Anonymous, anonymous, anonymous.

I say, "I'm not sure if—"

"You're not sure if this is for you. I promise it can help." She gestures up and down her frame. "Look at me. I'm a compulsive overeater, but I've abstained for four years."

Abstained? Seems like the type of word you'd hear from a shopaholic or a chronic masturbator.

Tina motions for us to follow her to the conference table. "You've picked a good day to start. Once a month we review the twelve steps and twelve traditions."

The table is full—ten women altogether. A woman whose pendant is lost between her breasts moves to make room for Reed and me to sit together. I put a hand to my chest, needing to feel the relative solidity.

A woman in a billowing floral blouse sits at the head of the table, her face pinched up like she's chewing on a Sour Patch Kid. Wearily, like a teacher in seventh period, she says, "Welcome to our new arrivals. Will you ladies share your books so the two can read when it's their turn?"

Even Reed's relaxed façade breaks here. He hates when our teachers ask him to read aloud. When we were placed in that kindergarten reading group, I was put there because I'd never been to school before. Reed, on the other hand, would soon be diagnosed with dyslexia.

I say, "It's fine. We don't—"

Tina speaks up. "I'll share with you."

This is like all those end-of-the-world movies where a meteor careens toward Earth. You want to get out of the way, but you can't. You want to stop it, but you can't. "I'll read for the both of us," I say. "My buddy's just here because I didn't want to come alone."

The woman at the head of the table shrugs. "Suit yourselves." She opens her book. "Let's begin by reciting the twelve traditions. Marilyn? Can you pass the boys one of the cards?"

The woman who made room for us passes Reed a laminated sheet. I want to tell him I'm sorry, that he can leave before he has to witness any of this. I want to tell *myself* I can leave. I *can* just stand up and leave, right?

I glance over the first of twelve numbered statements on the sheet, the words making no sense. We're mumbling. Reed's voice, my voice, they're mercifully lost beneath the conviction of those around us. "Our common welfare should come first; personal recovery depends upon OA unity. For our group purpose there is but one ultimate authority—a loving God as He may express Himself in our group conscience."

Is Overeaters Anonymous a Christian thing? The irony isn't lost on me. Mere minutes ago, I was wishing I could count on a god to make everything okay, but the fact that these women rely on God renders them all the more foreign. How could I have been so stupid? Maybe I shouldn't have relied on depictions in movies, which had me imagining that twelve-step programs were for social deviants and screwups, not people with closets full of Sunday hats.

We mumble through a few more traditions. All eyes turn toward me as we recite number five. "Each group has but one primary purpose—to carry its message to the compulsive overeater who still suffers."

All I have to do is stand up, I think. Reed will grin in his trouble-maker way and say something immature and horrible like *Guzzle balls, ladies!* and we'll be running for the sunlight above. But I don't move.

When we get to the end of the list, the woman with the sour face says, "If you want to share your personal stories while we review the steps, you can, but remember not to name any specific foods, as these may be trigger foods for someone else."

Trigger foods?

"My name is Susan and I'm a compulsive overeater. I've abstained for four days."

Oh God. Do we all say it out loud?

Susan examines her book. "Step one: We admit that we are powerless over food—that our lives have become unmanageable." I know her words apply to me, but something about hearing them from this woman in this place surrounded by these people—something fundamental inside me breaks. I look from one participant to another. The ruddy cheeks, the Stay Puft arms. Tina's goose-like neck, the slight wattle beneath her chin from some long-ago time before abstinence emptied her stretched skin. I resist the urge to touch my face or my arms. I concentrate on my hands, my decidedly thin wrists.

I try to slow my breathing as one woman after another takes her turn to read. I'm breathing too hard. Can they hear me? I'm not moving, but I feel like I need to slow down. Why can't I slow down?

"I'm Ann. I'm a compulsive overeater."

"I'm Carol. I've abstained for seven months."

"I'm Stephanie and I relapsed today."

One of the members—Lindsay? Sharon?—she tears up as she talks. "We admit to God, to ourselves, and to another human being the exact nature of our wrongs." It's like we've been banished here for a time-out, in trouble for getting fat. Reed squeezes my shoulder. Everything's fine. I'm fine.

It's my turn. Tina hands me her book. She points to the passage about the eleventh step. I open my mouth. Close. Open.

Tina whispers, "Start by introducing yourself."

My tongue could take a layer of paint off a wall. "I'm Brett." I shove the next words through. "I'm a compulsive overeater."

No, *no*. Why did I say it?

I'm afraid I might cry if I don't plow forward. "We, um . . . we seek through prayer and meditation to improve our conscious contact with

God as we understand Him, praying only for knowledge of His will for us and the power to carry that out." I make it through a few more sentences—words about hearing what God wants—before my voice fails.

The room is engulfed in a terrifying silence.

Then Reed takes the book from my hand. He picks up where I left off. He trips over several consonants and a vowel or two, but he doesn't look up or stop reading. He merely pauses to swallow, giving himself the time he needs to work out a troublesome word.

When he finishes, Reed passes the book back to Tina and she reads about the twelfth step. I don't know what she says. I only hear my own voice echoing in my head. *Compulsive overeater, compulsive overeater.* I'm seeing the look on Reed's face, like he's in pain for me. I put Reed through this nightmare, but he's still sorry for me and I don't want him to be.

I struggle past the ringing in my ears. Tina is saying something about "first time" and "scared." What is she saying?

"But now this is my favorite part of my week. I know there's one place in the world where everyone gets it, where I won't be judged. If I didn't have this, I might go off the deep end whenever things get stressful. This week, for instance, I had some struggles with my daughter. I want to bring her back to our meetings, but after her accident . . ." Tina smiles one of those fake brave smiles I'm becoming expert in. "Well, she's deep in her teen-rebellion phase."

A few light laughs.

"Anyway, I bought several trigger foods and just stood there in the kitchen staring at the grocery bags. Finally, instead of opening the door to addiction, I took those foods—one at a time—and placed them in the trash compactor."

I imagine the squishing sounds as a box of Bagel Bites is reduced to the size of a fifty-cent piece, the crunching noise as a box of Cookie Crisp sees its untimely demise.

"Each time I hit the compact button, I thought of one of you girls and told myself I'd make it until Wednesday. On Wednesday, I'd feel powerful again—powerful enough to be a mother to a teenager."

The ladies' smiles are playful, many glancing our way like they know exactly how it feels to want to put your kid up for adoption every once in a while.

"I was thinking," Tina says, "if I could make it until Wednesday, I could tell my friends what was going on and I wouldn't have to eat my trigger foods. Better still, when you brave women—" Tina glances to me. "People, I mean. When you tell your stories, I know I'm not alone. We all feel the same things and struggle in the same ways. Loneliness can act as a personal chef if you let it feed you."

Murmurs and nods.

A few others speak, but I can't bear to listen. I just want it to be over.

The circle stands and holds hands. Even at their annual Black Holes and Bonding Retreat, no one in the Constellation Corps would pull this "Kumbaya" crap. Should I run? I'm on my feet, at least, one step closer to escape. I glance to the posters of the beached rowboats, each so securely stuck in its bluff of sand that it might never ride the waves to freedom again. I'm thinking about what I said, those words I can never take back—*compulsive overeater*. It's far too late to run now.

Reed's grip comes stronger than I could have guessed, not moist and timid with the embarrassment I feel. Tina takes my other hand. The circle recites that famous mantra about God giving you serenity and helping you change some things and accept other things. I hate these words and I hate these women—these ugly, disgusting, *fat* women. Fuck them. Fuck this. All their talk about abstinence? It's like they're in a race to see who will break first, like they're competing to see who will fuck up and say *Hot Pocket* or *Little Debbie* and be banished forever.

When Reed and Tina drop my hands, I immediately start spelling on my thumb. My movements are warp speed. But the trembling won't stop.

Women mingle; some move toward the stairs. One flops onto the couch and thumbs at her phone. I'm not sure how, but Reed and I find ourselves at the table of pamphlets again, Tina at our side. "Please come back next week . . . Men never come back . . . There's a meeting in North Central that might have some men in it . . . Will you come back? If not here, maybe there . . . Please . . . Back . . ." She presses a thick manila envelope into my hands. "Reading about the experiences of other men helps."

"Uh-huh. Yeah." I thank Tina. I'm pretty sure I do, at least. Then I'm moving toward the stairs. It's almost over. It's almost done.

But then a figure emerges from the stairwell—rainbow jelly bracelets, hair as bright as Play-Doh. Oh no.

Mallory hasn't noticed me yet. She looks to Tina. "Ready, Mom?"

This is when I forget whatever word it was that made me think I could edit these panels out of my life. Even a noob knows you can't edit out panels once they're drawn.

CHAPTER FOURTEEN

The envelope of pamphlets Mallory's mom gave me rests between Reed and me in the cab of his Chevy—flap open, swatches of faded pastel paper peeking out. I'm trying not to look, but the package refuses to be ignored. I'm afraid of what lurks inside. Not that anything could be worse than the pointed and knowing look Mallory gave me just before I finally found the strength to run up the stairs. Who am I kidding? Strength didn't carry me up those stairs. Fear did. Mallory's arrival had me in full fight-or-flight, and somehow going all WWE on a roomful of ladies didn't seem like the more practical of my two options.

Reed pulls out of the church parking lot and accelerates, jostling the cab as he guns it west on Fort Lowell. The worst of the pamphlets slips from its manila prison: *To the Man Who Wants to Stop Compulsive Eating.* The pamphlet looks about a million years old, just like all those women sitting around the table back in the Methodist church. The paper is yellowed and bent, and I wonder how many guys have pulled this very pamphlet from the wall only to shove it back in the display because they were afraid someone might see them reading it. I still feel Tina's hands gripping mine, begging me to come back for the next meeting, telling me how not alone I am. But that's the problem, isn't it? They all saw.

They all know now, all those strangers who took turns crying or talking about abstinence or reading from that book they treat like a Bible.

The silence is underscored by the squeak of Reed's brakes as he slows for a stoplight. Any other time he'd be chattering nonstop about what new part of Thandie he got to heavy pet for the first time or whatever video game release date is coming up. Awkward silence isn't something Reed and I do, and somehow I feel bringing him with me tonight has harmed our friendship in a way I can't define, some way that makes my stomach hurt.

I crane my neck out the window, searching for the Condor boys. A warm breeze dries the beads of sweat from my temples. The air smells of exhaust and Rocco's Chicago Pizza, whose patio is only a few hundred yards from where we idle at Broadway and Treat. I will the scent away.

I turn my attention to Kid Condor. He should be just past the constellations of Hot Dog Jesus and Cheesy Gordita Crunch, directly east of Licorice Rope and Billy Bob's Big-Ass Bacon Burger, at the northern side of the Great Cool Ranch Dorito in the Sky. But I can't see him; the lights of downtown are a curtain drawn on all my pals residing past the exosphere.

Everything's okay up there—I know this—but my heart quickens anyway. Has that butt pimple Archer von Adonis struck again? Did he run Kid through with one of his light-year arrows, just as he did to Evelyn's neck? Kid is okay, right? I'm being stupid, thinking he might be in trouble; I know this. I know what's real and what isn't, that I'm being fanciful. That's the word Evelyn would use: *fanciful.* But I can't lose Kid Condor. Not tonight. Not after what just happened.

As Reed punches the pickup into gear and moves through the intersection, I lean forward, craning to see southwest, past the U of A and its football field, lights brighter than the daytime sun. Archer von Adonis should be somewhere over Wasson Peak, but he's nowhere in sight. I'm relieved to say I can make out the three points of the Great Cool Ranch Dorito, at least. If the Great Cool Ranch Dorito is there, that means Captain Condor is there, and if Captain Condor is there, that means Kid Condor is there—they all share the same westernmost star. Everyone's in place. Even Archer von Adonis must be right where he belongs. So why won't my panic ease?

I hear Ms. Finch's voice in my mind, something she said months ago. *Face reality, Brett; don't hide behind your fictions.*

But what if reality is worse than fiction?

Then face it bravely.

Archer von Adonis didn't make that hole in Evelyn's neck, did he? A tracheal tube did.

And so I set the Condor boys aside. I face my here and now. This panic? It's not for Kid. It's for me. Those women were horrifying fun house mirrors, and I didn't want to look. Why did I look? Why? A wail builds inside, pummeling my ribs. I put a hand to my chest, as if I could feel the vibrations.

Reed pulls a pack of Reds from his shirt pocket and props a cigarette between his lips. He lights up. The cherry glows too brightly—more pollution to obscure the stars. His mom is going to freak when she finds out he's smoking again. That's the point, though, isn't it? Reed takes his athleticism seriously; he doesn't actually smoke, not really. He's only smoking in anticipation of his mom's visit—so she'll pay attention, so she'll care.

The breeze through the windows lifts the hair at his forehead and blows his first puff around the cab and into the night. The incongruence leaves me feeling even more unsettled. Reed doesn't look like the type of kid who should have a cigarette in his hand. A trophy or a gold medal, maybe, something to affirm that his body is better than normal people's. I breathe through my mouth and think about what that talent agent said to him at the mall kiosk. He should call her.

I turn away, the look of him unbearable. He'll never respect me again, not after what he saw tonight.

Finally, he says, "The ladies were pretty cool, huh? Good mom vibes."

Cool? Were we in the same room? They were completely horrible. There's a lump in my throat, like a whole bag of Hostess Powdered Donettes all mashed together—dry as chalk and thick as kneaded clay.

"You all right, bud?"

Because of this lump, I know what will happen if I lie. I know what will happen if I tell the truth. So I just stare out the window, not saying a word as I watch the fast-food joints fly by on our way back to the apartment—Burger King, Jack in the Box, Carl's Jr., Eegee's. Jack in the Box again.

Reed presses me one more time, using his Scarface voice. "Dude? Brett? Talk to me, mang."

I want to tell him how afraid I am. I want to tell him that *hate* isn't a strong enough word for how I feel about myself, that I don't know the just-right word, that I need Evelyn because *she* would know; she'd have at least five just-right words for how loathsome I've become. I want to tell him I'm sorry for being like this. I want to beg him to forget everything he just saw. But I look instead to the Great Cool Ranch Dorito in the Sky and pretend he hasn't said anything. I imagine my sleek form rocketing through the fortifying ranch radiation, headed somewhere, anywhere, but here.

CHAPTER FIFTEEN

"Tell me about your week," Ms. Finch says. "Did you do what we discussed?"

The lump in my throat is back, bringing a bitter taste with it. How could she have done this to me? Sending me to that place with those awful women and their weird out-loud praying? I'm giving Ms. Finch what Evelyn would call *the cut direct*. I haven't said a word since I entered her office. I just dropped my backpack, took the bouncy-ball chair without asking, and arranged my face in the hardest configuration I could produce.

"Did you ask Reed to go with you?"

I try to play as cool as Captain Condor whenever he faces Adonis—the ease of a guy who sits *behind* the desk, not in front of it. Reed could pull this off with a pie sliding down his face, but I can't even force my gaze past Ms. Finch's Chuck Taylors. Why can't I possess even a drop of the no-fucks-given swagger of all truly dope-ass motherfuckers?

"Brett, part of helping yourself is being brave enough to try scary things. I know how brave you are. You know how brave you are. Did you at least keep your food journal?"

"Fuck my food journal."

I'm not sure what I regret more: that I'm too impulsive to maintain the silent treatment for even five minutes, or that the words sound almost soggy.

"I see you're hurting today, but taking this next step—going to a meeting—it will empower you. I promise."

Good. Let her think I didn't go to Overeaters Anonymous. Let her think I'll never go. If only I hadn't asked Reed to come along. He wouldn't have seen me for who I really am and I could pretend none of this was real. Afterward, I could have gone drunk drive-thru'ing all over North Central until the pain in my stomach hurt worse than those words I had to say. *Compulsive overeater.* I feel them everywhere I go, like a neon sign flashing above my head: *Hey, world, have you heard the news? Brett Harrison is a big fat compulsive overeater.*

Reed can never unsee my admission—the tremor in my hands, the tears swimming in my eyes—and of course he's trying to make me feel better, to make me believe my man card hasn't been shredded, but he'll never view me through the same lens again. I'll never be like him. How could I be? I'm Eating Disorder Boy, my superpower the ability to eat all the bad guys and hold them captive in my incredible expanding stomach—bank robbers and demented professors and mutant scientists, all drowning in the vodka I stole from Evelyn's liquor cabinet.

Ms. Finch stands and reaches for a notebook on her bookcase. She flips to a page containing several lines of scrawl. She chews on the cap of her pen as she paces the length of her office. Back and forth, back and forth. She stops, scribbles out a line, begins pacing again. I know what she's up to. When I won't engage, she merely refocuses on her work until it's time for me to go back to class. This was our modus operandi for the first several weeks when she started pulling me from fifth period. Talk about awkward silence. She might be on my shit list right now, but let no one accuse Ms. Finch of being a poor manipulator.

Since I've already royally screwed up my cut direct, I go ahead and take the bait. "What's that?"

"Did you know I'm a poet?"

I shake my head.

"Sometimes I write about difficult experiences I've had, things I still feel shame over."

I want to ask for more information, but I know Ms. Finch won't expound. The vulnerability river in this office only flows one way.

"This one's a bit of a rough one. I'm kind of nervous to share it with my critique group, but the more I engage with the subject matter, the stronger I feel; I feel more in control of it. Sharing with the group is actually the best part, even when I don't know if I really want to. Once I've shared with others, the subject matter loses its power to shame me. It loses its power over me."

Jesus. Could she be more obvious? Ms. Finch is just trying out a new way to manipulate me. And here an even worse thought dawns, a thought I don't want to explore: What if Ms. Finch has only *ever* been manipulating me? What if Ms. Finch isn't really a bro at all? That notebook—her "poetry"—it's probably just filled with notes about the head cases and juvenile delinquents she works with.

I set my jaw tight and cross my arms, sending a message Ms. Finch can't miss. Two can play the psychology game.

Ms. Finch sits and scribbles some more lines on her page.

Evelyn would be disappointed in me if she were here. *Brett*, she'd say, *the measure of one's character is in how he behaves regardless of how he feels.* Her voice held in place by the sponge pressed to her neck, she'd say through rasping exhalations, *Manners will get you everywhere in life. Don't forget that.* She's always telling me not to forget stuff. Since I moved in with Reed, I've missed Evelyn's constant reminders and gentle chastising. *Don't become a man when you can become a* good *man.* I miss all the ways she'd show me that she believes in me, that she's invested in my future. *You can do anything if you do it well.*

I glance to the obligatory inspirational poster tacked to Ms. Finch's wall and feel a little worse. The poster features a colorful picture of some nebula far, far away and the words *For a star to be born, there is one thing that must happen: a nebula must collapse. This is not your destruction. This is your birth.* Teachers go on and on about us empty-headed zoomers, how hollow our sentiments on social media are. But let's get real. Teachers were meme-ifying America with platitudes long before TikTok or Instagram came along to streamline the process.

How much longer before I can leave?

I reach for a squeeze ball in Ms. Finch's basket of *calm down, kid* stuff—fidget spinners and Slinkys and other such junk. I flex my hand as I bounce in place. Ms. Finch learned at some counseling conference that teen boys and toddlers need this sort of thing to help them calm their tits before they'll open up and talk about their problems. Who am I to prove her wrong? Bounce and squeeze, bounce and squeeze.

Ms. Finch sets her notebook aside and releases a long sigh. She's losing patience, but who cares? She's such a faker; I'll bet she's only half here anyway, just enduring the head cases long enough to get home to her hipster boyfriend for some Thai food and chill.

Finally, she says, "Okay, Brett, I can take a hint." She leans back and drapes one leg over the other. "If you don't want to talk about food, how about we talk about Evelyn?"

Have I mentioned yet that one of my superpowers is making a bad situation worse?

"I'm not talking about Evelyn."

"Brett—"

"I'm not *fucking* talking about Evelyn, okay?" I slam my fists on the desk, knocking the framed photograph of Toast to the floor. I rocket from the bouncy-ball chair, sending it careening into the filing cabinet. Ms. Finch flinches as I lob my squeeze ball at the window above her head. The ball barely makes a noise as it hits the glass and lands harmlessly beside her on the couch, but the look on her face . . . not fear. Disappointment. There's something in this look that makes me think myself a monster. Good. No one ever tried to help a monster.

I grab my backpack and storm out of Ms. Finch's office.

I set off in a run down the hallway, which is deserted but for some kid brandishing a neon-yellow hall pass and a shadow moving up the stairwell. Hall pass boy stumbles out of my way as I shove past him into the bathroom, which, mercifully, is empty. The cool blues and whites of the decor do nothing to calm the roiling anger that builds in my stomach and thumps in my chest. I slam a fist into a paper towel dispenser. *Goddamn, that hurts.* I feel like some roid-rage cliché.

I shake the pain from my hand and prop my arms on a sink, chest heaving. I stare at myself in the mirror. My face doesn't look right. I raise a hand to my chin, poke my neck, pinch the skin at my cheek. I crane side to side, examining my profile. Everything feels wrong. Everything feels too soft. Kid Condor is *not* soft. I lift my shirt and move my fingers over the flesh above my waistband, feeling the rippled red part where my belt buckle left an impression in my skin. You can see Kid Condor's abs. Why can't I see my abs?

I stumble into a stall, the door slamming, swinging. I let my backpack fall from my shoulders, books spilling from the open flap as it hits the floor. I lean into the toilet and try to throw up. I gag, gag again, but nothing comes up. My eyes water and my nose burns.

Stop it. I'm thinking, *Brett, you stupid piece of shit. Stop it. Stop this.*

But I don't want to stop. I try again.

Whatever's in my stomach burns the back of my throat but doesn't rise any farther. Nothing but spit swims in the toilet water. Leave it to me to screw even this up.

I sink to my knees, coughing. I concentrate on my breathing until its rhythm finally sounds normal. Two minutes? Five? I gather my books, replace each in my backpack. I pause when my hand brushes the cover of my food journal. I lift the book and trace the lines of Kid Condor's body, lines I could draw in my sleep. I lay my fingers over Kid's waist, measuring. Two fingers wide. Kid Condor's waist is two fingers wide.

Instead of slipping my journal into my backpack, I stand and sling my pack over my shoulder. As I step from the boys' room, I drop my food journal in the trash bin.

My backpack feels lighter.

I stride toward my next class.

I feel lighter.

CHAPTER SIXTEEN

Some nights, I'm startled awake by the sound of Kid Condor's crying. I'll be dreaming, right? And in the dream, Kid is floating in space, lost amid the thick wreckage of Monos, his home planet, the one Archer von Adonis destroyed. Moon-sized chunks and scorched bodies and planetary dust and single, frozen droplets of blood—all expanding in that silent way debris does in the vacuum of space when you watch this sort of thing in the movies.

The dream doesn't make sense, really. Captain Condor rescued Kid from this rubble when the boy was just a toddler, far too young to understand his fear or grief, but here in the dream, Kid is my age, fully aware of all that's happened. He bangs on the glass of his escape pod, pleading for help. Of course no one can hear him; no one's left alive to hear, even if you could hear screaming in space.

Kid rocks with pain, his arm scorched from an explosion that damaged his pod and sent him careening into the darkness. The fabric of his fly suit hangs in charred tatters at his shoulder; fibers stick to his skin where it burned. Kid clutches his inflamed bicep and calls out for his dead parents. He'll never forget the look on his mother's face when the flames overtook her: sorrow and fear. Not for herself, he somehow knew. Only for him.

Kid trembles. He always trembles.

The worst thing about the crying dreams—the part you probably already guessed—is that it's not really Kid who's crying. I mean, in the dream it *is* Kid, obviously, but outside the dream, the noises that wake me? These are *my* sobs.

Tonight, though, a different sound wakes me.

"Brett. Brett, dude."

I startle awake. My face is wet. My hand grips my arm in the same spot Kid Condor held his. The room is too bright, illuminated by the lamppost in the courtyard beyond the window, plenty enough light to realize where I am and what's happened. I grit my teeth. This dream crying is the worst kind because I can't fight it. I can't escape to my trampoline to be alone to do it. This is the first time Reed has heard me—or at least I hope it is.

From the bunk below, Reed says, "You all right, bud?"

I resist making the telltale sniffing sound that is sure to give me away. I wipe my nose on my shirt. "Yeah, I'm chill. I must have had a weird dream. I was . . . was I making noises?"

Reed swallows, the sound almost loud enough to echo. The hesitation can't be good. "It was like . . . you know when a dog gets kicked?"

I thought nothing could be more humiliating than what happened at Overeaters Anonymous, but I guess the universe really has it in for me.

Reed says, "We can talk about it if you want. You can talk to me."

All I want to do is say yes.

I say, "It was just a bad dream."

Reed's voice isn't as cavalier as I'm used to. "Would you just talk to

95

me? You're shutting me out, and it feels like shit. I'm your brother. I'll always be your brother."

This is the closest Reed has ever come to punching me in the gut. I kind of wish he *had*. *I'll always be your brother.* Evelyn said something similar when I was six and the adoption papers were finally signed. She took me out for ice cream at Hub downtown, which was my favorite because they had all those weird-ass flavors. She usually made me get mine in a cup because I've always been such a slob, but this time I got to have a waffle cone with two flavors—I picked s'mores and peach cobbler because, you know, age six. We sat on a bench at Armory Park and licked our cones beneath the night sky. Well, Evelyn licked hers. The evening was warm, even in winter, so I was licking the ice cream off my arm. I was just an ignorant kid—I know that—but I hate myself for what I said to her. Evelyn has always told me to be careful with words. *Words have power, Brett. Choose them judiciously.* I'm afraid of what I might have set in motion.

"Evelyn, how long before you die and I get my next mom?"

I glimpsed in Evelyn's expression a fleeting look she often gave me from my bedroom doorway when she thought I was asleep. This look was a mix of sadness and something worse, something I couldn't begin to identify until I was much older: pity.

Evelyn wrapped her arm around my shoulder. I rested my head against her, smearing ice cream on the crinkly fabric of her peasant top. She didn't speak right away but rather took the time to gather her thoughts. "Look up at the sky, Brett." She gently lifted my chin to be sure I was listening, a gesture she'd carry on into my teens. She pointed to the few visible stars, those bright enough to outshine even the light pollution downtown. I remember watching her finger move from one pinprick of light to the next, the motion connecting three of the brightest dots into a gigantic triangle. "Do you see those stars?"

I nodded.

"Well, we're made of the very dust that they're made of, and one day, long, long after we're dead, we'll *become* the stardust for a new star. We'll be together like that, shining forever and ever—well, at least for several billion years. Do you understand what I'm saying?"

My voice was filled with wonder. "We're made of *stars*?"

"Kind of." Evelyn laughed, even though I could see tears shining on her cheeks. "What I mean is that I will always be your mom and I will never leave you—ever. Nothing in the whole universe could stop me from being your mom. You are *my son*, and you get to keep me forever, okay?"

I wordlessly reached up and wiped Evelyn's cheek—more dirtying it than clearing her tears. Then I dove face-deep back into my ice cream, satisfied enough with an answer that made relationships seem irrevocable.

Reed means it when he says he'll always be my brother, but that doesn't make his words true—at least not outside the metaphorical sense that will one day see us from stardust to stardust.

I try to say, *I want to talk about Evelyn. Can we talk about Evelyn?*

I try to say, *I don't know how to fix this food thing.*

I try to say, *I'm ashamed.*

But I choke on the words.

"I'm good, really. Let's go back to sleep, okay?"

Reed's voice takes on an edge. "No, actually, it's not okay. I was there when . . . I know more than you think I do. There's no point in hiding from me anymore."

I can't bear this conversation, so I use what little I have to shut Reed up: anger. I feel like the Hulk, a monstrosity of pure rage destroying everything in my path. I growl, "Back off already. I don't need you trying to fix me all the time. It's annoying as fuck, and my private bullshit is none of your business." I'm saying the exact opposite of what I want to say, and I don't know why. "You couldn't understand how I feel, anyway. Your mom's perfectly healthy. All you have to do is act like a dick at school and she's right there again, wrapped around your little finger." Reed's mom flies in tomorrow, in fact.

"Are you kidding me? News flash: The entire world doesn't revolve around *you*. You're not the only person who's ever suffered, you know."

"Fuck you, bro."

"Fuck *you*, bro."

Reed's mattress creaks as he rolls over. I can almost feel the steam rising off him. The heat stings, and as I squeeze my eyes closed and try to fall back to sleep, I realize I'm still holding my arm, my fingers running over my scar, a remnant of a fire that blazed so long ago that I can't even remember the look on my birth mother's face when the flames overtook her.

CHAPTER SEVENTEEN

'm sitting in the back of AP English, two seats away from a sullen Reed, a configuration that was surprising enough to elicit several questioning glances. The other guys on the wrestling team, three of whom are in this class, like to call me Reed's husband, so it's a bit perplexing for them to see us avoiding eye contact. I already knew taking Reed with me to Overeaters Anonymous was the biggest mistake of my life, but what he said last night—that stuff about not being able to hide from him anymore? I can't believe he'd rub my nose in it like that. What the hell?

I feel like the Human Torch, every fiber of my body fuming. I do my best to douse the flames. I'm listening to our teacher, Banksie—"Name's Mr. Banks but y'all can call me Banksie 'cause I'm down with da cool kids, ya mean?"—as he spits some original rhymes about his favorite kind of cliché.

"Yo, this rhyme is kinda dumb. Ima have ya on da run. Banksie 'bout to blow dat mind, wif'a bunch'a idioms."

We students have been tasked with tossing out idioms at random for Banksie to weave into his rhymes, all part of his scheme to make our personal essays assignment "doper than bearable." He's no Hova, obviously, but he sure is quick. Maybe the guy's rap-battle skills—honed in his youth in Chicago's South Side—could have seen him to wild success on the charts if he'd continued rapping about the social issues he cares about instead of embarking on a life of steering impressionable at-risk youths like us. As it stands, the words of Banksie's raps fit hilariously with his nerdy button-down and Dockers look—*Yo, the language got some give, go on, split infinitive*—but the sharpness of them suggests we're in the presence of a well of untapped potential.

I thumb the Instagram feed on my phone, which is cradled in my lap, hoping for anything that will cheer me up. Looks like Teddy Masterson from my frosh pottery class finally came out to their mom. Double tap. Freya Lyon sprang for a Trenta at Starbucks this morning because she's *that bitch*. Double tap. I raise my eyes every so often and laugh at all the right moments the way a kid does when he wants his teacher to think he *doesn't* think his teacher *might* think he's on his phone in class. This is a game of mutually supposed ignorance students and teachers have been playing since time immemorial, and I've never met a big boss I couldn't defeat.

I scroll on until I'm assaulted by Thandie Gellar's radiant smile. Reed is there, too, leaning in, his lips brushing her shimmering cheek. That's right: Thandie's skin actually shimmers. Her caption merely reads This guy. I let my phone go dark.

My eyes rove over the pyramid chart of Banksie's favorite poets, an intricate configuration of lovingly framed headshots covering the better part of one wall. "Most aren't poets in the literal sense," Banksie explained, "but that only matters to those who don't listen when they speak." At the top is Banksie's favorite person ever, some friendly-looking grandpa dude in a clerical collar and bright purple shirt. Below, you'll find several rap and R&B artists—Erykah Badu, Jay-Z, and Salt-N-Pepa, to name a few—and a number of critical theorists whom Banksie is not allowed to assign, a detail he gave with an exaggerated wink to underscore that these people are decidedly not-safe-for-school and therefore cool as fuck.

I glance over a few names closest to me: James Baldwin, bell hooks, Audre Lorde, and the one I know best, Gloria Anzaldúa. It wasn't until Banksie "accidentally" dropped a book by Anzaldúa beside my desk that I truly understood what it meant to be a person of mixed indigenous and European descent, and why sometimes people like me don't feel that good about ourselves because there are still white people out there who manipulate us into thinking there's something wrong with our indigenous blood and our brown skin. The book really resonated because of memories I didn't like to think about. For instance, there was this one time when I was seven years old and this brat at my gymnastics class—populated with the kind of white kids easy to find in the Catalina Foothills—started calling me Del. "My name is *not* Del. It's Brett Isaias Harrison." I was in that bizarre phase kids go through where they need every total stranger to know their full name. "*Isaias?* What kind of name is that? Sounds like a sneeze, you ugly little turd. Your name is *Del*. Del, Del, Del." This escalated for a week or two before he finally used my full invented name: Del Taco. This kid was especially stupid to be so racist in Tucson, a city that remained Mexican even after it became American, a city in the heart of what Anzaldúa calls the borderlands, this vast stretch consisting of Northern Mexico and the American Southwest. Many of Tucson's festivals, including its biggest of the year, Día de los Muertos, celebrate our Mexican roots.

At the thought of Día de los Muertos, I can't help but be reminded of Evelyn. The Day of the Dead was always a huge deal in our house, ever since that first year I was in her care and she taught me to make sugar skulls and build an ofrenda to honor my birth mother. Día de los

Muertos is only five weeks away. Somehow I can't imagine us celebrating it this year.

I shake off these dark thoughts, refocus on the portrait of Anzaldúa. Thanks to her, I finally knew the name for what I was: *mestizo*. You can bet I loved teaching Evelyn my new just-right word (turns out she already knew it because English professors know everything, but she pretended to be blown away because it made her happy that *I* was blown away). She quickly bought one of those ancestry kits, which revealed that I'm part white—Welsh and Spanish, to be precise—and part Maya.

I was so floored by Anzaldúa's book because despite Evelyn's efforts to bring Mexican culture into our home, it still felt weird sometimes to be a brown boy raised by a white woman. Sometimes I wondered if I deserved to be there, in that big, beautiful house in the foothills. Sometimes it felt confusing and bad that none of my close friends were Mexican since I was too scared to try to *be* their friend. Just because I couldn't speak Spanish didn't mean I couldn't google the word the Mexican kids often called me, *pocho*, which is a pretty dick term for Mexicans who aren't "real Mexicans."

Anyway, for the gift of Gloria Anzaldúa, I adore Banksie. This doesn't make me unique. Everyone adores Banksie. He's the only teacher I've had who spends full class periods discussing BLM and the intersections of privilege. He talks about his experiences as a Black man and allows space for Black kids to do the same. "There are many things in this world more important than punctuation," he often reminds us. "Continually examine where your humanity lies on your value system, guys."

I'm pulled from my daydreams by a vibration in my palm. A new follower request pops up: @becoming_mallory. The sight of the notification has my stomach acid washing up my throat. Why would *she* be reaching out? And why now? I've successfully avoided her since our encounter at Overeaters Anonymous, which seems like quite a feat since I've caught her intensely and unabashedly gazing at me in Earth sciences several times. My finger hovers over the accept icon, but I can't quite touch it. I don't want to be friends with Mallory; I don't want to know Mallory. More than anything, I don't want *her* to know me. *Continually examine where your humanity lies on your value system.* Do I need to be nice to Mallory? The anxiety has me glancing at the clock. How much longer until lunch?

"Your turn, Brett."

I almost drop my phone. It catches in the spot where my thighs are beginning to rub together.

Banksie grins in the genuinely affable way he always does. "Your idiom is sure to be a winner. I can see how hard you've been brainstorming back there."

I'm blinking. "Uh, yeah."

Banksie sweeps an arm in a dramatic flourish. "Let us not keep the raucous groundlings waiting. The unwashed masses lust for their entertainment."

"Uh . . . You can't eat your cake and have it, too?" The words are out of my mouth long before I realize my mistake.

Sitting in front of me is everyone's favorite evil overachiever, Robyn Fletcher. She makes a quick little oinking sound, quiet enough to remain under Banksie's radar.

Robyn turns in her seat and gives me a predatory smile. "Don't worry, mouth breather. Only fifteen minutes until lunch."

Mouth breather? I'm not—

Then it dawns on me. The bigger insult here has nothing to do with the moniker. The fat boy just brought up cake. My recent troubles have led me stumbling into a whole new minefield. I'm thinking of Mallory's horrible nickname. *Mallory, Mallory, Miss Ten Thousand Calorie.* How long before someone clever brands me with a label far worse than Del Taco? A label I'll never live down?

What if they already have?

Reed sits forward and shoots me that look he's been perfecting since Overeaters Anonymous, the one that says *You ready to talk about your shit already?*

The badass seated between us, Ruby Orange—half-shaved head, pierced everything—snaps at Robyn, the type of whisper that leaves a handprint on the cheek. "Shut up, you fat-shaming little cunt, or I'll punch you right in your *dick*. That's your face, in case you were confused."

Fat-shaming.

Robyn gives Ruby a sour look and Ruby replies with a low growl. At the front of the room, Banksie remains oblivious, nodding to himself, composing my rap from scratch in the time it took for Robyn to drain my social bank account of every cent of currency. He plows into his latest masterpiece. "Yo, you wanna own dat cake, but you tummy rumblin' hard. Is you gonna scarf it down? Should you bury in da yard? Not a soul can have it all. Better make yer choice, boo. Don't be a chump; don't be a punk. Can't eat your cake and have it, too. Uuh, uuh, holla atcha boiiiiiiiiii."

The giggles erupt. Resident meatheads Devin Harper and Matt Shepp, who live for Banksie's raps, high-five. They're sure to mention him on their next YouTube recap. Tyler French, who's been covertly recording Banksie, thumbs his keypad with the super speed of Barry Allen. His roast-post should show up in my feed in three, two, one . . . There it is. #LMFAO. #savage.

But I'm not double tapping. While the rest of the class cracks up and Banksie turns the spotlight of his unwanted attention on Ruby (perplexingly, the idiom she comes up with is "You catch more flies with honey"), I'm thinking about how doubly screwed I am right now. I've just been knocked down a rung on the social caste system of high school, *and* I'm stuck writing a personal essay with my stupid idiom as its theme. I don't want to write about never having what you want because you've consumed it. I've walked into a trap.

A vibration in my palm again. Something's blowing up on Snap. Major drama going down on Insta, on TikTok, on Facebook (who uses Facebook?). Something big. I'm being tagged—relentlessly.

Half a dozen text notifications from people I don't even know.

Rustling around me as bodies move, fingers swipe. The room is suddenly alive and active, yet Banksie remains oblivious. Unlike in the movies, most of my classmates' phones are set to silent, so this moment of collective interest remains under the radar. Murmurs finally overtake Banksie's rapping as several more phones—some in backpacks, some in pockets—light up.

Oh God.

Faces turn toward me. Looks of sympathy, brows creasing in concern.

Robyn turns around and reaches for my hand. Why is Robyn touching me? Robyn never touches anyone; she floats through the halls like a hologram transmitted to a leper colony from a safe distance. She whispers, "I'm so, so sorry. If I'd known what you were going through . . . I'm here for you, okay?"

What?

I swipe a pop-up at random: Did you post this?

Another: Have you seen this????!!!!

Another: 🖤 🖤 ☹

Discord: This is Brett Harrison, isn't it?

Facebook: He's so brave.

Discord: I knew something was wrong. He's just been so different this year.

Comment: We have to come together for him.

Comment: His comic is fucking ridiculous, tho! LOL!

Comment: One look at his Kid Condor bullshit and you'd already know. Who writes a superhero who gains his power from cosmic Dorito dust? Fucking dork.

Comment: Don't be an asshole, Trevor. It's a DISORDER. He can't help it.

No. No, no.

I open Snapchat. Two girls from Earth sciences with bunny-rabbit filters on their faces: We love you, Brett! Kissy-face stickers, heart-eyes stickers.

Share. Like. Retweet.

I'm zooming in on the pictures—on Instagram, on Threads, on Snapchat. That's my handwriting, crinkled college-ruled paper.

#elevatetheconvo. #mentalhealth. #eatingdisorderawareness.

I'm staring at a page from my food journal, the one I ripped out but then reattached in Ms. Finch's office. The door is so far away.

Ruby grips my shoulder.

Her touch wakes my limbs. I'm seeing her phone in her hand. I'm seeing the same picture there that occupies my screen. A clattering noise. My desk. I've stumbled from my desk. I'm grabbing my bag. I'm running.

The door has already swung closed behind me when Banksie finally catches up with the moment, finally aware that something is off. He calls out, "Yo, yo, yo, homeboy! You need a hall pass!"

But his words are muffled by the pounding of my feet.

A stern-browed Mrs. Annalisa, my former English teacher, cries, "Slow down, Mr. Harrison!"

"Brett, come back!" It's Ruby's voice, a hollow echo somewhere behind me.

Pulse pounding in my head.

I stumble into a trash bin, send it catapulting into a bank of lockers. I stop short just before barreling into a group of drama girls reciting lines in the hallway. Terror burns on my face. I touch my cheek. Skin hot. They can *see* . . . They *know* . . .

"Brett? Are you . . . ?" The girl's phone chimes loudly. She looks down. Her friend peers over her shoulder . . . No. *No.*

I don't give them the chance to meet my eyes again. I'm already gone. I round a corner and burst through a set of double doors. I stumble down the patio steps and sprint for my parked car, not quite able to outrun the buzzing in my pocket, covering my ears against the dozens of expressions of sympathy and pity and admiration ringing through the halls and mercilessly quaking across the internet.

CHAPTER EIGHTEEN

I f you try to trace the photo, you'll only reach one dead end after another. Most people don't use a reshare app in Instagram, instead merely screenshotting and posting, so I've been relying on tagging to find out whose ass I have to kick. This just leads to my own account, everyone tagging me but not who they took the post from.

The detective work is punishing because it means I have to look at what I wrote—what everyone has seen—over and over again. It's like having to look at the gruesome crime scene photos of my own murder and being totally humiliated because for some reason I got murdered with my pants down:

I'm thinking about...
Um...
FML...
What am I thinking about?
I feel...
Ummmmmmm...Okay, so, I guess I'm just going to tell you
about what's been going on over the past couple weeks and you,

you know, you can tell me what you think, I guess. So Reed and I were distributing the new issue of Kid Condor the other day, giving the children what they want and all, and at one point we were running from the fuzz—don't ask why—I PLEAD THE FIFTH!—and I was messing up our grand escape because I'm kind of fat now and, I don't know, I guess not as spry as I once was, and it kind of made me realize just how heavy I'm getting and that feels bad. Uuummmmmm. I guess I feel guilty. Like, there's something wrong with me, like everyone's thinking I'm a fat loser but not saying it. I'm afraid my body might suck and that, like, I guess it should look different. Like, what if I'm ugly and will never get laid, which seems like a superficial concern when I write it down, but I think about this ALL THE TIME.

And I hate even looking at Reed, who's my best buddy, as you know, and who's hot, which you probably also know (I mean that in an objective way in case you weren't sure—people keep telling me I'm gay for Reed and I tell them so what if I am because gay is not an insult, you know?). Anyway, the other day there was this modeling company lady at the mall and she stopped Reed as we were walking by and she was like, Hey, bro (I'm paraphrasing here), she was like, Bro, you have that California look (whatever that is—what is the California look?), and she gave him her card but didn't introduce herself to me—she didn't even look at me, and I know I'm not hot but I'm still a person, you know? I just wanted her to see me. Girls never see me and most of the time I want them to, but then I'll get kind of sad about certain shit and I'm glad girls don't see me because I don't want anyone to see me, all of which is confusing. Uuummmmm. And then, we were eating pancakes for breakfast and I almost started crying at the table because I was afraid of being judged if I kept on eating, so I ate only two pancakes and then swiped a bunch of snacks at the gas station and hid in an alleyway so I could eat them without anyone knowing and so I could cry without anyone seeing (and I'm pretty sure I'm crying too much, or, like, too often, maybe?) because I think I might hate myself and I'm pretty sure I'm awful and I might be fundamentally fucked up because when I'm not forcing myself to eat less, I'm eating everything I can get my hands on and I'm hiding food and stealing food and I can't say any of this to anyone and I'm kind of freaked out to even write this, and then, uh, well, it was my birthday and I was thinking about Evelyn, and going to her house—which is what I want to do every day but NOT what I want to do ever again, and um, and I don't think I should write about her, and I did something pretty terrible involving fire and a box of chocolates that I don't want to write down, either, but I think it might confirm that A) there's definitely something wrong with me, and B) I'm a shit individual, and C) I might be a binge eater and I'm starting to think that might be a real problem. So, yeah, okay. I guess that's it.

CHAPTER NINETEEN

Ally Ford is crying on TikTok as she admits that she's been throwing up since she was thirteen.

On her Insta, Lindsay Xavier has gone live to tell the story of her battle with anorexia, a struggle that began when her ballet teacher would whack her in the stomach with a cane every time her belly extended past the point of concavity.

Mary Richardson just tagged me in a picture of her liposuction scars. She's already gotten over three hundred likes.

Jess Waterman and Penelope DeSantos want me to know I don't have to go through this alone. I've never met Jess Waterman and Penelope DeSantos.

Brodie Greene just posted a picture of us at his eleventh birthday party, our mouths blue with frosting, arms draped over each other's shoulders. @kidcondorcomics is #brave AF. #brettup, javelinas! Brodie Greene hasn't spoken to me in three years.

Robyn Fletcher has found a new pet cause to add to her curriculum vitae. When even one of us is suffering, we must encircle him in love! Too many heart emojis to count. I might just win her the election this year.

@becoming_mallory just sent me another message.

Allow Message? Allowing means @becoming_mallory will be able to send you messages in the future.

@becoming_mallory.

@becoming_mallory.

@becoming_mallory.

I hold my phone's power button down until the screen goes black.

CHAPTER TWENTY

One of Ms. Finch's favorite things to talk about is self-care. I'd heard the term before Ms. Finch started faking her friendship with me, of course—probably on one of those Oprah channel shows that Evelyn used to watch when I was a kid—but the concept flew under my radar until Ms. Finch asked me what I thought about it, if I understood what it meant and if I ever actively engaged in it. I tried to tell her I was too toxically masculine for such middle-aged-lady pursuits. "What? Like bubble baths and pedicures? Are you asking me to buy lavender-scented candles?"

Ms. Finch explained that all members of the animal kingdom, toxically male or not, engage in self-care because self-care is about respecting yourself enough to meet your needs. For humans, she said, this respect extends to celebrating who you are and setting aside time for the things you enjoy. "Sometimes," she said, "self-care does mean bubble baths— assuming you love bubble baths—"

"Oh, I do! I love them ever so much!"

"Okay, smart aleck. But self-care can also be about saying kind things to ourselves or dirt-biking, maybe gardening or going for a drive in nature—whatever makes you feel good."

I could see how self-care was a part of my life—at least where activities like drawing my comics or destroying Reed at *Super Smash Bros.* were concerned—but I got the sense Ms. Finch was worried that I wasn't caring about myself as well as I should. She asked me to do a little brainstorming. My homework was to generate a list of ways I might engage in self-care so I could more mindfully seek out such activities when feeling low or anxious. My list included stuff like spending time at the top of Tumamoc Hill and extreme trampoline air-drumming. It included reenacting scenes from *Scarface* with Reed for the millionth time because there's no such thing as reenacting scenes from *Scarface* too many times. It included sunsets and smoothies, a monthly tradition wherein Reed's dad takes us to Tito's Burritos for one of their killer smoothies before heading up to Windy Point to enjoy what is probably the best sunset in the Sonoran Desert, if not the world.

Eventually, my list expanded as I thought of other activities, like blasting classic Smashing Pumpkins while driving my clunker sedan. Getting to drive my own car now is pretty much the best thing that's ever happened to me. The last couple items that made my list were simply talking with Ms. Finch or writing in my food journal, even if that last idea turned out to be the worst thing that ever happened to me.

Tonight, I'm engaged in self-care.

I'm sitting on the floor of my old bedroom at Evelyn's house, back against the wall, rubbing the heel of my sneaker into the hole I burned into the carpet on my birthday. I'm trying to get the perfect fit, trying to make the hole disappear with my shoe. A rectangle of moonlight cuts my legs in half where it stretches across the floor, my feet framed, the rest of me hidden in darkness—hidden like the means of self-care I like most: this bottle in my lap. I uncap the vodka and grimace as I gulp down another mouthful of the liquid that looks so clean but tastes so dirty.

The thing about self-care is that it can be hella confusing. It's supposed to be about feeling good, right? Drunk drive-thru'ing isn't on my list, but goddamn if drunk drive-thru'ing doesn't make me feel good. This other notable exception, vodka, makes me feel awesome, too. So why do I feel guilty? Why do I have to hide what I'm doing from Ms. Finch?

My eyes feel kind of like strobe lights, but I take another drink anyway. I'm not sure if this sort of self-care counts—I guess that's what I'm trying to say—but I *want* it to count. I think it should count.

I peer through the window into the night sky. I can see the corner of Cheesy Gordita Crunch from where I sit. One time, Captain Condor had to save the entire solar system of its southernmost star from Archer von Adonis's solar destabilizer. That was rad.

I'm staring at the stars and I'm thinking about the stupid poster in Ms. Finch's office, the one about the nebula imploding. This is when the answer to my dilemma dawns on me. An implosion is necessary to make a star. How am I supposed to become my best self if I don't drink copious amounts of alcohol and go drunk drive-thru'ing? I mean, according to Ms. Finch's meme-worthy decor, I pretty much owe it to myself to tear it up, right?

Yes, this makes perfect sense.

I take another pull. I set the bottle down and grab my phone, which I've left face down on the floor. I turn the power on for the first time in several hours. I try to ignore the endless list of pop-up notifications, too many missed texts from Reed, far too many missed calls from Marcus, both worried because I never came home. I'm a dick for not telling them I'm okay—I know this—but every time I tried to open one of their messages, another notification would pop up and my hands would tremble; my stomach would churn.

Habit has me opening my Uber app when I note the satisfying lump of my car keys in my pocket. I don't have to Uber to the fast-food joints anymore. I can take myself. I shift my weight and fish out the keys.

It's here that a soft knock comes at my door.

I drop my keys and cap the vodka, shove it into my open closet, pull the door closed as Evelyn peers in. She attempts a feeble smile. "When did you get here, love? Was I sleeping?" She's forgotten to carry her sponge—or just not bothered since she thought she was home alone. "Why are you sitting in the dark?"

I'd like to laugh, as I so often do, at the farting sounds the words make as they escape from the hole in Evelyn's neck, but Evelyn always says that the best type of laughing is the joyful kind, and I don't feel any joy tonight, just defeat and a depth of shame I can't quantify.

Evelyn sits beside me, arranges her oxygen tank and her tubes. I hate these artificial appendages—Evelyn the Adonis experiment. *Put them behind you*, I think. *Better still, leave the tank in the hallway.* Perhaps Evelyn can read my mind, because she stands again, pushes her tank into the hallway, then reseats herself. In the dark, Evelyn almost looks fully humanoid. I imagine her face without plastic jutting from it. She's rosy and well rested, not pale and hollowed. Her eyes are bright and alert in that way that always makes me feel listened to, like I'm the most inter-esting person on the planet. My imagination is stretching to its limits tonight, but the effort is worth the small comfort of seeing what I want to see.

Evelyn puts an arm around me and I rest my head against her. Since most of the power behind her voice leaks from the hole in her neck, her speech is little more than a whisper. "Gracious, it's late. Why aren't you at Reed's? You have school in the morning."

I touch the screen of my phone. 12:46 a.m.

"Something happened." I'm slurring. "I don't . . . I'm embarrassed." Maybe I'm not slurring but I only think I am? Either way, it's the saying out loud—or the trying to say out loud—that gets me. This is becoming a trend. Tears build behind my eyes. These days it seems my tears can come as quickly and with as much destructive force as Aqualad's hydrokinesis. I'm white-knuckling it to avoid being swept away. I grimace with the effort it takes to hold my feelings inside.

She says, "It's just us here. It's all right."

I know what she means. She's trying to tell me it's okay to cry. But I'm still afraid to. What might I say if I just let go of myself in front of her? I cover my eyes with my hands as the first sob breaks through. "It was a bad day."

Evelyn holds me as tightly as she's able, which makes me cry all the harder because I can't even feel her. I clutch at her nightgown, as if the firmness of my grasp were the only thing holding her here. When the worst of my hitching eases, I slide down and lay my head on her lap. She strokes my hair. "My sweet boy. I'm here. I'm right here."

Maybe it's the alcohol loosening me or maybe it's the darkness or maybe it's just because I need her so badly tonight, but for some reason I really, really want to believe what Evelyn is saying, even if I know it isn't true. I know she *wants* her assertion to be true because *I* want it to be true, but I'm having to live without her, and nothing she could say can change that.

What if I could pretend to believe, though? Maybe just for tonight? If I pretend Evelyn really is here for me, I can tell her anything and she won't judge me or be ashamed of me. I can pretend she'll be able to help.

I squeeze my eyes closed—tight, tighter. *I didn't want to tell you about this . . . this problem I've been having.* Articulating it—even if only in my head—brings on a fresh wave of tears. I power forward anyway. I imagine telling Evelyn about what I've been doing with food—the drunk drive-thru'ing, the counseling from Ms. Finch, the trying Overeaters Anonymous and wishing to be vaporized because it was so awful and humiliating. I tell her that sometimes when I look at Reed, I'm overcome with envy and I'm not sure if that envy makes me hate myself or if it makes me hate him. I tell her I tried to write about my feelings in a food journal but because I'm dense as fuck, someone found what I wrote and posted it to the internet and now there's this relentless outpouring of love and support—there's this "important conversation" I've inadvertently started—and I can't bear to be this person everyone feels sorry for. I just can't stand it. I tell her that I hate the word *brave* because suddenly the word is associated with me, but it's not true or accurate or chosen judiciously because it doesn't apply to me at all. I'm the opposite of brave. I'm the biggest coward I've ever met, but how do I tell people that? How do I make them see the truth? How do I tell them that I wrote that page because I was too cowardly to say any of those things out loud, even to myself? How do I tell people that what I wrote was private? It was *mine* and no one else's, but they took it and they're making it theirs and I hate everyone, most of all myself. And how am I supposed to go back to school? How? I tell her I wish everyone were bullying me because at least then I wouldn't have to be the tragic poster boy for eating disorder awareness. I wouldn't be the reason all these girls at school are "Bretting-up" and owning their anorexia or bulimia or maybe just the fact that they overate at dinner two weeks ago, because what I do, this thing I'm most ashamed of, this

118

thing I can't fucking talk about and this thing I can't stop crying about, is, evidently, all about them.

As I imagine telling Evelyn this awful stuff, I try to picture her responses—I try to put brilliant and soothing words in her mouth, try to figure out what she could possibly say to make me feel better—but nothing worthwhile comes. Evelyn is silent. Of course she's silent. And all the while I'm still thinking about food, imagining how great a milkshake would taste right now. I need a milkshake. I need a cheeseburger. I need onion rings. I need, need, need.

When I finally speak for real, my voice comes out hoarse from crying. "I should go. I should try to get some sleep." What I mean is, I'm tired and I'm thinking my belly should feel as heavy as my eyelids. What I mean is, I'm more hungry than tired, but Evelyn doesn't need to know that.

I reach for my keys.

Evelyn places her hand over mine. She says, "Not tonight, Brett."

Not tonight?

There's something in Evelyn's voice that makes me wonder if I said everything out loud, if she knows that I'm drunk right now, if she knows what I want to do, this thing I shouldn't do drunk, this thing I shouldn't do at all, no matter how desperately I try to justify it. Did I say everything out loud? Does Evelyn know everything?

Evelyn says, "Just sleep, my sweet boy."

For once, the sound of her voice and the comfort of her touch is enough.

Evelyn says, "Just sleep."

And so I do.

CHAPTER TWENTY-ONE

I take a tentative bite of my PB & J. Feels like I just bit into a glue stick. I scrape the roof of my mouth with my tongue, take another bite. Swallowing is a chore. I haven't eaten since breakfast, so I'm famished, but even these two bites leave me sick. I'm hiding behind the arts building, in the alcove provided by the rarely used emergency exit, my new favorite hangout during lunch period. I can't bear to be seen right now under any circumstances, but I'm sure as hell not going to be seen eating. The din of students in the courtyard on the building's west side still freaks me out. After school, in my car, I can truly be alone. I'll eat then.

I slide the sandwich back into its Ziploc and send it sailing toward the trash bin about five yards away. Nothing but net. The basketball team is really sleeping on me.

This spot is pretty appealing as there's a shaded area of patio against the doors and a calming view of a planter bed filled with cacti and three impressive agaves. A tiny lizard darts past my foot and into the shade cast by a barrel cactus. He must come here to hide, too. Our school is massive—there's like three thousand students—so you'd think I could find a clique that eschews the internet, maybe some Quakers. But even people who don't know me stare now. Signing up for the witness protection program is the only option left to me.

I see her shadow and hear the *click-clack* of her heels before her lithe body rounds the corner. My heart quickens and I freeze in place, a fawn in the path of a predator.

Robyn Fletcher.

"Excellent," she says, clapping her hands together. "I thought I'd find you here. You're always trying to sneak away unnoticed, but you're quite noticeable now, as I'm sure you're aware."

Robyn's pleated skirt is characteristically short, which at least gives me something pleasant to focus on as I avoid eye contact.

"My eyes are up here, Brett."

My gaze flits back to the lizard (he's doing little lizard push-ups now, God bless him). Sensing danger, he turns and skitters off.

Robyn expertly kneels and folds her legs beneath her, a well-practiced yoga routine perfected to avoid flashing the countless horny boys she attracts. She pulls a small Tupperware container from her handbag, opens it, and begins gingerly chewing on a floret of broccoli. Where's the rest of her lunch?

Robyn Fletcher is a tricky case. Her ruthlessness and cruelty are legend—she could be your classic eighties-movie bully, one dimensional and one-note, a Johnny Lawrence from *The Karate Kid*, for sure—but when she's not insulting "troglodytes" like me, she's vehemently protesting the use of plastic straws or posting about her work with Habitat for Humanity. I want to believe her activism genuine, but I'm pretty sure her every move is calculated. There's the real Robyn, whose meanness can't even be explained, and then there's the Robyn on paper, who wouldn't look out of place alongside Malala Yousafzai and

Greta Thunberg. Has she come to make fun of me or save me? Which Robyn will I get today?

"I'm here with a proposition you're sure to want to take advantage of, but let me start by saying I'm moved by your bravery in posting that picture."

She thinks I'd willingly humiliate myself? I open my mouth to correct her, but her voice is the type to drown out all others, even without a bullhorn in hand. I marvel at how affected her diction is when she goes into politician mode. Today's Robyn is a far cry from the girl who called me a mouth breather last week. Normal people just don't talk like Robyn Fletcher.

"Who among us hasn't felt these insecurities but been too ashamed to reach out for a helping hand or a shoulder to cry on?"

You, probably.

"Yet just look how many have been stirred to action by your vulnerability."

Now I get to enjoy a lecture on how I'm a role model to girls everywhere. Rad.

"It was wrong of me to poke fun at your body—I understand that now—and I'm taking an uncomfortable but necessary personal inventory, committing myself to real change and allyship for those in recovery."

Recovery from what? Can one recover from social annihilation?

"And though I can't truly understand the depth of your experiences or those of people like you, I believe that together we can become the change we want to see in this school."

Someone should slap some cuffs on this monster for sullying the image of Mahatma Gandhi by paraphrasing him.

Robyn finally closes her mouth, though only because she's taken another bite of broccoli. I've never had a real conversation with Robyn—not because there's no such thing but because I've only ever been a target of her ridicule. I'm not sure how to handle her now, but my anger over the past few days leaves me wanting to be as real with her as she is fake with me. "Look, I don't know what you think you know about me, but you have no idea what you're talking about. Plus, you're kind of a dick, so . . ."

It's alarming but mesmerizing to see how effortlessly Robyn drops the caring-and-concerned act. Her expression clouds over like Storm's when a battle is about to begin. I've played a card she didn't expect. The game has changed. "Fine. I'll level with you. Ever since you put out that garbage comic book of yours, your social status has plummeted."

This seems like a gross exaggeration, but it still stings. My incredulity must show, because Robyn says, "How many times has Reed had to defend you? How many threats has he had to make to keep the wolves at bay?" Robyn smiles at my confusion. "You don't know? The work he does on your behalf?"

Too late to hide what my face has already given away. She has the upper hand.

"You really don't know, do you?" Her eyes light up as she puts together what I'm only just realizing myself, what surely can't be true but *feels* true. "Because he does it behind your back—to protect you. That's sweet. He's a good husband, that one."

I'm staring at the concrete now. My heart thunders. I want to hide my devastation from Robyn, but she's far too formidable a big-bad. I never should have tried to defeat her in my weakened state.

She puts a hand on my arm. I'm too stunned to shake her off.

"I don't say these things to hurt you, Brett. I say them because I need you to understand that there's an opportunity here. We can help each other. Through me, you can enjoy a rehabilitation of your image. You don't have to be the childish weirdo artist kid who spends way too much time drawing bulging male bodies in banana hammocks anymore."

"It's not like that. I—"

"Instead, you can help me lead a new club."

"But—"

Robyn actually puts a finger to my lips to shush me. I hate that my body responds to her touch. I can feel the heat in my cheeks—and in other places. Of *course* if a girl was finally going to touch me erotically she'd be a supervillain hell-bent on destroying me. That makes perfect sense.

"I've already handled everything, talked to Mrs. Annalisa yesterday. She's agreed to advise. Our eating disorder support club will have everyone forgetting about your dorkariffic comic book. Of course we'll have to come up with a name that's not so depressing. Healthy Plates Club, maybe. We'll need a hashtag involving the word *wellness*."

"People like my comic." The words taste stupid. "Well, some people do."

Robyn's expression suggests I'm the most pitiful kitten ever to be rained on. "Mm-kay, sweetie. Let's say they do. They'll still like you more if you become the face of a movement to promote healthy relationships with our bodies here at Tucson City High. You don't even have to do anything but show up—plus, you know, talk about your bullshit. Should be easy since you already got the ball rolling in such attention-seeking fashion."

"Are you *high*?"

"I'm chillingly sober, Brett. I want class president and you want . . . how did you put it? To be seen by girls?"

"I didn't mean it like that."

"Who do you think is going to join this club? All those nose-picking masturbators reading your comics?"

I'd never give her the satisfaction of knowing as much, but Robyn has hit a nerve. After Overeaters Anonymous, you couldn't drag me to a club like she suggests. I don't want to be surrounded by girls talking about their girl problems. I don't want to have girl problems.

"Plus," she adds, "I'm guessing you don't want to hide back here to eat your lunch for the rest of your high school career. Image is all about spin. You can keep being the pathetic crying kid or you can be a hero. Isn't that all you've ever wanted? To be that Kid Condom character you draw all over everything?"

Yet another reason to hate her. I'm never going to be able to unhear *that*. "Why me, anyway? If I'm such a loser, won't I just bring the club down?"

"People need a narrative that inspires. Look at me."

"You told me not to."

"Look at me but not in a pig way."

I begrudgingly obey. After all, I couldn't look at Robyn in a pig way if I tried. Everything about her repulses me now.

"The club members will be nice to me, sure, but people need someone to look up to who's more like them, someone who gets their plight. It boggles the mind, to be sure, but you've caught the public's imagination. For the first time in a long time, people are into you—or at least they *want* to be—and since we're not playing games with each other, I'll be perfectly honest. I'm nothing if not opportunistic. You're a bandwagon, and I'm jumping on."

Robyn stands and smooths her skirt. She drops her Tupperware into her handbag and pops a mint into her mouth. "Seriously consider my offer, Brett. I'll meet my goals one way or another—it's kind of what I do.

But you? You only get to be Jesus until the next big thing comes along. Capitalize while you can."

Robyn spins on her heel and clicks away, each stomp reverberating like a gunshot. I stand, a little dazed by an encounter that proves just how ill-equipped I am to deal with girls, especially demonic ones. It's not until the bell rings, signaling the end of lunch period, that I realize I'm standing over the trash bin, eating the sandwich I threw away twenty minutes ago.

CHAPTER TWENTY-TWO

There's this memory that's been playing on repeat in my head all afternoon, making it impossible to concentrate in any of my classes. In this memory, Reed and I are thirteen—so, total dorks, obviously—sitting cross-legged on my trampoline in the dark, lit only by the dim glow filtered through the sliding glass door of my house. We're laughing like fools, which makes me feel especially accomplished because I've thought up this event, this game we're playing, to make Reed feel better. Today his mom finally moved out, and though neither of us has said a word on the subject, I know he's hurting.

"Shots, shots, shots, shots, shots, shots, shots, shots!"

Reed pumps his fist in the air as I rip the foil from a little plastic condiment cup—the kind you get with your chicken tendies at Jack in the Box. I tilt my head back and down the viscous substance inside, gulp the tangy slop and laugh in triumph as I lick the container clean. I toss the spent cup dramatically to the sand beside the trampoline, where it joins a pile of other cups, and affect my best Scarface voice. "You got good stuff here! Class A *shit*!" The *Scarface* theme, "Push It to the Limit"—a machine gun of synths and squealing tires and gunned engines—plays on loop in my mind, and I'm pretty sure this faint feeling in my head, accompanied by the gurgling in my stomach, must be what it's like when you get too drunk. If there's a limit, I'm pushing it. This game is called Ranch Shots, and the churning in my stomach suggests Reed is going to win.

Reed grabs another cup from the box of ranch dressings between us, which I scored as Scarface might: through bribery and extortion. Lego enthusiast and Pixy Stix peddler Tad Sherman owed me big-time after I let him cheat off me on our geometry test. After some intimidation and negotiation, his big brother was able to smuggle the box out of the Jack on Speedway where he works, his pocket well lined and Tad's debt paid.

"Shots, shots, shots, shots, shots, shots, shots, shots!"

Reed gags as he chokes down his shot—maybe his twenty-fifth?— but he doesn't disqualify himself by giving up or puking. He tongues the inside of the cup, even makes a big show of slowly licking the underside of the foil. He tosses the cup at me. "Buttermilk House Sauce, suck my dick!"

I pull back the foil from another cup. The smell is too much. I close my eyes and breathe through my mouth until the nausea passes. The grin on Reed's face is the type you'd see on Archer von Adonis when he's bested the Constellation Corps. He knows he has me, but I'm not going down without a fight. "Okay. Okay, all right." I hold the cup as high above my face as possible, hoping the breeze might save me from the smell. I tip and squeeze the cup so the dressing falls into my mouth in one gelatinous blob. The dressing no longer tastes like ranch but a swampy slime of oil and chemicals. I gag once, twice. I swallow.

Oh no.

Ranch's revenge is coming. Ranch's revenge is here.

I spring forward—sending Reed somersaulting backward—and flop onto my stomach. My torso hangs over the edge of the trampoline. I grip the metal frame tightly and spew as noisily as I can. I've been gored in battle, all moans and death dramatics.

Reed clutches at his stomach, rolling with laughter. Between gasps for air he cries, "Haha, loser!"

Another wave of vomit hits the dirt. I scrub my forearm across my mouth. Is it over? Tell me it's over.

It's not over.

My body undulates as Reed gains his feet. He bounces once, twice. "Frog splash, motherfucker!" He crashes down on top of me, squeezing another spurt of toxic ranch up my throat and into the dirt. Reed's laughing, laughing. Let's see how funny he thinks he is when I shit my pants on him, the jackass. But even as my stomach cramps again, even as I dry heave a few more times, spitting and panting, I know I've killed it tonight because Reed is so happy. The way he feels can't last—soon enough the reality of what's happened will show up to frog splash him in the feels—but for this small window of time, I'm the hero. I'm the guy who's saved him from what his mom has done, and I think Captain Condor would issue a commendation for my valor.

I shrug Reed off and roll onto my back, stare into the night. "Good game, bro." My breath comes shallow. "You destroyed me."

Reed flops down beside me. "You bet I did."

We lie like this for several minutes, a comfortable silence.

Finally, Reed says, "She's not coming back, is she?"

It's not quite dark enough to hide what we both don't want me to see, what I can hear in his voice, despite his efforts to hide it.

I don't dare look at him. I have to pretend I don't know he's crying, right? I want to lie to him. I want to say his mom has just made a mistake and that she's sure to realize how miserable her life is without her family and she'll be home before the end of the month, but this separation has been coming for some time, despite Reed's steadfast denial. Today, Reed's mom boarded a plane to San Diego, where a guy who's not Reed's dad waits for her.

I say, "She'll visit. I'm sure she will."

"No," Reed says. "She won't."

I want to give Reed a hug, or maybe tell him I'll always be here for him, but I'm stopped by a force field that seems to grow from inside me. We've already said too much, I think—we've already broken the rules of being men somehow, though I'm not exactly *sure* how—and if I say the wrong thing or if I try to touch him, it'll only make things worse.

Reed sniffs only once, as if his problems could be solved by a Zyrtec. "It'll be okay."

"Yeah," I say. "For sure."

I want to reach for the box of ranch shots, but it's too late now. I've really tried, but I can't fix this, which seems wrong because isn't that what men are supposed to do? Fix stuff?

After several minutes of silence, we're startled by the sound of the sliding glass door gliding on its track.

Evelyn says, her voice normal because there's no hole in her neck yet, "Guys, it's time for Reed to head home."

I immediately start whining. "But you said he could spend the night."

"I know, love." Now Evelyn's voice is decidedly *not* normal. Her words sound strangled. "I'm sorry to do this, but I've gotten some news. There's something important I have to talk to you about, something that shouldn't wait."

I feel a familiar pang in my gut, not the kind that makes me want to hurl more ranch into the dirt but the kind that makes me want to run. And though I don't know it yet, this is the moment my whole life changes. It's here I forget about trying to fix things for Reed. I forget that maybe even he struggles. I forget, I want to believe, not because I'm the most selfish person on the planet, but because Reed is such a goofball, always up for trouble and adventure, always so positive, always . . . I forget, perhaps, because from here on out, Reed is the one always trying to fix things for *me*.

CHAPTER TWENTY-THREE

Usually when I need cheering up, I go straight to Smashing Pumpkins' *Siamese Dream*—"Today" is the hero we need, not the hero we deserve—but after fuming over my encounter with Robyn Fletcher all afternoon, I'm not as interested in soothing as I am in stoking. I want to feed a monster who doesn't live in my stomach, the monster who lives in my heart and mind. This particular monster dines on "Bullet with Butterfly Wings" from *Mellon Collie and the Infinite Sadness*, Billy Corgan's angry-boy masterpiece.

I'm blasting the song on repeat in my headphones as I sit hunched over the desk in our bedroom, a practical hand-me-down made of particle board and laminate situated under the watchful eye of my new Captain Condor standee and a floating shelf populated with a few dozen WWE action figures. I slam my pencil down and furiously grind up what's left of my Hi-Polymer eraser, rubbing it into my sketchbook as if to start a fire. It wouldn't be so bad if my sketchbook went up in smoke, actually. My new Adonis studies—his blocky face contorted in a cruel sneer—are trash. I can't count how many times I've drawn his sharp, geometric features over the years, yet for some reason I can't get him to look like himself. Where am I going wrong?

I stride to the closet and grab my sturdy plastic document tube of official Constellation Corps Universe model sheets from its perch on the top shelf. I return to the desk, pop the tube open, and push my Prismacolors out of the way. I reverently unroll the Adonis sheet—big enough to cover the work surface—and weigh down the edges with a few action figures. This sheet, like each of the others, is a silky slab of Mohawk Superfine bearing my signature below the official gold-foil seal of the CCU, which is embossed with the Great Cool Ranch Dorito in the Sky emblem (yes, I had these stickers custom-made online). My model sheets are treated like precious treasure maps, which, to an illustrator, they essentially are. The sheet bears a dozen Adonis expressions and twice as many poses. I compare today's drawings to the masters. Is the problem in the cheekbone? The width between the eyes?

I yank open the top desk drawer, the one that still functions. (When I moved in, Reed gave me this drawer and kept the broken one below for himself.) I rummage until I find my compass and protractor, then take a few measurements in my sketchbook. I hate to prove teachers everywhere right when they say geometry matters, but I go ahead and lay my protractor over Adonis's face on my model sheet anyway and open my phone's calculator app.

The jaw is definitely not as wide in my new sketches. Plus, the slant of the brow is too high and the bridge of the nose too short. What the hell? Am I imagining it or . . . does Adonis seem kind of younger than he is?

I pack my document tube away. I've just picked up my pencil again—determined to get my ratios right—when Reed clamors into the room, home from wrestling practice. He dumps his gear on the floor and flops down beside it, lies on his back, eyes trained on the ceiling. He plays with the collar of his tank top, an unconscious gesture he always makes when he's anxious. He says something, but I can't hear him for Billy Corgan's screaming at the end of *Bullet*'s bridge.

Reed turns his head and mimes removing headphones.

Pulling myself from between Billy's wails feels like being yanked from under a security blanket. I don't know if I have it in me to face Reed—not after what Robyn Fletcher said, not after the words Reed and I had last Monday night, just before my journal page hit the internet and my world imploded. But it turns out it's really hard to avoid someone when you live together and share just about everything. I've only avoided a conversation this long because Reed's mom was in town for the week. Now she's gone again. My roommate's back.

He says, "It's not as bad as it seems."

Usually, I'm the first to correct Reed when he uses a pronoun without an antecedent, but he doesn't have to spell the *it* out. The *it* is all anyone is talking about. At the very least, Reed is on my side again, our fight forgotten. So why do I want to body-slam him?

Prompted by my expression, Reed works harder. "Look at the silver lining: Now that your issues are out there in the world, there's no need to hide from them. Maybe now you can handle your shit. And everyone's being super supportive. They want to help you. No one's talking trash—well, a few people are, but I shoved them up against the lockers. There shouldn't be a problem now."

But there *is* a problem. *This* is the problem. I'll go ahead and correct myself: Reed's incessant protection of me is the problem, a problem I didn't even know I had until today.

Or did I? How many times have we tortured Marcus with *The Karate Kid* since I moved in? How many times have we ordered pizza with extra sauce because that's the way I like it? How many other ways has Reed deferred to me? Favored me? Gone out of his way for me?

My drawer is still open. I slide it in, slide it out, the path smooth and silent. Reed's drawer? It hangs half on the floor, its contents spilling at my feet. The evidence is everywhere I look. He even took the rap for me with Dean Ricamora over our covert comic-booking, didn't he? Jesus, this is humiliating. No wonder his buddies call us husbands.

I say, "What do people really think of my comic books?"

Reed props himself on an elbow, startled. "What do you mean?"

"All those people who trash them behind my back, they don't bully me because of you."

"Well, no, I mean, sure, some douchebags—"

"I'm not stupid. I know what people say about the Condor boys." I point to the glowing review of my flagship issue, framed on the wall. "How did you get Ajay to write that?"

Now Reed is sitting on his heels, fully engaged in a fight he didn't know he was having. "What the actual fuck? Why are we talking about this?"

"It's a simple question."

"I had nothing to do with that! I don't even know Ajay!"

"You're always protecting me, treating me like an infant! You did something! Just tell me!"

"If you don't want to be babied, maybe you should stop acting like one! Your food bullshit? Just a lack of self-control. You're as self-indulgent as a child. Look around you, bro. Everyone else is growing up, but it's like you got stuck at thirteen!"

Reed knows the number is a sore spot for me, the year Evelyn's doctor first called with bad news. How could he say that knowing what he knows?

"You've always been immature—and you get a free pass because of being an orphan and shit—but you're growing pathetic. I *warned* you that the food stuff in your comic books was cringe—I fucking *told* you—but you wouldn't listen!"

I feel like that meme you often see where the woman is looking perplexed and all the complicated equations are floating around her head. Puzzle pieces that might never have revealed themselves are falling into place. A clear picture of my friendship with Reed forms. It doesn't look the way I thought it did. I now see the real reason Reed discouraged me from putting my name on my comic books. It had nothing to do with hype or buzz. He was *embarrassed* for me. And worse, he was trying to save me—*again*.

I snarl, "How about you stop with the favors? I never asked for your help. I don't need it, and I don't want to be your fixer-upper anymore."

Reed hops to his feet in that annoyingly athletic way that always makes me feel like a slug. "No prob, bro." He taps his chest and shoots me a peace-out sign as he strides from the room. The front door slams, footfalls on the stairs down to the courtyard. Probably on his way to mix saliva with Thandie Gellar. The girl *I* worshipped. The girl *I* wanted.

It's here I realize I'm trembling, my finger frantically spelling out expletives on my thumb. I grab my hand to quiet it, then peer up. On the wall, just to the left of my review, hangs a snapshot of Reed and his mom, taken a couple months ago when he visited her in San Diego. They're standing on a beach, a breeze lifting his mom's hair. Reed sports a fresh neon-red sunburn, his skin a classic shade of fried white guy. I glance from the picture to my failed sketches. Glance up, down again.

And I finally see what's wrong with my sketches.

The resemblance between Archer von Adonis and Reed is uncanny.

CHAPTER TWENTY-FOUR

My old bathroom at Evelyn's house is far too white, blinding even when lit by nothing but waning afternoon sunshine. When I was eight, Evelyn and I painted the whole thing deep blue with planets and galaxies, moons and meteors and all that stuff. I was already a budding artist, so the murals didn't turn out as crappy as you might expect. We stuck plastic glow-in-the-dark stars all over the ceiling until it was bright enough to brush your teeth with the lights off. I meticulously arranged the stars just like they look in the night sky: the Great Cool Ranch Dorito surrounded by all the other constellations I loved.

This project came about after Evelyn figured out why I was still wetting the bed. It wasn't because I didn't wake in time but because I was afraid of the dark and didn't want to venture even the few yards from my bed to the attached bathroom. Evelyn had put a night-light in there, of course, but it cast spooky shadows. Evelyn thought perhaps if I made the room friendly, if I made it a place where Captain Condor and his pals might hang out, I wouldn't be so freaked to go in there at two in the morning. As always, she was right.

Now if you run your hand along the stark wall, you can still feel the ridges of the planets just under the surface. I never should have painted over them. I never should have removed the stars. Why did I remove them? Why did I paint the bathroom so painfully neutral?

Sometimes I ask myself questions I don't want to answer. This is one of those times.

I shake off my memories and focus on what's important about this bathroom, the thing that's still here. The toilet. I'm a man on a mission, and this time I'm not going to screw it up. I've just eaten a whole pizza, a bag of Doritos with salsa, and a pack of Reese's Peanut Butter Cups. My guts could rip open at any moment. It's time to get serious about this barfing business.

I can't get what Reed said yesterday out of my head—that part about lacking self-control. What if I can prove him wrong? I'm thinking of my idiom—you can't eat your cake and have it, too. I've been chewing on the problem all day, wondering if I can work up the courage to solve it. What if I can eat but *not* eat? I've been telling myself I don't know why I tried to throw up after my meltdown in Ms. Finch's office, but that's not true. I know exactly why. Every time I look in a mirror, I know why. What if I could keep bingeing but not get fat? No one would know there was a problem with my eating—I mean, there wouldn't really be a problem then, would there? I wouldn't have to consider seeing a thera-pist as Ms. Finch suggested. I wouldn't be like those miserable women at Overeaters Anonymous anymore. As pissed as I am at Reed, I have to admit he pointed me toward the solution, which has been waiting right under my nose—bully to him for once again playing his role as my hero to perfection.

I hop in place, psyching myself up like you might if you were about to head into the ring for a prizefight. "You got this, killer." I shake my nerves out through my arms, my wrists, my hands. "You can do this, beast." I pound my chest a couple times, slap my face.

I lean over the toilet bowl—not too close. The toilet is sparklingly clean, but it still feels wrong to stick your face in a place where your butt is supposed to go. "Okay. Okay, okay." I prop myself with one hand, take a breath, and try to force my binge up. I cough, cough again. My eyes water. I take several heaving breaths.

Puking is easy when you're sick—an inevitable projectile explosion you can't keep up with. So why is this so hard? And why does it hurt so bad? Feels like someone's taken a cheese grater to my tonsils. Nothing of substance has come up, but my stomach acid is eager to make an appearance.

I lean forward again. More gags, more coughs. The whole process is louder than I expected. I imagine Evelyn in her room, asleep—she's always asleep—and I do my best to be quiet.

I dry heave again.

Nothing.

Again.

Again.

And finally it's happening. My stomach bends as my binge rockets out of me. It's so much messier than I expected. Nearly as much makes it onto the toilet as into it. I guess there's a reason to stick your face all the way in the bowl.

The heaves ease and I sink to my knees, trembling. These efforts alone have exhausted me, but I can still feel the pressure in my stomach. I've committed to puking until that bad feeling goes away. The smell alone is almost enough to ease the process. I close my eyes—they're watering too much to see anything with clarity anyway. I want to avoid the smell but it's *in* my nostrils.

As I purge more, purge harder, I stop thinking so much about completing the mission, about being a killer or a champion. Instead I think about Reed and that just-right word he said yesterday: *pathetic*. This word has no place in this activity—I'm handling my shit, right? Isn't that what he wanted me to do?—but the word still trumpets through my mind. I think about how Evelyn would feel if she were to walk in and see me doing this.

I wish I'd thought this through sooner.

There's a rustling sound. The wheels of Evelyn's oxygen tank?

God, I'm stupid.

I spit and wipe my mouth. I scrub my eyes with my forearm and quickly gargle at the tap. My eyes are bloodshot, teary. I look like this kid from my eighth-grade drawing class, Danny Cavanaugh, just after he and Hal Garza got in a fistfight: face red and mottled. I flush the toilet, but there's no hope of wiping down the seat or the floor in time. I whip around and bolt from the room, slamming the door closed behind me. I wipe my eyes as best I can. Sunglasses on? Sunglasses on. What the hell am I doing? I push the glasses up to sit above my forehead, wipe away a fleck of something half digested from my shirttail. I lean against the wall like I'm James Dean or something and wait for Evelyn's face to appear in the bedroom doorway.

But the noise is gone. One second, two. Nothing. I pop my head into the hallway. Evelyn's not there.

Evelyn's not there.

I leap out of my skin at a knock at the front door—three sharp, confident raps.

Who would come here?

I stealthily slip down the hall and into the foyer, keeping my back to the wall to conceal myself from any prying eyes that might peer through the narrow window by the door. Perhaps I can catch a glimpse through the peephole and hold my breath until the visitor leaves.

I carefully move into position to spy on my assailant.

Oh God.

The colorful form that fills the peephole's view is far too familiar. That hair that always makes me think of a My Little Pony. Just the sight of her wrings my stomach again. I can still smell what I've done, the evidence stuck in my nostrils, burning in the back of my throat.

I turn on my heel, prop my back against the door, and hold my breath.

"Open up, Brett. I know you're in there."

Silence.

"I followed you here after class let out. I know about the stop at the QT, and the other stop—at Dominos."

Stalker much?

"I know what you're doing in there."

Please tell me Mallory hasn't installed hidden cameras.

"Binge eating is seriously problematic, Brett."

The bingeing is only the half of it, so perhaps the barfing is still my secret.

"Brett. Open up."

Who does Mallory think she is, anyway? An expert on shoving food in your face or something? Is this why she's been doggedly after my attention ever since my food journal hit the internet? Robyn Fletcher's words flash across the ticker in my mind, that stuff about being a role model. If this is what Mallory wants, she has another think coming. I'm not like Mallory at all, and I'm sure as hell no role model.

"Just go away," I say. "We're not friends, okay?"

"Of course we're not friends, asshat. We barely know each other. This conversation would be simpler if you opened the door."

"I'm not home."

"Well, that much is obvious."

Does she know I don't live here anymore? I'm overcome with a visceral need to get her out of here. Get her away from the house before she realizes . . . I squash the thought before it overwhelms me. I say, "If I promise to be out in five minutes, will you go wait in your car—or whatever vehicle you've used to stalk me like the creeper you obviously are?"

Her voice is laced in suspicion, which is aggravating since I'm the one being stalked by a toxic fangirl right now. "All right. But don't try anything funny. We have business to attend to, whether you like it or not, and you're not going to avoid me any longer—this is just how it is. Accept it."

I assume Mallory is talking about stripping my flesh and wearing me as a coat, but since I can't be sure, I have to admit my curiosity is finally piqued.

Back in my bedroom, I'm tying my shoes when I note the neon puke spatter on the cuffs of my jeans. I've succeeded in getting rid of my binge, so why does the sight of how I've done it leave me so disgusted?

I quickly flick the random chunks of food away, give my whole body a once-over, until I'm sure no one would suspect what I've done. I gather my wallet and keys. On my way out, I glance to the bathroom door, picture the messy toilet beyond. I should clean up before I go, but I'm listening to the silence in the house. I'm thinking about how badly I need to get Mallory away from this silence. Tomorrow, when I'm sure to give this whole procedure another try, is soon enough. For now, my mess can wait.

CHAPTER TWENTY-FIVE

The first thing about Mallory I don't want to see is the dried blood on her biceps from where she picks at her skin. The surface of her arms and chest—the part that's visible above the neckline of her tank top—is inflamed and rough, a dimpled landscape of some faraway moon. The next thing I don't want to see is the thick flap of belly fat that hangs over Mallory's thighs, halfway to her knees. The third thing I don't want to see—and I don't even want to say it because it feels bad to say it, like, I feel like a dick for saying it—is the extra flesh on Mallory's back, which the jerks at school refer to as her "back boobs." The jerks only use this term when Mallory is close enough to overhear them.

I don't want to look closely at Mallory and I don't want to even *think* about what I'm seeing because all this stuff I don't want to see—it makes me sad for Mallory. Even worse than that—and I really don't want to say this part; this is the part Ms. Finch would tell me to go to the mat for myself to say—is that these aspects of Mallory's body *scare* me. What if one day, many chicken tendies from now, I have to find shirts that will make room for a hanging belly? What if I never see my dick again? What if I have to figure out how to fit in chairs with back boobs? These shitty thoughts lead to even shittier ones. Boobs on the back might not be as bad as boobs on the front. What if I'm a virgin forever because girls won't want to move my belly aside to have sex with me?

When I look at Mallory, legs splayed out as she sits on the tiled floor of her bedroom, back against her unmade bed, my gaze moves immediately to the rainbow cascade of her hair, which, under these scrutinizing circumstances, actually makes me smile—and kind of makes me want the cheap cupcakes you get at the supermarket, the airbrushed ones made of loads of delicious hydrogenated oils and adorned with plastic rings. When Mallory motions for me to drop my backpack and sit across from her, my eyes settle on any part of her body covered in clothing, a wardrobe thoughtfully curated by someone with a fly sense of midnineties alt-rock style (the nineties are the best musical decade, and I'm happy to fight anyone who disagrees). Mallory's outfit—composed of ripped-up plaid pants, Doc Martens, and a tank top screened with the words *Totally 100% Unicorn*—also makes me smile, so I try my best to see these things instead of the stuff I don't want to see.

Mallory says she likes to sit or lie on the tile the moment she gets home because it helps her cool down after doing anything in the unbearable heat. I relate. Reed and I often jump in the pool at the apartment complex fully clothed before getting in his pickup to drive anywhere.

Just being in Mallory's bedroom—situated on the north-facing side of a pretty sweet pad on the Eastside—has a cooling effect. Shaded light filters through the window, and the whole room is dimmed by the pictures papering the walls and ceiling, most torn from magazines or printed off the internet. I can tell the room is painted princess pink because the color peeks out here and there and is prominent wherever lengths of architectural trim cut into Mallory's epic collage.

The pictures are another thing I don't like to look at. Each features a fat lady. Some are wearing bikinis and some are naked—not, like, in a porn-y way, but, you know. Some of the pictures are just body parts—just faces, some of them—like from a L'Oréal ad or whatever. Glued or taped between the bodies, sometimes written directly on the skin with Sharpie, are all sorts of positive phrases. These affirmations aren't quite the type you'd expect to see painted on a plaque hanging in a white girl's house—*live, laugh, love* and all that—but more specific. One catches my eye. *You're beautiful. It's society that's fucked up.* That one's kind of nice; it sounds like the type of thing Gloria Anzaldúa would say if her mouth was as foul as mine. Plus, it rings true. One of the safest places to look at Mallory is in the eye because she *is* really beautiful, like she could be one of these ladies from the Neutrogena or Olay ads on her walls. She's got these remarkably thick eyelashes, even though I'm pretty sure she isn't wearing any makeup to get them like that. Unlike the skin of her arms, Mallory's face is smooth and clear, like she's never had a pimple in her life, and her smile is way more interesting than those of most girls because she's got this chipped tooth in the front. Come to think of it, her chipped tooth also makes her seem like a total badass, which, judging by the fact that she's managed to drag me here, must be true.

The next message to catch my eye kind of makes my stomach hurt. *Everything is going to be okay.* I think of the scabs on Mallory's arms. I think of my fight with Reed. I think of what I did at Evelyn's an hour ago, and I know the platitude is a lie. I swallow in an audible way. How many lies does Mallory have to tell herself to survive high school and whatever other shitty things happen to her? This thought makes me think about the lies I tell myself; it makes me think about the *ways* I tell myself lies, and I want to stop thinking.

Mallory reaches beneath her bed and pulls out one of those beat-up metal toolboxes you'd expect to see under a construction worker's arm. "My dad wanted to give this to his son someday. He had three girls."

The lid creaks as Mallory opens it. The box is not loaded with hammers and wrenches but art supplies—inks, cutting gouges, a brayer.

"You're an artist, too?" I ask.

Mallory rummages around until she emerges with two putty knives. "Printmaker, yeah. Mainly relief and intaglio. Screen printing is for athletic people."

I don't even know what intaglio is, but I like the sound of it—ancient, arcane. I file the word away for use in my comics somewhere.

I say, "Are we making art?"

"Maybe another time."

I assume I'll have little say in whether there will be another time, so I figure I'd better get comfortable with Mallory as soon as possible. I force myself to look at her belly. I want to look at it until it doesn't scare me. The overhang almost touches the floor between her legs. There's just enough room underneath to stand a quarter on its edge.

Mallory catches me staring. "I can pose for a photo if . . ."

I quickly glance away. "Jesus, sorry. I didn't mean . . ."

"It's okay. Take it in. It's called an apron. Not all fat people have them. I'm special."

"Apron?"

Mallory grins at my discomfort. She lifts her belly, hefts it as if judging its weight. "Well, officially this is known as a pannus stomach, but yeah. In layman's terms, an apron."

"Apron. Okay, that's . . ." I'm nodding, nodding, taking the time I need to process. "Okay, yeah, I mean . . . I get it."

Mallory laughs. "Now show me a cool part of your body. Fair is fair."

I feel the redness in my cheeks. "I don't know if I have any parts as special as an apron, but if I discover something worthy, you'll be the first to know."

"Deal." Mallory hands me a putty knife. "Now, down to business. No one can know about what we're doing, okay? If you breathe a word of this to anyone, I'll chop your balls off and wear them around my neck."

Who wouldn't be charmed by such threats?

"You're probably wondering why I've brought you here. I'm not about relying on men for anything, but I'm swallowing my pride because I need your skinny privilege to accomplish a task I'm too fat to accomplish myself."

Skinny privilege? "Maybe let's dispense with the cryptic lead-in and get to why I've got a putty knife in my hand."

"We're going to scrape my pictures off the walls, all of them. I want nothing left but the ugly shade of gender conditioning underneath."

Of all the possibilities spinning around the roulette wheel in my mind, this was not where I expected the ball to land. "Okay?" The question mark is all over my voice. "But why do you need me, exactly?"

"Because you need this, too. I don't expect you to get it right now, but you'll understand in time."

I resist sighing in frustration. I might be known for epic daydreams and fanciful reveries, but I've never met a dramatist quite as dedicated as Mallory.

I say, "Okay, I'll stick a pin in that inquiry for now, but *skinny privilege*?"

Mallory stands, rolling onto her knees first to do so, and retrieves a stepladder resting behind the door. "You're going to handle the ceiling and anything I can't reach from the floor or bed."

My confusion must appear on my face because Mallory releases an *ugh*—like, an actual *ugh* you could spell out—and grabs me by the wrist. I drop my putty knife and she pulls me down the hallway, past a bookcase filled with old VHS movies and battered children's board games, into a small bathroom decorated in that cowboy-themed way you sometimes see in houses on the Eastside, houses where moms don't have full-time jobs. A vision of Mallory's mom flashes before my eyes. I shove my hands into my pockets to rid them of that feeling of her squeezing them, begging me to come back to another Overeaters Anonymous meeting.

Mallory gestures to the toilet, which looks somehow wrong for a toilet in a house full of women. It takes a moment to register that the seat isn't merely lifted up. The seat is altogether gone.

I cock my head, open my mouth. Close, open.

Mallory says, "I broke the seat, dork. My dad is bringing another one home tonight. If I break that stepladder, I could break my ankle."

My laugh is reflexive. "Damn, girl." I shake my head, catch my rudeness a moment too late.

Mallory punches me in the arm, packing more of a wallop than I might have guessed. I cry out and grab my bicep. The damage must not be too damning, though, because Mallory is laughing, too.

Mallory says, "In case you haven't noticed, I'm what's known as a super fat. This chip in my tooth? I fell down the stairs last year because I couldn't see where my feet were landing."

"Whoa."

"Yeah. So I'm going to need you to handle the ceiling. Can you do this for me, tiger?"

I kind of like that she just called me *tiger*. "Scraping your ceiling with my skinny privilege. Got it."

On our way back to Mallory's bedroom, I hold short at the bookcase, enthralled by the stacks of eighties and nineties action-adventure films—familiar names like *The Goonies*, *Die Hard*, and *Back to the Future*.

Mallory says, "My dad actually has a VCR. He says the movies are better this way, but a dinosaur *would* say that. I think he only holds on to them to pass them down to that son he's never going to get. I've watched them all. A few don't suck."

My eyes rove over the titles, so many that some tapes are shoved in lengthwise, stacked on top of those standing on edge.

"My God." I kneel to get a look at a title I couldn't miss wedged on the bottom shelf. I lovingly slide the tape from between its companions to survey the precious relic. *The Karate Kid.* Original UK edition. This must be hella rare. The sleeve doesn't feature the familiar cover image of Daniel LaRusso and Mr. Miyagi looking into each other's eyes, which is what shows up whenever we stream the movie on Marcus's Amazon account. No, this sleeve is composed of incredibly realistic watercolor images from the film: Daniel poised to kick ass, Mr. Miyagi looking proudly over his shoulder, plus some smaller vignettes from the movie. It's a good thing I'm already kneeling; otherwise, my knees would buckle.

"It's yours," Mallory says. "If you want it."

The shock and joy are too much. "I couldn't."

"Who hasn't heard you blathering on about your favorite 'superhero'? My dad won't miss it. I certainly won't. What a stupid plot. Teaching a kid karate through unpaid labor? Gross."

I'm nerding out so hard. I don't even care that I don't have a player for it. "Really? Oh my God. Reed is going to shit—" Here's when I remember that Reed isn't exactly the friend I thought he was. The thought sobers me. "Well," I say, my enthusiasm at a respectable level, "you've just won yourself a picture-scraping slave for life. Let's do this."

We return to Mallory's bedroom. I set my precious treasure aside and prop the stepladder in the corner opposite Mallory's bed. She sits on the floor and leans under her desk, begins picking at a section of wall you wouldn't even see when standing.

"Can I ask one more question?" I say.

"Maybe. Your voice is annoying, though, so try to keep it short."

I reach for a loose edge of Scotch tape and pull. "Why do you want to scrape off all these women?" I want to ask why these pictures are even here to begin with, but maybe the economy of a single question will yield answers to others.

Mallory takes a deep breath, not out of annoyance, I think, but as a way of measuring her words. Finally, she says, "Because I don't need them anymore."

Another answer that only leads to more questions. I figure I should shut up for now, though. Mallory doesn't want me to speak; she only wants me to *do*, so I set to scraping at the ceiling, bits of paper falling around me, as delicate and peaceful and unexpected as snow in the desert.

CHAPTER TWENTY-SIX

I'm emptying my half of the closet.

Jeans and dress shirts. Cargo shorts and tighty-whities and T-shirts, everything pulled from its hangers or drawers. I dump Punisher shirt after Green Lantern shirt after Deadpool swim trunks on the floor, carelessly, as if none of these items mean anything to me. Only my sock drawer gets a stay of execution. Well, that and the suit hanging under plastic in the closet's blackest corner. It's the first suit I've ever owned. I can't bear to look at it, let alone touch it, so for the purposes of today's exercise I'm pretending it doesn't exist.

Minutes pass—six, seven, maybe. Mount Cotton-Poly Blend grows.

Once my closet is bare, wobbling hangers finally still, I stand back and eye the summit, map the various routes to the top, the pitfalls that would bring certain death to any microscopic mountain-climber foolhardy enough to scale these craggy peaks.

I think about the purge I helped Mallory with. I couldn't understand why she wanted to get rid of all those women and positive messages on her walls, but I'm dwelling on what she said—*I don't need them anymore*—and I think maybe I get it. Maybe these women were heroes for her—or at least inspiration—and she's grown out of them. This got me thinking about my clothes, so many emblazoned with the colors and symbols of my own heroes, and how few I still wear because I've grown out of them—in the literal sense, I mean. Getting fat happened as a frog boils to death. Gradually, and then all at once. One day I was wearing my favorite X-Men tank top—it's got these kick-ass Wolverine slash marks through the logo—and then I no longer fit into my favorite X-Men tank top. I'm kind of confused about what I'm doing right now, but I think I should stop thinking and just do it.

I strip naked, certain I have at least an hour before Reed gets home from practice. I toss what I was wearing on my bed—the keep pile. I grab a Venom T-shirt from the cliffs of Mount Cotton-Poly Blend and pull it over my head. Too tight. I yank it off and toss it at Captain Condor's feet—the discard pile. I grab a pair of the Flash briefs. I'll be lucky if these make it over my thighs. They do, if barely. Keep? I try to imagine making it through a day with my junk choked in this death grip. I might want children someday. Discard pile.

I grab a button-up and then a button-down and then a pair of gym shorts. I sort methodically, stomping on my thoughts, afraid that maybe I don't really like this activity, that maybe what I'm doing is nothing like what Mallory was doing, afraid to think because thinking too much might bring my work to a screeching halt.

I suck in my stomach and shove myself into one article of clothing after another. I fumble with buttons that close at the neck but don't want to cooperate around my middle. Though the air-conditioning is set to a comfortable temperature, I'm sweating by the time I reach for the final article in the pile, a *Love and Thunder* T-shirt Evelyn bought me only last year. This was the last time she took me school shopping, an activity I'd face a firing squad of light-year arrows to avoid, but she loves.

Loved.

Loves.

As I drop the shirt in the discard pile, my breath comes heavily, not so much from exertion but from the effort it takes not to think too hard. There's a familiar tingling in my sinuses and a growing pressure behind my eyes. I look to the clothes on my bed, the pile only a third the size of the pile at Captain Condor's feet, and release a small, involuntary moan. I'm staring at the image of Stormbreaker on my Thor shirt and the thoughts I don't want to think are crashing through, as if the weapon could make rubble of even psychic walls in a single throw.

I'm thinking, *It's not too late to put it all back in the closet.*

I'm thinking, *If you keep throwing up, you'll probably fit into these clothes again by winter break.*

I'm thinking, *You could lose the weight even faster than Fat Thor did in that Enya montage.*

I'm thinking, *You're all right; you're all right; you're all right; you're all right.*

I'm thinking, *Evelyn can't take you shopping to replace any of this.*

I'm thinking, *This is bullshit.*

I'm thinking, *I can't do this.*

I'm thinking, *You have to.*

I'm thinking, *But I don't want to.*

A wail builds in my throat.

You're all right; you're all right; you're all right; you're all right.

I can't say why—because what I'm doing seems more than a little weird—but suddenly I drop to the floor, stretch my body out, and slide under the mass. I crawl into the smell of my detergent, an allergy-friendly brand Evelyn picked for me when I was little (the one Marcus had to repeat the name of several times when he took over guardianship). I engulf myself in the memories these clothes carry. Wedged between my heroes and the floor, I exhale a deep, slow breath and concentrate on their weight instead of my feelings. It slows my heart and compresses my frenzied mind to stillness.

I feel lost.

I feel enveloped.

I feel crushed.

But my tears recede.

I could fall asleep right here, but what happens when Reed finds me naked under a pile of clothes? I allow myself a few more minutes, as many as I dare, and then I release an exhausted sigh and rise out of my heroes. I slough them from my chest and pull them from my eyes. I step from beneath them to retrieve the roll of garbage bags from the lowest pantry shelf. I unroll three bags, label them with masking tape—*regular stuff*, *superhero shirts*, and *trash* (because I'm pretty sure no one wants my underwear, regardless of how lucky they'd be to own them)—and then, my thoughts and feelings firmly in check, I sort my clothes for the Goodwill and replace the meager leftovers in the closet.

CHAPTER TWENTY-SEVEN

Mallory tips my trash bag of superhero T-shirts over her bed and gives it a shake. A cascade of primary and secondary colors, emblems, insignias, and symbols bursts forth—most familiar to the casual Netflix viewer, some more obscure. They stand in stark contrast to the soft, feminine colors of Mallory's bedroom—a sensory invasion: too bold, too garish, too *boy*. Beside them, I drop the batting and the bolt of electric-blue fabric we just scored from the reclaimed bin at the craft store. Evidently, we're turning my T-shirts into a comforter.

"Ever used a sewing machine?" Mallory asks.

"No, but something tells me I'm about to."

"Everyone should own a sewing machine, if only to upcycle."

"Upcycle?"

"Make something new out of the old or used. It's actually better than recycling because it skips the energy wasted in processing. We're doing our part for the environment—and paying our respects to the exploited sweatshop workers who made these T-shirts."

I laugh. "Where do you get this stuff?"

Foraging through the pile, Mallory freezes, fixes me in a stare that could stop a bunny's heart. "Pick up a book, Brett." She turns, reaches for a volume on her bookcase. "Actually, start with this one." The book jacket features a picture of a broken high heel, symbolic, I assume of the broken nature of the fashion industry. It's unlikely I would ever be caught dead reading a book with a ladies' shoe on it, but I nod enthusiastically anyway. Maybe I can hide the book inside the pages of the latest *Young Justice* and at least give it a try.

"Everything we're wearing right now was made in sweatshops filled with women and children. If you're shopping anywhere but a thrift store, you're an asshole."

I make a mental note to never underestimate Mallory's wokeness. Just being around her makes me want to be a better person. I'm glad I agreed to come over this afternoon. When she invited herself to hang in my hiding spot at lunch today, she asked what I was up to after school. I don't know much about girls, but I *do* know questions like these are always a trap. I couldn't tell her I was planning to drop my clothes off and then eat myself sick, so I just said I was running to the Goodwill and then heading home to destroy the dreams of the weak in *Apex Legends*. (I'm not as strong without Reed, but together we've won a handful of times. We lost our shit that first time, pretty much tore the bedroom apart in our revelry. Reed even did a flip off my bed.) Mallory is incredibly perceptive—another interesting girl thing. Aware of how miserable I was, she poked me in the arm. "Spill it."

"It's my superhero T-shirt collection. I've spent a really long time curating them—a few are even vintage. But, you know, I'm kind of gaining weight, and most of my clothes don't fit anymore, so I'm trying to be a man about it and donate them to some other comic book nerd in need. I don't know. It kind of feels bad."

Mallory leaned in, like I'd said something important without knowing it. "First off, stop being a man about anything, especially your emotions. You're smart, and obviously have a broad vocabulary. Do better than 'bad.'"

I laughed and shrugged, taken aback by such an unexpected critique. "Uh, all right. I guess I feel sad?"

"I want more than a single syllable, caveboy."

"I feel . . . ashamed."

"Good."

"And cheated."

"Excellent—not that you're feeling that way but that you said it."

I grinned, surprised that Mallory could make me feel proud of myself through such simple means, and maybe even more surprised that it would occur to her to do so. Evelyn would like her. I wished I could take Mallory to meet Evelyn, but that thought led to other thoughts I didn't want to think about, so I boxed the thought up and buried it deep in the moldy catacombs of my mind.

"Second," Mallory said, "you don't have to give up what you love just because your body is different now. You're not going to the Goodwill later. You're coming to my place."

You couldn't have paid me to hang with Mallory even a few days ago, yet I couldn't deny that the thought of another afternoon with her bolstered me. She's a mystery, something new to unravel. Only one concern had me hesitating. "Will your mom be there? I kind of ghosted her OA meeting and I'm afraid she'll think I'm a dick."

"I've been ghosting those stupid meetings for months now. Those meetings aren't for you. They aren't for anyone."

Of course I agreed. Until my food journal hit the internet, that meeting was set to go down as the most humiliating event of my life. But something told me Mallory could say so with authority, like she understood things I didn't. "How do you know?"

157

Mallory's expression clouded over. Maybe there were things in her life she didn't like to think about, too. Finally, she said, "My doctor says so—well, not in so many words, but she was the first to endorse me no longer attending. My mom shit a brick—there was a glorious screaming match—but what could she do?"

With every morsel Mallory revealed, I wanted to know more—why would a doctor tell someone so fat that she shouldn't abstain from her trigger foods?—but I sensed I needed to be patient. Mallory might be the stalker in this arrangement, but I'm the one who needs to earn her trust.

"Anyway," she continued, "I wouldn't subject you to my mom. When she's not at OA, she's at Bible study or taking my sisters to ballet or Girl Scouts, gymnastics, whatever—all the tortures I've grown out of. She's a tornado who sucks up anyone in her path. I think she avoids being at home because she's afraid if she has a minute to herself she might use it to eat."

We laughed together, which kind of made me feel like a jerk, though it was worth it to be taken into someone's confidence.

Now Mallory hands me a pair of scissors. "We're going to cut along the seams to separate the fronts of the shirts from the backs, but we need to be careful about it. We want clean, straight edges. We want them to retain the shape of a T-shirt."

We sit on her bed and set to destroying my beloved collection. Not destroying, I remind myself, *upcycling*. I thought this part would be painful, like murdering my friends, but instead it feels like performing surgery to save them.

After we have a pile of several panels, Mallory shows me how to thread the sewing machine—simpler than it looks—and sits beside me while I attach one shirt to another, altering the orientation so the pieces almost fit like a puzzle, some shirts oriented upright, others upside down.

Mallory says, "We'll fill in gaps with the scraps from the backs of the shirts once the fronts are all put together."

At first, it's pretty tricky to keep my lines straight. I guess I'm a lead foot, because Mallory encourages me to let off the foot pedal until I'm more adept at guiding the fabric. It pulls like a car with alignment issues, steered by a mind of its own.

The whole process is super satisfying, and it's not long until we have a large rectangle of attached shirts, big enough, I'm guessing, for a queen-sized bed. Mallory produces a tape measure, the kind you'd see in the tiny hands of Cinderella's mice. She shows me how to measure and cut a backing and border from the bolt of blue fabric. I'm so engrossed that I actually startle when my phone vibrates against my thigh. A text from Reed. Will I be home for dinner? Neither Reed nor Marcus polices my comings and goings, but they do check in with me when I disappear for hours on end. I realize I haven't thought about food since I arrived at Mallory's.

"It's okay," Mallory says. "We can finish another time."

"No." I shake my head and tap out a perfunctory message: Be home late. "I want to finish tonight." Heat rises in my cheeks and I give Mallory a sheepish grin. "I mean, I can't wait to sleep under this bad boy, so . . ."

Mallory smiles in that full-bodied way you might if no one were watching. I've never seen her smile like this before. I make a mental note to ensure she does more often.

I drop my phone on the bed and sit on the floor beside her. We've got the blanket laid out now, a layer of batting between the T-shirt panel and the backing panel. Mallory shows me how to thread yarn in a pattern across the blanket's surface. "This keeps the batting from moving around."

As she works, I snip the lengths of yarn and tie them into knots.

Mallory says, "So you live with Reed, right?"

I'm immediately afraid of this conversation. What if easy questions lead to hard ones? But Mallory is starting to open up to me. I owe her the same.

"Yeah. I moved in with him in January—after my mom started going in and out of the hospital." I surprise myself with my next words, more than I've given anyone outside my immediate circle. "Lung cancer." It's impossible to think about Evelyn without tearing up, but I swallow my feelings, determined to survive a few sentences of conversation without crying. "I was visiting her when you followed me the other day. That's her house, my old house."

Mallory nods but doesn't press for more. Instead she says, "Must be pretty fun, living with your best friend."

I grimace. "It was, or I guess I thought it was, but things are kind of . . . I don't know. We're having marital issues, I guess."

Mallory's body quakes. "So the rumors of your torrid gay romance are true?"

I'm laughing, too, enough to screw up my knot. I untangle and start again. "Not true, I'm afraid, but they might as well be with the level of drama we're twisted up in. First he steals my girl—"

Mallory punches me in the leg.

I cower and spike my voice with a healthy dose of melodrama. "Violence is never the answer!"

"Women aren't possessions, Brett. Also, I want names."

I roll my eyes. "Perfectly-independent-woman-who-don't-need-no-man Thandie Gellar."

Mallory's eyes widen. "Oh yeah. I can see how that would sting."

"To be fair, he didn't know I was crushing on her. I was too embarrassed to tell him because I knew she was way out of my league."

"And what league would that be?"

Mallory's question takes me by surprise. Doesn't she know? Her expression suggests we aren't moving on until I give her an answer, so I stumble through the first metaphor that pops into my mind. "Well . . . I mean, I guess you could say Reed is a Peter Parker, right?"

Mallory stifles a guffaw but nods for me to go on. "I can't wait to hear this one."

"Okay, so, you know, the Peter Parkers of the world, right? They're the ones who get the MJs . . ."

The evolution of Mallory's expression is not encouraging, which should shut me up but instead makes me talk faster.

"And I mean, like, I guess what I'm saying is that if *Reed* is the Peter, I must be the Ned Leeds—the good MCU one, not the shitty Hobgoblin one, obviously—which is kind of spookily uncanny since Ned isn't just the chubby one but the *of-color* one, the sidekick to a white thirst trap, and, I mean, I guess I'm getting off track because obviously that's just a technical detail since MJ is Black and it's not really about race, right?" I have a feeling Mallory might tell me there's definitely something about race going on because she's much smarter than me, and my own heart is telling me there *might* be something about race going on, and I kind of think maybe Gloria Anzaldúa would agree, but I don't want to think about that right now, so I plow forward before Mallory can respond and I say, "I mean, I love Ned and all—everyone loves Ned; he's dope as fuck and super cool, obviously—but, I mean, he's just the guy in the *chair*, you know? And the guy in the chair doesn't get the . . ."

And this is when it dawns on me. Ned absolutely *does* get the girl, a really hot one who dresses—I'm disturbed to report—a lot like super-villain extraordinaire Robyn Fletcher, which kind of makes her *not* hot? What the hell?

"So what you're saying is that you're a guy in a chaaair?" Mallory narrows her brow and draws out the final syllable to underscore how ridiculous I must sound. "And as such you're not good enough for Thandie? Is that the thesis?"

I'm so disoriented by my own train of thought that I don't know how to respond. Ned is with *Betty Brant* in *Far from Home*. How could I have forgotten that?

Before I spiral too far into territory I can't begin to navigate, I deflect. "I mean, I'm not sure my league is really what's important to the fight. The real problem is that Reed keeps going out of his way to protect me, catering to me all the time. I guess it's because of my mom, but . . . it's just annoying, like we're not equals anymore or something. I don't need protection, you know? I'm not fragile." Even as the words leave my mouth, I know they're not true. This crying-every-five-minutes thing, the puking thing, the drinking thing—all the things.

Mallory sets the yarn aside and begins tying with me. "There are worse things you can do to a person than love him too much."

Mallory's words knock me off-kilter. "Huh?"

"Reed loves you."

"The gay thing is a cool joke and all, but we're not actually gay for each other."

"Oh my God." Mallory busts up and shakes her head sorrowfully. "What are we going to do with you, my poor wayward boy?"

I raise my hands in surrender. "Okay, I'm clearly missing something. Let's have it."

"What does being gay or straight have to do with love?"

"Uh . . ."

"Reed loves you, and you love him. A lot of kids don't have someone like that in their lives."

I wonder if Mallory is speaking from experience. The possibility bowls me over. What would I do without Reed? Where would I be right this minute if not for him? I pick up my phone. He hasn't texted back, maybe because I was rude or maybe because neither of us is the best at writing texts. Under Be home late, I type, But maybe we can play Apex Legends when I get home if you're still up.

Several minutes pass with no response. It's fine. We've both behaved like dicks, but when guys fight, we get over it in no time. I feel a lot better having taken a step to set things right.

Mallory and I reach for the final length of yarn at the same time. "It's your masterpiece," she says. "You tie it."

I carefully twist a tight knot, then hop to my feet. Mallory joins me, lifts the blanket above her head so I can get a good look at what we've done. It might be the dopest thing I've ever seen. Now instead of being in one of my favorite T-shirts, I can be under *all* of them.

I spy the *Love and Thunder* shirt, the last one Evelyn bought me, prominently placed in the center. I'm thinking about that scene in the movie where Jane turns to stardust, and I feel too misty to talk.

Mallory gets it. Her empathic powers are dialed to their highest setting. So she lightens the mood, wrapping the blanket around my shoulders like a cape. "Fly, my little Avenger."

We laugh, and I wonder if maybe I could.

CHAPTER TWENTY-EIGHT

Shortly after arriving home, I exit the bathroom I share with Reed, my eyes still red, face blotchy from puking. I'm not too worried about anyone noticing. Marcus is at the factory, like always, and it looks like Reed turned in early; it's only ten o'clock, but our room was dark when I poked my head in. I'd hoped for a chance to apologize for freaking out, and just for, I don't know, being so hard to be buddies with lately, but I guess my apology will have to wait until morning.

I'm wired from my epic upcycling project with Mallory, and I've successfully rid myself of the In-N-Out I had on the way home—lending new irony to the burger joint's name—so I think I'm going to spend a couple hours on my stupid idiom essay. It's due next week and I haven't written a word.

I step into our bedroom and beeline for the desk, my path illuminated by the light following me from the living room. The shadows cast a sinister pall over Captain Condor's rigid countenance. I should turn the standee around if I'm going to be throwing up at the apartment. The expression on Captain's face has always been one of fatherly pride, but lately there's something about the hardness of his jaw and the black voids behind his mask that make me feel judged, like Captain might shake his head with disappointment if he could.

I grab my notebook from my drawer and turn to tiptoe from the room when Reed's reading lamp flares to life. The light is feeble, yet the effect is blinding.

"I know what you're doing."

Reed speaks from behind an issue of *Doom Patrol* propped open on his chest. He lies casually on his bunk, one arm draped off the side of the mattress, legs crossed. Tank top, boxer shorts. Relaxed, comfortable—states of being that are only mildly familiar to me anymore. If he was reading, why was his light out? Has he been waiting to ambush me? Dramatic much?

I pretend I don't know what he means—maybe because I *can't* know what he means, at least not for sure. Is he talking about what I think he's talking about? I say, "I'm working on my essay. Have you started? It's due next week." After only a moment's hesitation, I add, "You can give it to me to edit for you . . . if you want."

Reed doesn't look up from his comic book. "I'm not talking about homework. You know what I'm talking about."

My chest constricts, like when you go extreme trampoline air-drumming on a winter night.

"You could at least do a better job of cleaning up. I don't want to see that when I lift the toilet seat. I found some on the wall."

I've been careful, haven't I?

Captain Condor's rich voice echoes in my mind. *You left the evidence on purpose.*

No, of course I didn't. Why would I do that?

Superheroes stand for truth, Brett.

165

It was an oversight. I cleaned up and then . . . maybe I missed some, but . . .

Reed says, "If you want to pull that shit, I can't stop you. God knows I've tried. But I don't want to know about it, and I sure as fuck don't want to see it."

I'm scribbling furiously on my thumb. "Sorry." This is not the type of apology I had planned, and it's all the harder to say because it seems the apology I wanted to say has no place in this conversation.

Reed sits up, swings his feet to the floor. "Your apologies aren't worth shit. Have you even seen Ms. Finch since your food journal went public? You're getting worse. I figured once your disorder wasn't a secret anymore, you'd do something about it, or maybe Ms. Finch would *make* you do something, but here we are with your barf on the wall, so . . ."

The realization hits so fast and so hard that I actually stumble backward. I'm saved from falling by the desk behind me. Reed *knows* me; he knows how ashamed I am of all of this—yet he keeps talking about how *good* it is that my secret's out, how productive, what a lucky break, just what the doctor ordered to light a fire of change under my ass. In a split second, I'm seeing what I've missed.

I lunge. Reed yelps as I shove his shoulders into the mattress and straddle him. I pound him in the face with my balled fist, not so much a proper punch as an awkward Hulk smash. I've never hit someone before, so my form is questionable. Blood gushes from his nose. I'm screaming, "*You* posted my journal! *Why?*" I get in a second strike before the pain in my hand registers, jolts reverberating up my arm in throbbing waves.

Despite the pain, I aim for another strike, but Reed has finally caught up to me. He grabs my arm mid-smash and twists his body, throwing me roughly to the floor. Nailed to the carpet, I writhe and buck, but there's no hope of besting a wrestler at his own game. I use the only weapon left to me and spit in his face, which seems fair enough since he's bleeding on mine.

"Stop it! Fuck!" He shifts forward on my chest to hold my arms down with his knees. His hands freed, he scrubs his face with a forearm, lifts the front of his tank top to stanch the blood draining from his nose.

"Get the fuck off me!"

"Calm down!"

"Get off!"

"Calm down!"

"Fuck you!"

"Fuck you!"

My breath heaves, and I think I could puke again, what with Reed's entire weight resting on my chest. I try to jerk free once more, but the effort is only half-hearted. I'm the one who got the punches in, if you could call them that, but somehow I feel like I lost the fight.

I relax my limbs, let the adrenaline drain into the carpet. The moment it's gone, a familiar emotion rushes in to take its place. *Don't start crying*, I think. *If you start crying* . . . I grit my teeth until the wave passes.

Reed rises off me. He staggers backward to sit on the edge of his bed, shirt still pressed to his face. I sit up, mop his blood off with whatever's on top of the dirty laundry pile.

Through panting exhalations, he says, "I was coming up the stairs that day when I saw you burst into the boys' room. I was headed there myself, but when I got to the door, I heard you punch the towel dispenser. I know when I'm in a towel-dispenser-punching kind of mood I need to be alone, so I waited outside the bathroom until you left. I figured I'd ask you what was up later, after you'd cooled off—not that you'd have told me."

The bitterness in his voice is so palpable I can taste it—then again, I may just be tasting his blood.

"So I went to take a leak and I found your journal. I didn't know what to do with it. I wasn't going to do anything. I just wanted to talk to you. You think no one could possibly understand what you're going through, but I'm a fucking *wrestler*, dude. You wouldn't believe the fucked-up shit I've seen guys do to make weight. But then you wouldn't talk to me, and I knew you were shook from that OA meeting, and I thought if I—"

"You thought wrong."

A bitter laugh. He shrugs. "Yeah, well, it turns out trying to help you yields nothing but shit consequences, which is exactly what Thandie warned me about. I thought I knew better. Consider me punished."

He talked to *Thandie*? About *this*?

"You know, I got kicked off the wrestling team when I took the rap for our covert comic-booking. Didn't have that info filed away in your little self-absorbed head, did you?"

My shock must speak for itself.

"I've been pretending to go to practice because I didn't want you to feel bad."

"I *never* asked you—"

"You didn't have to. That face you're making right now? That wounded one? You make it *all the time*, and I can't stand it."

Reed rises from the bed, brushes past me. He's in the living room by the time his final words reach me. "Coming at me with that *sorry* shit. Stop being sorry and start being different."

Brett Harrison

Banksie

AP English

8 October

Idiom Essay Rough Draft

Sometimes You CAN Eat Your
Cake and Have It, Too

I was maybe seven years old the night I learned my first lesson about ~~barfing~~ vomiting. I'd eaten some contaminated tomato sauce and woke in the dark with severe food poisoning. The one thing I remember about the whole ordeal, the detail that stuck with me, was that it was so violent and so sudden that my puke actually hit the wall opposite my bed. I was just lying there fully asleep, and suddenly my insides were flying across the room as if my stomach were a slingshot. I didn't think that sort of thing was possible outside of horror movies, and I really wish I hadn't had reason to find out otherwise. The more meaningful lesson—the lesson I should have taken to heart—was that puke has a way of getting and staying everywhere. For months afterward, you could still spy the random pink spatter crusted on the drywall, flecks ~~Evelyn~~ my mom missed when she cleaned up after me.

Now I know ~~hella~~ many things about puking that I wish I didn't know.

First, doing it takes commitment because your stomach doesn't want to cooperate. You'll have to gag and gag, which makes your eyes water so aggressively that you'll question if your body is merely reacting physically or if you're crying because you feel so ~~shitty~~ bad about yourself. It's probably a little of both. When the puke finally comes, it hurts, as if you did a few thousand sit-ups. Your face will hurt, too. It'll feel like your eyes are going to pop out and blood is pummeling your forehead. Every time you ~~spew~~ puke is another gauntlet of physical discomfort to run. Will you make it to the finish line? [Note to self: How will Banksie feel about rhetorical questions?]

Another thing I wish I didn't know about puking is that puking can burn ~~the fuck out of~~ your throat in a lasting-damage kind of way. You'll walk around with the raw throat of a head cold or like you're about to get a head cold. The intensity of the scratchy throat is affected by what you ate and when you ate last. Basically, ~~tossing your cookies~~ vomiting feels like someone's dousing the inside of your head with Drano.

The acid can get up in your nostrils and burn them, too. Puking leaves your sinuses clogged and your nose stuffed. Even your snot will smell like barf. Everything will smell like barf. [Note to self: Is barf too colloquial a word? What about snot? Does it matter in a personal essay? Am I allowed to colloquial the fuck out of this?]

Regarding the smell, expect puke to get all over your hands—and sometimes your feet and clothes. No matter how thoroughly you wash your hands, they'll stink for hours afterward and you'll live in fear that others will smell the sourness, which you're actually growing used to. You'll be afraid people will know what you're doing, that they'll talk about you on the internet because, evidently, you're way more compelling than you ever wanted to be. Each time you throw up, you'll look in the mirror at your red eyes and your burst capillaries and the snot and saliva hanging from your face, and you'll watch the tap water wash away the painful gunk coating your hands and forearms, and you'll feel judged, like your man card has been permanently revoked—because boys don't do this, do they?—and you'll wash your face and rinse your mouth. You'll rinse again, and then again, because it seems you can never get rid of the rotted taste sticking to the roof of your mouth. And pretty soon you'll start doing that thing your English teacher always talks about, the thing he told you you're not allowed to do in your idiom essay, that thing where you shift into second-person pronouns as a way to distance and protect yourself from stuff that makes you so uncomfortable and so ashamed that you can't bear to speak about it directly, so ashamed that you can't bear to say the word "I" in relation to it.

You'll attempt to write an essay that tells the truth because you're getting so tired of your lies and your denials and you're not sure you can keep this secret anymore because you might be more afraid of what you're doing in your bathroom than you are of what might happen if you fess up to what you're doing in your bathroom. In this essay, which will grow more meta with every line, you'll attempt to illustrate that you can, in fact, eat your cake and have it, too. All you have to do is leave traces of your cake on your bathroom wall or on your T-shirt or under your fingernails. You can carry your cake with you always—or at least until your ~~best bro~~ roommate finds traces of it beneath the rim of the toilet and calls you out and you write this garbage mess of an essay and you sit here staring at the wall forever because even moving seems like something you could screw up royally, until finally you gather your strength and tear these pages from your notebook and you burn them because you've met Reed, that traitorous taint licker, and you know it's not safe to wad them up and toss them in the wastebasket beneath your desk. Fuck.

CHAPTER TWENTY-NINE

'm lying drunk on my trampoline, watching the sky for shooting stars and wondering where Evelyn is. I've been at it maybe an hour and clocked three shooting stars (meteors fall more often than people realize; you just have to have the patience to look). Each flaming meteor that burned out earned me another flaming gulp of vodka. My supply dwindles. What will I do when I down the last drop?

I cradle my bottle in my armpit and check my phone for the millionth time. Nothing. I've texted Evelyn several times with no response:

> I came to visit but I couldn't find you.

> Where are you?

> Hollaback, girl.

> You're out way past curfew.

> Seriously, tho.

> Talk to me.

> I need you.

> Please text back.

> Please text back.

> Please text back.

I wasn't going to burden Evelyn with my fight with Reed. I was fully prepared to make up some lie about how much fun we had getting up to fill-in-the-blank mischief. I only wanted to be near her. I wanted her to give me a hug so I could hold on just a little longer than I should but not long enough to rouse suspicion that something is wrong, that everything is wrong. I wanted to talk to someone who doesn't believe I'm an asshole or a loser, maybe even thinks I'm the greatest kid in the world.

But that person isn't here.

I flip through the barren Rolodex in my mind, looking for a comforting place to land. Marcus is not the nurturing type; we've never once talked about my feelings. I think about my various buddies, all of whom have been hanging out with Reed since I disappeared from the social landscape at school. None of those friends would ever talk about feelings, anyway. Ms. Finch was my best bro for such needs, but even she's a stranger now. I rub my belly. Maybe I should eat something.

And then there she is, filling the landscape of my mind, a burst of color in a night too black. I rock forward into a seated position and text Mallory:

> Hey, so I'm drunk and everyone hates me.
> Wanna come talk about our feelings?

I know Mallory is guarded, and maybe I haven't earned enough trust to talk about *her* feelings, but she also really cares about people and doing the right thing, so maybe if I'm someone in need . . .

The response is nearly instantaneous:

> You at Reed's? I don't know where that is.

> Actually, I'm at my old house, on my trampoline.
> There's no gate or anything. Just come around
> back and you'll find me.

When Mallory rounds the south corner of the house, I plaster a genuine smile across my face, which, I realize, is probably hard to see in nothing but the relatively distant light from the neighbor's back patio. I wave. "Get up here, girl."

Mallory looks dubious. "Why are you in the dark? I almost tripped on the pavers getting back here."

I lift my arms to showcase the sky. "The darker the better."

Malloy takes in the starscape. "Nice. But I'm not getting up there."

"Dude. Not cool." I hop to a standing position. The vodka bottle rolls at my feet. I place my fists on my hips and give Mallory a stern look. "Get up here yesterday."

Mallory's words come matter-of-factly, which stings more than if they'd been judgmental or disappointed. "I don't think I like you when you've been drinking."

My buzz drains immediately. I flop back into a seated position. "I'm sorry."

The moment the words are out of my mouth, I'm cringing, bracing for the response I got from Reed yesterday. *Your apologies aren't worth shit.* But instead Mallory extends her arm. "Give me the bottle."

I relinquish it, suddenly anxious to see as much distance between me and that bottle as possible. Mallory sets it on the patio steps. Will she just keep walking? I release a breath I didn't know I was holding when she turns and rejoins me at the edge of the trampoline.

"It's safe up here," I say. "It can hold you. We don't have to jump, just sit."

"It's too high."

I grab the metal frame with one hand and flip over the edge, landing cleanly on the ground. I lace my fingers together and hold my arms beside Mallory's legs. "M'lady."

"Brett . . ."

I give her an encouraging nod. "Just a little boost."

Mallory shakes her head and sighs, a sure sign she's resigned to her fate. "If I break anything, I'll have the surgeons transplant it from *your* body." She grabs the trampoline frame and shoves herself off the ground. Her torso skids onto the mat, and she only lightly kicks me in the face while trying to gain her bearings.

"Radical." I leap up to join her, and we awkwardly roll toward the center of the mat, limbs tangling. We laugh as our bodies crash into each other, release a few squeals as we right ourselves, finally sitting across from each other, me cross-legged and Mallory sitting as she does on the floor, her legs akimbo to leave room for her apron.

"That was the most action I've ever gotten from a girl," I say. "You're welcome."

Mallory's arm juts out to slap me, but I'm too quick. I perform a reverse somersault, leaving her on her back again.

When our laughs wane, I look to Mallory, hoping she'll say something. Anything will do. Some social-justice-warrior thing or feminist thing. But instead she sits quietly, an expectant look on her face. She must have learned this trick from Ms. Finch—or maybe this isn't so much a Ms. Finch thing as a girl thing? Whatever the case, I know what I have to do. I was the one who asked her to come. I can't chicken out now.

I say, the words tasting bitter, "It was Reed who posted my journal page, the hottest literary sensation at Tucson City High. I'm sure you've read it."

If Mallory is surprised at this information, she doesn't show it.

"I was going to apologize to Reed, you know, for being pissed at him when I shouldn't have been, but then he . . ." I have to tread lightly. I don't want Mallory to know I'm throwing up. Do I want Mallory to know I'm throwing up? "Um, he started yelling at me about how I'm not getting help—you know, for the bingeing—and how it's messed up that I stopped seeing Ms. Finch. She was helping me, trying to, at least, but I screwed that up. And then he said something about how he thought I'd change now that I have no reason to hide what I'm doing, and that's when, I don't know, I just knew it was him, he was the one who posted what I wrote. Only Ms. Finch was supposed to see it, and . . . it was awful and embarrassing and he was my best friend . . ." I'm shaking my head. "God, I'm sorry. You don't want to hear all this." I release a long breath. Whatever meager reserves of stoicism I might be clinging to go with it. I grab my face to hide my tears when they come. I don't even know why I'm crying most of the time anymore. Because I'm hurt? Because I'm afraid? Because Evelyn was supposed to be here and she wasn't here?

She wasn't here.

Instead of speaking, Mallory begins rolling the dozens of jelly bracelets from her wrist. In the dark, they're leached of their intense rainbow colors, yet it still seems like Mallory is stripping away some of her vibrancy as each plastic ring hits the trampoline mat. In seconds, her wrist is naked. She thrusts it toward me, twists her arm to catch the meager light so I can see . . . ? Oh no.

Two ridges of skin, paler than the rest, rise from Mallory's otherwise-smooth wrist. I know immediately what these scars mean, and the sight of them makes me cry harder.

Mallory speaks softly, her words measured. "This happened this summer, just after school let out." She holds her wrist to her body, not so much to hide it as to cradle it. "Yet again, my mom and I were fighting on the way home from OA. I was only attending because she threatened to take my car away if I didn't. As you can imagine, she's the great abstinence success story. Hasn't touched sugar in four years, not since she decided it was finally time to get rid of the baby weight *once and for all.*" Mallory underscores her words with a dramatic fist pump and the inspiring inflection of a general addressing her troops. "I mean, who doesn't eat sugar? Like, ever? And she has to walk into those meetings with *this* beside her"—Mallory gestures to her body—"making stank face the whole time in front of her friends. I said some nasty things I regret, or maybe I don't regret, I'm still working that out, and she said . . ." Mallory's jaw seems to harden. I didn't recognize until this moment just how strong she is. "She said that she'd rather have no daughter at all than an embarrassment like me."

"Oh my God."

Mallory blocks my words with her hand. "I want to be clear about something. I didn't do this because I wanted to die. I *don't* want to die. I did it because living was too hard, because every day felt like a

178

fight—with my mom, with everyone at school, even with myself . . ." Mallory looks to her hands. "Especially with myself. I didn't know how to win the fight, or even how to keep fighting."

I'm nodding, wiping at my eyes. If Mallory can tell me this story without crying, I can at least try to be strong as I hear it.

"I don't know you well. I don't know what makes you tick or what has led to your bingeing. I didn't know if you had anyone to talk to, anyone helping you, but I'd give anything to have had someone, because . . . because maybe if I had, I wouldn't need to cover up these scars on my wrist. I have a doctor now—and a dietician and a therapist. I have all these people helping me see myself and my life differently. I feel like a fighter now. And I wanted to make sure you had someone. So don't apologize for opening up to me, okay?"

"Okay."

"Promise you'll talk to Ms. Finch?"

I nod some more, eyes trained on Mallory's wrist, still hidden from view. "I'll try."

And then I do something I can't even explain. I reach for Mallory's hand. I lift her wrist to my mouth and gently kiss her scars, like Evelyn used to do whenever I'd crash and burn on my scooter. I hold Mallory's hand in both of mine and force myself to look her in the eye. "I'm really glad you're still here."

She smiles, her eyes finally welling. "Thanks, nerd. Me too."

"You want to watch for shooting stars with me?"

We lie side by side, waiting for those split-second bursts of light. In between, I point out my favorite constellations and tell Mallory about some of Kid Condor's more memorable adventures in their star systems. Mallory laughs and comments, both poking fun at me and admiring my creativity.

After I'm spent and we finally fall silent, Mallory says, "Brett? We shouldn't be here, should we?"

My silence is answer enough.

"You want to ride shotgun to Yogurtland? I've got reward points to blow. If we leave now, we should make it before they close."

I hope Mallory hears the smile in my voice. "Yeah. Yes, please. That sounds dope."

As Mallory navigates the winding lanes of the foothills, her car descending into Tucson proper, I realize, for once, I'm not feeling guilty to be heading toward a late-night snack. I realize, for once, I won't be eating alone.

CHAPTER THIRTY

Mallory swipes her arm across the shelf here in aisle twelve of the Grocery Bargain Barn, Tucson's first stop for end-of-the-line nonperishables and once-fresh produce. I jump out of the way as a tower of identical boxes of kids' pasta, each emblazoned with the words *Macarrones con Queso!*, crumbles, the cardboard bricks tumbling into our cart like the rubble of a city destroyed. Evidently, several dozen boxes aren't enough for whatever it is we're doing on this glorious Saturday, because Mallory is immediately on her hands and knees, gathering the boxes that overshot and hit the floor.

"Help me, dweeb." She hands the boxes to me.

Dweeb is what passes for a term of endearment to Mallory, and after she was there for me when I was feeling so low, I figure I can roll with that.

"We need every box," she says. "Don't let a single one go to waste."

Are we going to eat all this? It's pointless to ask Mallory questions—I will only know what she wants me to know when she's ready for me to know it. I wouldn't mind plowing through these boxes, if that's the plan. My insatiable stomach monster has been stirred to life by the familiar siren call of the boxes' color scheme—the primary-blue and neon-orange tones of a thousand dinners past. Could we actually eat all this? Could

I throw it up without Mallory finding out? Every time I puke now, I start crying, and it's getting harder and harder to convince myself I'm doing the right thing.

I step to the shelf, collect and drop several stacks of boxes into the cart.

All Mallory told me about the day's agenda is that I'm playing the role of assistant in a printmaking project. I'm failing, though, to see a connection between our shopping trip and any form of art making beyond the macaroni necklaces kids string together in kindergarten.

I load the last of the Macarrones con Queso! into the cart and reach for the name-brand stuff farther down the shelf.

Mallory stops me. "We're not paying an extra eight cents per box to line corporate America's pockets. Fuck the oppressors. My art is for the proletariat."

I'm too embarrassed of my ignorance to ask what a proletariat is, but since I'm with Mallory, I don't have to. As she steers our cart past last year's Lunchables and deli meats, she tells me about her favorite graphic guide to Marxism. "You'll love it because it has lots of pictures."

We angle past an endcap featuring trendy-looking sunscreen that's surely little more than moisturizer these days, to the aisle housing cooking and baking supplies. We find what looks like a tub of Crisco—a knockoff brand, of course—and load three tubs into our cart.

"Perfect," Mallory says. She examines a messily scrawled list in her pocket sketchbook. Stars and stripes are drawn haphazardly around the page's edge. The title of the list reads *Fat American*.

She nods. "Uh-huh. Okay, yeah. Got that. Totally have some of those." Mallory's smiling with her whole face, that rare kind of smile I'm one of the few privileged enough to witness. "I think we're ready."

She turns the cart toward the front of the store, holds short. Her smile disintegrates as she reaches for the phone perched precariously in her bra. She rolls her eyes. "Ugh, gross. One sec." She swipes to answer, puts the phone to her ear. "All good, Dad. Yeah. I'm with my girlfriends. You know, shopping, girl stuff. Uh-huh. Okay. I'll be eagerly awaiting your call. Yes. Got it. *Yes. YES. Bye.*"

We're on the move again. Mallory lifts her arm, indicating her rainbow wrist. "Ever since, he calls me literally every hour when I'm not in direct sight or at school. He knows treatment's going well, but he still acts like I'm determined to end it all at any moment."

"That blows, but it proves he loves you."

"You got me there, kid."

"What's treatment like?"

"I see my doctor once every three weeks, my dietician and therapist every other week. More often at first. I still attend two group therapy sessions a week, one about food and another called a process group. We make a lot of art that shows our feelings. My extracurricular activities used to be limited to hanging out at the community press every day after school or being dragged against my will to OA. Now, besides my shifts at Jack, I've got a reserved seat both onstage and in the audience for the Mallory show twenty-four seven."

"That sounds overwhelming."

"At times, but I love it, actually. Dr. Hug is pretty much my favorite person ever."

"Dr. Hug? Really?"

"The most aptly named doctor on the planet, probably."

Every time I think about my promise to Mallory—the promise to reconnect with Ms. Finch—my insides fill with Slinkys. Everything Mallory says sounds terrible—will Ms. Finch pressure me into doing all those things? What if it's worse for me because of the puking? I think of Evelyn and force myself to think the just-right word: *purging*.

Whatever may come, a promise is a promise. After our talk on the trampoline, I devised a plan for getting back in Ms. Finch's good graces. I'm not off to a great start, though. After spending the last two afternoons visiting nurseries all over Tucson, I failed to find the perfect visual aid. It's a stroke of luck that Mallory needed to visit a grocery store, because I think I know what I can buy instead.

"I'll meet you up front," I say. "I gotta grab something."

At the cramped checkout stand, a young clerk doesn't even make eye contact, let alone comment on the contents of our cart. He passes one box of macaroni and cheese at a time across the scanner. The woman waiting behind us taps her foot conspicuously, sighing at regular intervals, each exhalation louder than the last. I don't blame the clerk for not speeding through the process. The Grocery Bargain Barn—whose façade really does look like a barn—seems like the kind of place where futures come to die, and perhaps the clerk just doesn't want to die alone. The tag on his shirt reads *Carson's my name. Saving with a Smile's My Game.* A poster of a rooster with bulging shopping bags under his wings hangs behind Carson's head. *Cock-a-Doodle-Dooooo Not Pay Full Price!*

When he's bagged the last of the boxes, the vegetable shortening, and the tiny jar of Kalamata olives I added to the conveyor belt, Carson finally looks up, not with a smile but with the hollow expression of a zombie. "$46.73."

I've never gone shopping with a girl before, but I watch enough TV to know I'm supposed to pull out my wallet. Hand in pocket, clamp down, hand out of pocket. Nailed it.

Mallory actually stomps on my foot. "Instead of lecturing you on the oppression of women through financial dependency, I'm assigning you a book report on *A Room of One's Own* by my favorite author, Virginia Woolf. You've heard of her?"

I don't dare speak for fear that the truth will slip out: that I only know the name because it was prominently featured on the bookcase housing Evelyn's favorite moldy old texts used to torture college kids.

The impatient woman behind us is actually smiling now. Mallory turns her attention to Carson. "You've read it, right?"

Perhaps a neurological disorder has deadened Carson's facial muscles. He moves his blank expression to me and then to Mallory and then back to me. "$46.73."

"Okay, then." Slowly, Mallory pulls several bills from her bra.

As we steer our cart through the sliding doors, Mallory uses her sternest voice and says, "I'll expect a thousand words on my desk by nine a.m. Monday morning." Her grin couldn't be more triumphant. Saving with a smile, indeed.

CHAPTER THIRTY-ONE

I don't know how to say this without sounding like a total pervert, so I'll just say it: Mallory's boobs are pretty epic.

It's an hour or so after our adventure at the Grocery Bargain Barn, and I could never have anticipated our mac 'n' cheese art project would lead to this: Me, Mallory, Mallory's boobs, all chillin' on the poolside patio in her backyard. I'm staring at said boobs and I'm telling myself to stop staring because surely staring makes me a creep, but I can't stop staring because I've never seen real live boobs up close. Mallory isn't exactly naked right now—she wears a bright yellow pair of thong panties—but she may as well be. Her skin, the color of the delicious pink Hostess Snoballs I sometimes eat by the boxful, seems to redden further in the merciless afternoon sun even as I stand here awaiting directions.

"Brett."

Do I hear something?

"Brett."

That's my name.

Mallory slaps my cheek.

I shake my head and blink, the spell broken. My words come as more of an exhalation than speech. "My God . . ."

Mallory slaps me again, the clap reverberating.

"Come on!"

"You said you could handle this. If you're going to be my assistant, you need to act professional."

I *did* agree—when a girl asks if it's okay to take her clothes off in front of you, you don't say no. At least I had the good sense to confirm that Mallory's family would absolutely *not* be showing up this afternoon. Tina may be the supervillain in Mallory's life, but she looks like a kindergarten teacher, the type of woman who doesn't use curse words. I don't want to imagine the humiliation if she were to step out onto the patio right now. Mallory's dad is at work, and Tina and Mallory's sisters are in Las Vegas at some convention for fat women that Mallory used to attend but doesn't want to attend anymore. "Not because there's anything wrong with the event," she explained. "It's pretty cool, actually. I'm just . . . moving in a different direction with treatment. I want to be a person who happens to be fat, not a fat who happens to be a person."

Now I avert my eyes and kneel on the concrete, where we've laid out our art supplies in the shade of a patio table. An open tub of vegetable shortening and a box of latex gloves stand beside two shakers—the kind you'd use to dust pastries with powdered sugar. Each is filled with orange cheese powder from the dozens of boxes of Macarrones con Queso! we bought this morning. On the table rests a thin stack of paper—Evolon, Mallory called it. Each sheet is maybe a yard wide by two yards long. This is super-fancy stuff—a world away from even the Mohawk I like to use when I'm treating myself. Mallory ordered her Evolon on a roll and cut it to size herself—it kind of looks and acts like fabric.

Mallory snaps on a pair of latex gloves, passes a pair to me. "Okay," she says. "I'll do my front and you can do my back."

"You mean I don't get to touch your boobs?"

Mallory gives me a dirty look and mutters, "Lose my number." But even she can't hold her laugh in.

We dip our fingers into the vegetable shortening, taking generous globs. "From neck to knee," she says.

I try not to tremble, but I can't help it. This is a lot more than I bargained for when I volunteered for this project. Mallory is more assured than me—or at least she's better at pretending—and I can't help but wonder how she's doing this. Could I do this? I'm not sure I would want to take my button-down off in front of her, even though it's sticking to my back with sweat and the breeze might be nice.

I touch Mallory's neck with the tip of my index finger.

She grabs my wrist and lays my full hand on her shoulder. "Brett. Get over it. It's just a body."

Easy for her to say. I've never touched a girl like this, and I fear my hesitation was an admission of my embarrassment. Yet why am I the embarrassed one? Who just gets naked in front of a guy like it's no big deal?

"Would it help if we treat this like a lesson in printmaking?" Mallory turns around, gestures up and down her frame. "Think of me as merely a plate on which ink is applied." She rubs shortening into her clavicle. "I'm what's known as the matrix. Repeat after me." She speaks very slowly. "Mayyytrix."

"Matrix, okay."

Mallory turns around and I get to work on her back. My mechanical movements relax into something more fluid as she speaks.

"A matrix can be anything you're going to print—usually carved woodblock or linoleum, or a copper plate with an image etched into it."

I reload my hands with shortening. "But how will we print your body—your matrix, I mean—without ink?"

"The shortening is standing in for ink. There are many ways to ink a matrix. I've even inked copper etchings with berry juices."

"Dope."

Mallory's voice is a bit brighter when she talks about printmaking.

"My teacher once treated us to pie on critique day; then, after we cleared out of the lab, she pulled the paper plates from the trash and printed whatever was stuck to them for our print exchange." She shakes her head in admiration. "Such a baller move."

Mallory's lesson is so lulling that I almost forget I'm going to have to apply shortening to her butt. *I'm about to touch a girl's butt.* The vegetable shortening is like an electric conductor. The smoothness of Mallory's skin sends a charge through me. This is unprecedented. My arousal is distracting, but maybe if I keep talking, it'll pass.

"What's a print exchange?" I ask.

"It's when a bunch of printmakers decide on a theme and everyone makes an edition of prints for the exchange. I've got a whole portfolio upstairs full of cool shit from killer printmakers. I even got my hands on a Zena Foss recently."

The name means nothing to me, but I make a mental note to ask to see it when our hands aren't greasy. "It's cool that you make a lot of stuff for free. I like giving away my comics."

"Printmaking is very democratic."

I'm on my feet again, so Mallory pulls her hair up to ensure unobstructed access to her shoulders. I try to ignore the scabs from where she's picked at her skin.

She says, "It's a great place to belong and get along. Not competitive or elitist."

"Comics are like that, too. Hella collaboration and loads of support for each other's work."

"It's awesome making art with friends."

The subtext isn't lost on me. Are we friends? Until the past week, I hadn't imagined Mallory the type to befriend anyone. In Earth sciences, she just seems like those sad sleepwalker people in antidepressant commercials. I feel kind of sick thinking about the images of Mallory I once held in my mind. I was only seeing what everyone saw, what we *thought* we should see. But she's so much more than those scars on her wrist or the scabs on her arms. These details support the narrative I've always assumed but contradict the image of the self-assured artist who would show me her boobs on our fourth hangout and then slap me around for enjoying them. The more I learn about Mallory, the more confusing she becomes.

Evelyn's voice comes pounding between my temples. *Never reduce a character to an archetype, Brett. People are gloriously complicated. You're gloriously complicated. That's what makes you a person, not merely a human.*

Evelyn conveyed this lesson while critiquing one of my earliest stories about Captain Condor. It was then, when I was maybe twelve years old, that I realized Archer von Adonis needed to have a heart, too, that maybe he only ever became evil because Captain hurt him deeply in a terrible mistake back when the two were best buds as cadets in the Constellation Corps.

Suddenly, I'm seeing Adonis looking more hurt than evil. Or is that Reed's face?

I wish I knew how to stop thinking.

I walk around Mallory to check our work, dabbing shortening in spots we've missed. I stand back and give her a thumbs-up.

She cracks up. "You should see your face right now." She tosses her gloves aside and lays one sheet of paper on the ground. As if my hands weren't just on her butt, she says, "Don't check out my ass while I pull the print."

She kneels at the edge of the sheet and sprawls out flat on her stomach, like you might on a beach towel, laughing at herself. She affects the voice of a studious narrator of a nature documentary. "Not fearing the desert heat like her fellow cetaceans, the great white land whale suns herself in ecstasy."

I'm laughing so hard I'm struggling for breath. I can't believe Mallory is comfortable enough in her skin to poke fun at her size. How does she do it?

She says, "Hold the paper down, will you? Keep it perfectly still if you can."

I drop to Mallory's side and use my hands and knees to secure the paper while she rises back to her feet.

She passes a powder shaker to me. "Be generous. You can never have too much cheese." I think of the waitresses at Olive Garden, ever poised with a cheese grater in hand to pile parmesan on top of my food. I think about how often I ask the waitress to stop cranking the grater before I really want her to. Like the clothes I dropped off at the Goodwill, the shame of such a thought doesn't fit in Mallory's presence.

We lose our shit on the cheese shakers, slapping the bottoms with our palms, coating the paper in a thick layer of cheese dust. The whole thing is hella weird but also hella fun. Like, really fun. I'm laughing so hard, in fact, that I cough violently, choking on a cloud of cheese. I fall on my back, giggling, losing my shit like Scarface just after he snorts a line of cocaine. My giggles infect Mallory with giggles. I wipe the dust from under my nose. When was the last time I felt like this? Certainly not around Reed. Not at Evelyn's. Even extreme trampoline air-drumming can't make me feel like this anymore.

Finally, we pull ourselves together. "Time to see the finished print," Mallory says. Before I can dive out of the way, she lifts the paper and gives it a gentle shake. Cheese takes flight, coating the patio like the neon pollen of the palo verde trees that line the fence. I tousle my hair, a nuclear-orange dandruff falling on my shoulders.

Mallory examines her work with a critical eye, then with the loving gaze of a historian in the presence of a precious, ancient document, the way I used to look at my comic panels before Reed became a bad guy—or *I* became a bad guy?—and Kid Condor started feeling too sad to fight evil.

She says, "Goddamn, I'm amazing."

She isn't wrong. The orange blob is distinctive enough to suggest a body but abstract enough to invite closer examination. Up close you can see details of Mallory's physicality—the void of her belly button, even her nipples. The print begs to be touched—is it rough like sandpaper or soft as velvet?

We quickly set up another sheet to print the back of Mallory's body. Another success.

"You want to do one?" Mallory asks.

"God no." I look down at my stomach, which is pushing against the buttons on a shirt that only just escaped eviction during the great purge of my closet. "Nobody wants to see this printed and hung in a gallery." The words are out of my mouth before I've registered their effect. Jackass.

Surprisingly, Mallory doesn't get mad at me. Instead she says, "I've applied to have a room in the student gallery all to myself in a couple weeks. I'm going to put on a show that glorifies my body, even if doing so speaks to the identity politics I'm trying to rise above."

How many nuggs could I buy if I had a dollar for every time Mallory says something that goes over my head? Ms. Finch tells me my precociousness is remarkable, *even for a self-involved teen with a mind for drama*, but I think Mallory has me beat in the smarts department. "Say more."

"The show's going to be called *Fat American*. My tagline is 'You're an American. Be an American.'"

"Fat American." I grin. The whole thing makes me uncomfortable, but I think I understand it.

Mallory explains anyway. "Diet culture teaches us that we're supposed to look a certain way, right? But look around. The most American body type a person could strive for is mine. Well, maybe not mine but at least yours."

Did Mallory just accuse me of having the ideal body type?

I say, "I'm sorry about what I said, about no one wanting to see a print of my body. I didn't mean to insult . . ." I take a breath, hoping to keep my foot on the ground instead of in my mouth. "Like, I guess I mean there's nothing wrong with your body." It occurs to me that I could be the only boy in my school who, at this very moment, is in the presence of a nearly naked girl. Am I lucky? Should I express as much? I release a nervous breath. "I like your body."

Mallory gives me a smile I can't define—a look that might be pitying or even sad. She sets to hanging her prints from clips on the pergola. "You don't like my body, Brett."

"*No*, I do. I mean, your boobs are . . ."

"Don't say awkward shit you don't mean. You're *afraid* of my body. It grosses you out."

"No, it's just—"

"It's okay to feel your truth."

Is it, though? It doesn't feel okay. Mallory sounds a lot like Ms. Finch right now, which might have reassured me before Ms. Finch and I had our falling out. I think about my jar of olives and hope my plan to win back Ms. Finch works. I want to talk to her about the body in front of me. I want to understand how I can feel aroused and repelled and afraid and comforted by Mallory's body all at once. Oh, and patriotic. I want to understand how a mouthwatering print of Mallory's body could possibly make me love being an American.

I'm not sure why, but I feel like I need to do the unthinkable for Mallory. I channel my inner Kid Condor and lift the shirttails of my button-up, just a few inches.

Am I really doing this?

Before I can chicken out, I pull my shirt over my head and drop it to the ground.

I stifle a shudder. I'm too pale, too soft. I don't look how I'm supposed to look, and I must be a freak because my body isn't normal.

Mallory's voice comes gentler than I knew it could. "You don't have to."

I stare at her, determined to hold her gaze until I stop feeling like a sideshow attraction. I feel the air as it enters and exits my chest. I feel the sun on my skin. I want to reach for my shirt and put it back on. But I don't. I just stand here looking at Mallory while Mallory stands here looking at me.

Finally, my hands go to my waist to fumble with the button of my deck shorts. Time to go all in. I pull the zipper down and the shorts fall to my ankles.

Mallory makes a high-pitched noise. Her hand flies to her mouth. Is she . . . ? Holy *shit*. Mallory is trying to stifle a laugh. Mallory is *laughing* at me. What the hell?

"Dude!" I cover my crotch with one hand and awkwardly grab at my shorts with the other. I only manage to look more foolish. "I'm trying to be vulnerable here!"

"I'm sorry. God. So, so sorry. Genuinely, fully one hundred percent sorry." She's still cracking up. "It's just . . . *Superman* Underoos? The T-shirts I could wrap my brain around, but this?"

I look down at my bright red briefs—my favorite pair, and one of the few to survive the purge. I'd forgotten I chose them today. The adrenaline drains from my body. Miraculously, all the awkward feelings go with it. "My Superman undies make me feel powerful, okay?"

I'm seeing the movement of my stomach as I laugh, and it doesn't look quite so strange. It just looks like a stomach when you laugh. My thighs don't look too pale—a *wrong* kind of pale. They just exhibit the particular farmer's tan of a mixed-race kid—all deep bronze where the sun touches me every day and a warm, reddish tan where my clothes block the rays. I snap the yellow elastic at my waist and raise a finger to underscore the seriousness of my next words. "These bad boys are staying on, though. You're not getting me into a yellow thong, no matter how pathetically you beg."

Mallory grimaces, sticks out her tongue. "Thank Christ for that."

I kick my shorts aside and hand Mallory a fresh set of gloves. "Don't enjoy this too much. Remember, as a certain printmaker . . ." I think of Evelyn and strive to choose my words more judiciously. "As my printmaking *friend* taught me, this is *not* the hella-sexy bod of a high-flying superhero, okay?" I affect the nasal tone of Ms. Weathers, the crankiest secretary at Tucson City High. "This is a mayyyytrix. Can you say it with me, Mallory? Repeat after me: Mayyyytrix. Mayyyy—"

This is when I go tumbling into the pool. I register the cool water before the shove that sent me into it. Before I've even broken the surface, Mallory cannonballs in to join me. We crow and squeal, shoving each other under, splashing in an epic water fight, my spirit, for once, as buoyant as my body.

Brett Harrison

Banksie

AP English

13 October

Idiom Essay Rough Draft—Take Two

To Have. Not.

　　Like most kids, I went through an Animal Planet-obsession phase around the age of eight. I was certain I was going to supplement my income from my job as "lead astronaut" of NASA by moonlighting as the host of a <u>Bindi the Jungle Girl</u>-type show where I would get to hang out with numbats and three-toed sloths and tapirs, all while teaching kids that animals are precious and should be conserved and respected. Thinking I might want to save an animal myself, my mom introduced me to this organization where you could donate the contents of your piggy bank to adopt an endangered animal of your choosing. I'd been adopted recently, and the experience was all-around awesome for me, so I was eager to pay it forward and provide a loving home to an adorable baby orangutan in need.

　　You can imagine my disappointment when my package arrived from the adoption agency, not a massive wooden crate marked FRAGILE and FROM BORNEO in large stenciled letters, plenty of air holes drilled in its sides, but merely a thick manila envelope. How had they stuffed my beloved Rocco into such a small package?

　　When the contents of the envelope were dumped on the living

room floor and the reality of my guardianship set in, I threw a massive tantrum and cried myself to sleep, my glossy color photo of Rocco and the offending thank-you letter from the adoption agency propped against the lamp on my nightstand.

When they say you can't eat your cake and have it, too, what they're really saying is you can either have or NOT have—simple as that, nothing in between. But my experience raising Rocco proves otherwise. Rocco was my good boy, but he WASN'T. I never even met the guy—and that limbo, that in-between, meant nothing truly satisfying could come from the arrangement. After all, it wasn't long before my glossy photo of Rocco was shoved under my bed with all the toys I didn't want to properly clean up—neglected, forgotten, our relationship eroded and meaningless.

Recent events have me wondering if life only ever proves my idiom wrong. How can I be afraid of Mallory's body but also excited to touch it? How can Reed be dead to me if he's right there sleeping in the bunk beneath mine every night? How can I inspire others who struggle with food to be brave when I'm obviously a coward? How can I lash out in anger at Ms. Finch when I'm the dick in our relationship, not her?

"You can't eat your cake and have it, too" is a lie people tell themselves to make life seem less confusing and scary—as if all you have to do is make a choice and a safe, reliable reality will follow. This lie is untenable, so how am I supposed to write a decent essay about it? How can I see the idiom at play in my life when it reeks of more bullshit than even a scammer adoption agency that would cheat a child out of twenty dollars of his hard-earned allowance?

CHAPTER THIRTY-TWO

I actually braved the courtyard for lunch today and have no intention of throwing up my corn dog, plus I'm on my way to make things right with Ms. Finch, so I guess you could say I'm having a pretty dope day.

Have I mentioned yet that one of my special talents is speaking too soon?

I'm nearly to the counseling office when I spy Robyn Fletcher charging toward me in the crowded hallway before fifth period. The instinct to run is so intense that I turn on my heel and smack right into a bank of lockers. Chuckles, murmurs. I reach for my pocket, which is weighed down by my jar of olives. I breathe a sigh of relief. My cargo shorts are dry, the jar still intact.

Robyn calls over the din of voices. "Brett! Damn it! Don't make me run in heels!"

It's not that Robyn can't take a hint. It's that she's entitled enough to only acknowledge hints that support her own aims or fit her own narrative. There are no delusions in Robyn's world, merely exclusions. I'm reluctant to admit that this could be the one thing we have in common.

I steel myself, turn to see a smile so white and so wide that I'm wondering if Robyn shouldn't audition for a role on Shark Week. Has she had her teeth whitened since last we spoke?

"Based on the fact that you haven't liked a single one of my tweets or responded to my DMs, I'm assuming you're still foolishly disinclined to take me up on my offer, but I'm giving you one last chance. I'm prepared to cut you loose in favor of someone else, someone with far more potential." She gives my cargo shorts a disdainful look. "Someone who knows how to dress herself, at least—so decide now."

Who could Robyn possibly be after? Who among the throngs of students who spoke out seemed to *stand* out? While it's a relief to know her interest in me is waning—and being free of her really would make this a super-dope day—my curiosity gets the better of me.

"Who are you thinking of?"

"The ten-thousand-calorie girl. You know her, right? Rumor has it she tried to off herself this summer. She's perfect."

"I'll do it."

Robyn's face is as elastic as the best of the theater thugs', yet her shock appears entirely authentic.

"I'll do it. I'll lead your club." It's hard not to growl the words—hard not to knee Robyn in the crotch—but I think of Mallory and force myself to speak calmly.

"O-okay." This is the one stammer I'll probably ever get out of her. I savor it.

"I have a single condition. Nonnegotiable."

Robyn smiles. I've just sweetened the deal. It's not so much the winning she loves; it's playing the game. "I'm listening."

"You leave Mallory alone. You don't look at her. You don't speak to her. You don't speak *about* her. That rumor you heard? You don't spread it."

Myriad expressions pass over Robyn's face. She's calculating. Recalibrating. Spinning new information to her advantage. This all happens in the time it takes to tie a shoe. She lands on sympathetic admiration. She reaches out to touch my arm. "Our hero falls on his sword. I do declare. Maybe you really *are* just like Kid Condom."

I yank my arm away, skin crawling. The reality of what just happened sinks in. I protected Mallory—and that feels good; at least I think it feels good—but at what cost? Suddenly, I need to get to the boys' room. I need to throw up. If I can just empty my stomach, I'm thinking, I'll be okay. But no, I'm supposed to see Ms. Finch. I don't want to talk to Ms. Finch with barf breath. I don't want to throw up. I don't want . . .

Robyn spins and strides away, heels drilling into the polished concrete flooring. The enthusiasm in her voice would be inspiring if it wasn't so nauseous. "We're going to change lives, Brett. I'll be in touch." She looks over her shoulder. "And *do* respond to my DMs this time, will you?"

CHAPTER THIRTY-THREE

Ms. Finch regards the bottle of olives I've placed on her desk, a hint of curiosity in the twitch of her brow. She doesn't question, merely folds her hands and looks at me expectantly. She could make this easy if she wanted to. Besides Evelyn, Ms. Finch is the most brilliant person I know, so she must be aware of why I'm here. I glance past the olives and the framed picture of Toast to be certain my impromptu visit isn't actually written on her desk calendar: *Receive groveling and heartfelt apology from Brett Harrison on October 14.* Ms. Finch could tell me she gets it, that she understands why I acted like a total dick last time I saw her, but I don't deserve such courtesy, and I don't want it. I want to man up—or human up, as Mallory would say. I want to be as brave as Captain Condor might be if he hurt someone he cares for.

I try to ignore the sour taste burning in the back of my throat. "I bought you some olives."

Nailed it.

Ms. Finch merely stares.

Okay, try harder. I look to the potted succulents on Ms. Finch's bookcase. Maybe this will be easier if I avoid eye contact. I put my hands in my pockets and rock on my heels. "Apparently, you can't buy an olive branch at the grocery store. They don't have them at any of the nurseries, either. I tried everywhere. I don't think olive trees live in Tucson. I don't know where olive trees live. Greece, probably, right?"

"Are you trying to tell me something, Brett?"

I knew this would be hard, but I didn't expect that my nostrils would start tingling or that my eyes might well. The act of crying has grown too familiar, but I can't quite make sense of why I'm having to hold back tears right *now*. I'm not talking about any of the hard stuff, the stuff I refuse to talk about. When I went over this apology in my head, it played out pretty simply. I was just supposed to walk in here like I owned the place and set the olives down triumphantly with a super-fat grin and Ms. Finch was supposed to laugh because she appreciates my cleverness and then I'd be like, *Do you forgive me?* and she'd be like, *I'll cherish these olives for as long as I live*, and then we'd pick up right where we left off.

Real life never plays out like my fantasies.

I open my mouth but only manage a feeble "Uh . . ." I scribble furiously on my thumb. "I'm super grateful for you, and I'm hella ashamed of what I did, and I'm so, so sorry and hope you'll forgive me, and it's not an excuse because what I did was so gross, but I was super sad—super embarrassed, I mean—because I *did* go to Overeaters Anonymous, and it was legit the worst thing that's ever happened to me, and I was so humiliated and I blamed you, but it wasn't your fault and I know you were just trying to help me, and I know you don't like the other f-word, but I think that might be bullshit because you *are* my friend and—" A sob bursts from my throat. "Are you still my friend?" I rub my eyes and sink to the couch. There's something wrong about this arrangement—me on the couch and Ms. Finch statuesquely poised on her bouncy-ball chair. We're in the wrong spots, and I wish she'd come around her desk and give me a hug, but of course that wouldn't be appropriate. I wonder if that makes her as sad as it makes me.

"I forgive you."

Ms. Finch isn't grinning or laughing like I saw in my imagination. Instead she looks like she might cry, too, even though she's probably not allowed to because she has to seem all neutral and unaffected by anything. I hate seeing Ms. Finch like this. I don't want her to be sad for me—I don't want her to have reason to be sad for me—but maybe if she's sad, it means she understands and still cares. "Can you tell me . . . can you say that you understand?" I shudder. "Please understand."

"I understand."

About a million things are swirling in my head: Evelyn and Robyn and Reed and Mallory and that unbearable thing Mallory did because she felt like no one loved her. This disorder would shame Evelyn if she knew about it. This disorder turned me into a pawn for Robyn's evil machinations. It nearly ruined my friendship with Ms. Finch and completely destroyed my bromance with Reed. I've lost too much. I don't want to lose anything else. I don't want to have a life where no one loves me. I don't want to be too sick to be loved.

Just when I'm supposed to stop crying and suggest we make olive finger puppets to lighten the mood, I blurt, "I threw up before I got here." Despite my conviction, I'd reel the words back in if I could. Now that they're actually out there, they're staring at me and taunting me and I'm afraid of them. So I cry. I cry and cry and cry. I cry for minutes—three, five? I cry noisily, but I can't stop.

Ms. Finch just waits until I'm ready to try again.

"I've thrown up nineteen times in, I don't know, two weeks?" I grab a tissue—you're never more than an arm's length from a tissue in this office. "It's not what you think it is."

Ms. Finch says, "You need to say what it is. I know you don't want to, but you need to."

"I *can't*. I don't want it."

Ms. Finch nudges me gently. "Don't want what?"

"The *word*. I have enough words."

"Words don't define you. They are not who you are. The words merely define behaviors."

"The word you're thinking of isn't even accurate. I've only done it a few times. Only when I've binged. It's not like my teeth are falling out or anything. Do I look like I've missed any meals?"

"This isn't about how you look. It's about what you're choosing to do and why you're choosing to do it."

"I'm not bulimic." I shake my head. "I'm not."

Ms. Finch gives me her nonjudgmental face, the one that makes me so uncomfortable that I always have to keep talking when she makes it.

"I'm not." I hate how weak my voice sounds, how defensive. "I'm *not*."

"Okay, you're not. But you are purging after you eat. You're telling me this for a reason. What's the reason?"

I give Ms. Finch a pleading look. I want this to be over. I started it, I know, but I just want it to be over now.

Ms. Finch glances to the ceiling and bites her lower lip. She looks like she's thinking of the solution to a tricky equation. Finally, she says, "Who, to your reasoning, is the most successful comic book writer or artist?"

The question yanks me so far into left field that I wonder if I blacked out for a second and woke up in a different conversation. I still feel pretty soggy, but my tears dry up almost immediately.

"Anyone you deeply admire. There are no wrong answers."

"Well, um, obviously Stan Lee." I realize I'm shredding a wadded tissue, which seems disgusting, so I shove it into my pocket. Also disgusting. "A total god among men. He invented most of the best characters and basically changed the face of comic books forever."

"Did he do all this alone?"

"No, I mean, no one runs a company alone, right? He had plenty of creative collaborators, too. Everyone knows Steve Ditko and Jack Kirby, also gods."

"So Lee had to ask for help when he was stuck? Creatively or with a business decision?"

"Yeah, I guess that's true."

"And would you say you look up to Lee? Is he a role model?"

I nod vigorously. "Hell yeah. He was tits." The words aren't out of my mouth before the enthusiasm drains from them. I feel my face fall. I mean what I've said, but I'm finally catching up to Ms. Finch's game. I know why we're talking about Stan Lee. Crafty woman. I'm crying again, too, because even though I want to be as brave as Captain Condor and as wise as Stan Lee, saying what I need to say next—saying what Ms. Finch wants me to say—is really, really scary. I'm afraid of whatever might happen after I say it, afraid of the unknown, and maybe mostly afraid of the questions pummeling my mind: What if this disorder is it for me? What if I can't be fixed? I shove the words out anyway. "I . . . think I need some help." I grit my teeth, but there's no damming my sobs.

Ms. Finch releases an audible breath, like she's relieved. Again, she waits patiently while I cry.

"I'm ready . . . for the help you described. Like, a therapist, right?"

"You'd start with a therapist, yes, one who specializes in what you're going through. The therapist can help you decide on a plan of treatment."

Treatment. Another word I don't want. I'm thinking of what Mallory told me at the Grocery Bargain Barn. Is binge eating a disease? Is throwing up my food a disease?

"I'm scared."

"I know, and that's okay. Good, in fact. It means you're doing the hard work on yourself. Facing the hard things is always scary. If it wasn't, we wouldn't have to be brave."

I'm nodding.

"I'll have to talk to your guardian, all right? There's no way around that."

I don't want to say anything ever again, so I just nod some more in resignation.

"It's settled, then. You can stay as long as you need to, until you're ready to go back to class. Then I'm going to make some calls and we'll get this figured out. Sound good?"

I spread out on the ratty, pilling couch with my shoes on and everything. I close my eyes, hoping to ease the throb in my head.

I wake with a start, almost fall off the couch when the awkwardness of my vulnerable position hits me. The more painful blow comes a moment later when I remember what I admitted to and what I asked for.

Ms. Finch looks up from her computer. "Twenty minutes is all. You can still make it to sixth period if you're ready."

I run my hands down my cheeks. My eyes hurt and my sinuses feel clogged. I spy my jar of olives. It sits on Ms. Finch's bookcase, near her Ruth Bader Ginsburg bobblehead. I'd like to smile but it feels like my cheeks are made of clay.

I stand and sling my backpack over one shoulder.

When I reach the door, Ms. Finch stops me. "Brett . . ."

I glance back.

I expect her to give me her signature line. *Are you proud of you?* Instead she says something that feels a million times better. "I'm proud of you."

CHAPTER THIRTY-FOUR

I'm kind of wishing Marcus were a deadbeat.

We're sitting, just the two of us, on the couch in the apartment's living room, staring at the scattered *Sports Illustrated* magazines on the chipped coffee table. I know why we're here, and I'm not sure I can bear it. We're about to have what Marcus called a *man-to-man*—timed, it seems, to coincide with Reed's imaginary wrestling practice, which is only still happening, I assume, because Reed would rather have his hands all over Thandie Gellar than be anywhere near me.

Marcus could sit across from me in his favorite sagging armchair, but I'm pretty sure he doesn't want to make eye contact. Please tell me we won't have to make eye contact.

There's a quaver in Marcus's voice, not the emotional kind but the uncomfortable kind. He clears his throat. He swallows. He clears his throat again. He reaches for a pen on the coffee table—the one Reed uses to draw strategically placed dicks on all the magazine covers—and begins clicking the tip out and in, out and in. Finally, he says, "I owe you an apology, Brett."

Oh God.

"When I agreed to take you in, I made a promise to your mother."

Oh God, oh God.

"That I'd love you and take care of you like a son."

Please stop talking. Please stop talking.

"That I'd be there for you when you need me."

Please stop.

"But sometimes I fail at my job as a dad."

Stop, stop.

"Reed's been in so much trouble lately." Marcus shakes his head, clicks his pen. *Click, click. Click.* "He misses his mother is all. It's not an excuse." Marcus stares wistfully into the blank void of the television screen. For a moment I dare hope the conversation might end before he brings it back to me. "And then you . . . I knew something was wrong." He slides the pen into his shirt pocket, the tip still out. "But I didn't know how to approach it, so I didn't try, and that was cowardly of me."

Why won't he stop talking?

"I should have known how to talk about it. That's my job as a parent and I failed you."

Stop fucking talking.

"But I can do better now, okay? We'll tackle this thing together. I've put in a request to switch to day shift so I can be around more. Maybe we can cook dinner together, start eating together like proper families do—not just on Sundays. Believe it or not, I was a great cook once upon a time. I can teach you . . . if you'll let me."

I'm thinking about the expertise I've kept under wraps, that *I* could teach *him* how to prepare Mexican cuisine. I stare over the peninsula into the kitchen, see a flash of us working together in the claustrophobic space. I watch as Marcus ribs me about whatever ridiculous thing I said to a crush at school that day. I see us making a mess while I teach him to roll flautas. I'll start there because any clown can learn to roll flautas.

I'll be really patient, and maybe even Reed is there, and maybe he wants to learn, too, and before you know it maybe Marcus will be putting his own signature spin on a mole verde and Reed will be begging for more of my chickpea-and-chorizo tostadas with elotes followed by a cinco leches cake for dessert. But then the vision slips away and I'm seeing Evelyn and me making messes in *her* kitchen, and I can't even bring myself to nod. I think I'm going to be sick, and not, for once, on purpose.

"Your counselor explained some things to me, about your problems. If I'd known it was like that . . ." He scrubs a hand over his stubble. "I should have known, and I didn't, because . . . maybe because I didn't *want* to know."

Marcus puts a hand on my shoulder.

His touch makes me want to cry. My tears wouldn't surprise anyone at this point, but I've never cried in front of Marcus. I'm not starting today. I won't do that to him.

"I bought some books. I'll learn, okay?"

I'm staring at Victor Wembanyama on the cover of *Sports Illustrated*. He leans casually against a wall, looking downward at the camera from above like he knows all about me and wonders what's wrong with me. I glance from Victor to the other guys on the covers, all these guys who don't look like me.

Marcus says, "I know you don't want to talk about this with me— God knows I barely spoke two words to my father when I was your age—I get that. But I set up an appointment with a therapist who knows how to help, a Dr. Bradford. We'll go see him next Tuesday, all right?"

Marcus just keeps phrasing everything in the interrogative, as if putting a question mark at the end of every sentence is going to elicit a response.

"I know you don't like to talk about your mom, but promise me you'll try. You need to talk about her. Maybe try writing about her before the appointment?"

I stiffen. I know Marcus means well, but he doesn't understand what he's asking, how insurmountable, how impossible his request. I visualize myself saying all the things he thinks I need to say in some richly paneled shrink's office, and I know I need to escape this conversation. I need to be alone because I need to cry—the tears are coming and I can't stop them.

I try to pull away, but Marcus holds firm to my shoulder.

"Let me do my job, Brett."

It takes a split second to understand what Marcus means, but in that instant I see myself as Kid Condor just after his planet was destroyed. I see the fear in my eyes. I sense how alone I am in the universe. I see myself drifting farther and farther from the life I knew, one of safety and love and promise and hope. I see the unknown and I see the dark. And I don't want to be alone.

I lean in and wrap my arms around Marcus. The pen in his shirt pocket grates against the side of my head, but I don't care. I'm overwhelmed by the strength of Marcus's arms and the warmth of his body because he's alive and heavy in the way only the vital are—not like when Evelyn hugs me—and I feel safe for the first time in months, maybe years.

Tomorrow, we'll go on like none of this happened. Marcus will act like a man again and I'll act like a man again, and we'll pretend that Marcus is just a dad who's too harried to really be involved and I'm just a boy who would never cling so tightly to anyone, especially a man who isn't even my real dad, but for right now, I just give in and allow Marcus to prop me up as I cry. In his arms, I feel just a little less afraid. In his arms, I think just maybe I'm going to be okay.

CHAPTER THIRTY-FIVE

When I pop my head into Ms. Finch's office to relay the news about my appointment next week (spoiler alert: she already knows), I linger, working up the courage to ask for advice on something I didn't know was on my mind until now.

Taking the hint like a pro, Ms. Finch says, "Something else?"

I move for the couch, drop my backpack and sit on the edge. "Actually, yeah. Can I ask you about something we haven't talked about before?"

"Sure. What's up?"

"Well . . . say there's this girl you've started spending time with—I guess in your case a dude, right?—and let's say your hangouts are kind of awkward at first and then sort of friend-zone-ish, and, like, you're not really attracted to the guy, or maybe you are but you don't know it. But then, after a while, you start to realize just how grateful you are for the person, and then a supervillain threatens this person, and it's, like, instantaneous: You realize you can't bear the thought of this girl you like—this guy, I mean—getting hurt. You want to protect him, maybe you'd do *anything* to protect him, and maybe you didn't know you liked him like that—romantically, I guess—because maybe you don't. Maybe you're just confused. How would you know? Like, if you liked the guy? Or like, how would you know if the guy liked you, especially because the guy is kind of aloof but, like, maybe he also took his shirt off one time and asked you to rub him down with vegetable shortening, which was, I don't know, kind of arousing?"

Ms. Finch is white-knuckling it not to laugh, and it occurs to me that I might be embarrassing myself right now. I give her a sheepish grin.

She says, "This conversation would be much simpler if you phrased your question in the concrete rather than the hypothetical."

"So you know Mallory Clark, right? From the drive-thru?"

"Not personally, no, but in the context of your life, yes."

I lean forward and prop my elbows on my knees, hands clasped, appreciating the safe view of the carpet tiles. My thoughts drift to Ned Leeds in the MCU and how he ends up with his Robyn Fletcher doppelgänger, Betty, and I'm wondering if I would choose someone who looks like that over someone as amazing as Mallory. I kind of think I might choose a Mallory every single time. I say, "I think we might be falling for each other without knowing it, and I feel kind of bad because— Mallory's even told me this—she told me that I'm not attracted to her body, that I'm afraid of it, which in some ways is sort of true but also definitely not true, and I'm not sure what that means, like, if she's right, but I think . . ." I let out a long breath, just a few extra seconds to think. "Okay, yeah, so I *do* know that I don't *want* her to be right." I glance up, smiling triumphantly. "I like Mallory."

"It sounds like that's new information for you."

I nod vigorously. "New as of two seconds ago, yes."

"The only way to know if someone likes you back is to ask. The most respectful thing you can do for Mallory is tell her how you feel, as honestly as you can, and ask if she feels similarly. Listen carefully when she speaks—that'll help you be respectful of her answer. It can be easy to hear what we want to hear instead of what's actually being said."

"But what about her body? What if she's right about it not being attractive to me?" Mallory's words are echoing in my mind: *You're afraid of my body. It grosses you out.*

"Telling someone you like them isn't asking them to do anything physical. If Mallory likes you in the same way you like her, you can see what that feels like and talk about how you might want to bring physicality into the relationship. Most people start by holding hands or kissing. When they're ready, most do more. But any act of touching should always involve enthusiastic consent, so listen to your body, and pay attention to her body, the things she says and the things she might be feeling but not saying. If you feel that enthusiasm on both ends, trust it. If not, it's okay to be honest with Mallory about that, too."

"I don't want to hurt her."

"Honesty and kindness are not mutually exclusive. You're a very articulate person. If it comes to it, you can tell Mallory the truth in a gentle way, and you can be sensitive to her feelings. I'll expect nothing less."

I'm nodding, gears turning, the plan for telling Mallory how I feel already forming. I want it to be special, so I'm going to take her to do something hella radical she's never experienced before. The arena-sized drums and sweeping synths of "The Glory of Love," the far superior theme song to the far inferior film, *The Karate Kid Part II*, buffer the walls of my mind. Themes of courage and honor, of being a hero to the one you love, pretty much the most epic ballad of all time.

"Brett? You still here?"

"Yes. Sensitive, gentle. Cool." I stand and gather my backpack.

"And Brett . . ."

I linger at the edge of Ms. Finch's desk.

"These developments are exciting, but you're about to embark on very important work with your new therapist. Make sure you're able to give it the attention it deserves, all right?"

Knowing what I do of Mallory, that she can actually help me stay focused, I answer with confidence. "You got it."

Fist bump. Nailed it. Peace out, Finch.

CHAPTER THIRTY-SIX

When we pull into a parking space at the medical center across from Tumamoc Hill, Mallory shoots me a look that says *I hope your death is painful*. Because I'm not totally clueless, I expected such resistance. Beyond a desire to surprise her with wacky hijinks as she often does me, the look on Mallory's face is reason enough to have kept our destination secret. The plan is to show Mallory that just because she's a super fat doesn't mean she can't enjoy the awesome views of our beloved Old Pueblo. She can do anything she sets her mind to. I'll be right there, cheering her on when it gets steeper toward the top. If Mallory can conquer Tumamoc Hill, she can conquer anything. It will feel good to be able to die a hero having given Mallory this gift.

Better still, once we're at the top, I'll say some stuff and she'll say some stuff, and maybe I'll put my fingertips on the small of her back like Reed did Thandie, and then, I don't know, maybe we'll have a first kiss that involves Mallory's lips instead of her scars.

I've timed our arrival to get us to the top of the hill just as the sun sets. The heat is more bearable this time of day, and while the view is always incredible, seeing the city lit up at night is my favorite way to experience Tumamoc.

Mallory quickly exits the vehicle, not because she's eager to get started, I imagine, but because staying in a parked car in Tucson can be a death sentence. At least the car smells good. In anticipation of hosting a special guest in the passenger seat, I actually cleaned out all the fast-food trash that's accumulated since I got my license. I bought a fancy air freshener that attaches to the vents, too. Hopefully it's powerful enough to counteract the effect when the trash begins piling up again—probably starting tomorrow, if I'm being honest.

She hoofs it—a good sign. But not toward the trail—a bad sign.

I hop out of the car. "Hey, wait!"

Mallory heads down the road leading back to the city, her footprints distinct in the shoulder of rust-colored dirt. She calls back. "I'm getting a Lyft. This was cute and all, but I'm out."

I rush to catch up, match Mallory's pace—quite a clip for someone so averse to an easy hike. I spin and stumble, almost skipping backward so I can look at her when I speak. I put my hands up. "Give it a chance. You'll like it, I promise. It's not even that hard."

"Stop talking, nerd." Mallory keeps walking.

"The path is paved all the way up to the observatory. You won't fall and twist your ankle or anything."

Covered in a crude layer of asphalt, the path up Tumamoc eventually tightens to allow only a single service vehicle to pass. You'll see a lot of people on the trail, especially at cooler times of day, but I've never once seen a vehicle. More than anything, this is an easy, if steep, walking path for the casual lover of nature or partaker in moderate aerobic activity.

"I said no."

Frustration creeps into my voice. "Come on, *please*! Do it for me! I've done everything you've asked of me!"

There's this pained look on Mallory's face, closer to the face I see in Earth sciences than the one I've grown used to admiring whenever we hang together. She releases a pent-up sigh. This is the sound of me winning. She says, "We stop when I say we stop."

"Absolutely." We'll stop when we've reached the top, but Mallory doesn't need to read the fine print right now.

"And you don't say anything if I go slow."

"I like slow."

"And you're carrying my water."

"Who says chivalry is dead?" (Mallory, probably, but I give my backward cap a little tip anyway to prove today's commitment to good old-fashioned male values.)

Mallory looks to the ground and shakes her head—there's still a chance she might change her mind. She turns to survey the hill, a hand perched on her hip. We stand in this moment of indecision for just a second too long. My chest deflates. It's over.

But then, without another word, Mallory trudges toward the car, where my backpack—loaded with water and peanut M&M's—awaits.

I yank my fists down in a show of triumph. "Yes! You're going to love this, I promise."

I grab our gear and we cross the street. Seeing how pissed Mallory is, I figure I should keep my trap shut for the first several minutes of our walk. This is difficult, but I know I need to respect her experience.

Mallory sets the pace, which is not actually slow at all. She ignores the glances she gets from ladies in skintight athletic wear and guys whose shirts are twisted around their heads like sweatbands. I don't. I don't want Mallory to know I'm aware of something that might embarrass her, so I only give onlookers angry Scott Summers eyes when Mallory won't notice. I see these glances and hear the accompanying murmurs pretty much everywhere we go. I know what these jerks are thinking, and I want to blast them to mists of gore.

With nightfall approaching, the groups and pairs of hikers begin to thin, most only moving down the hill. As her audience scatters, Mallory eases into the walk, even snapping pictures here and there of the abundant yellow senna, the occasional bursting fairy dusters, and the wolfberries dotting their hearty stalks of bright green brush. She smiles when she thinks I'm not looking. We're maybe a third of the way up the hill when she turns to take in the view of Thimble Peak.

Because it's Tucson, not because we're fat, we're both drenched in sweat. I guzzle half a bottle of water, pass one Mallory's way. Maybe it's safe to engage in conversation, even if I question whether we have the breath for it. I've had Mallory's treatment on my mind almost constantly, and I want to know more about it. Has Mallory's team helped her lose weight? Do they talk about trigger foods and addiction like at Overeaters Anonymous? I haven't told Mallory about my own appointment yet. Maybe because I don't want anyone to know until I'm 100 percent certain it won't lead to more humiliation.

"So, like, what's the deal with your treatment? Please tell me it's not like OA."

Mallory steps off the path and sits on a boulder by some impressive cacti. The area is completely shaded, as we're on the east side of the hill. I join her.

She reaches down to massage her calf. "I don't know if you're ready to know about this yet, but I'm just going to plant a seed in your brain right now. You don't need to do anything with the seed. It might even be better if you try to avoid the seed for now. It can just sit there in your humble little brain garden until the day comes when you might be ready to water it."

This conversation hasn't gotten weird at all.

"Maybe the easiest way to describe what I'm learning in treatment is to tell you what I'm *not* learning—not anymore, anyway."

Characteristically cryptic. I have to admit I like the drama.

"My mom, monstrous as she is, is not actually a bad person or a bad mom. She's merely a victim of diet culture."

There's that phrase again; Mallory first uttered it during my print-making lesson. "Diet culture?"

"It's a whole thing. Too immense to be unraveled in a single conversation. I'm still unraveling it myself and I've been in treatment for over four months. But I will tell you the first lesson you need to learn, especially because you're a man. Diet culture, which is rooted in white supremacy and capitalism, teaches women that they're supposed to look a certain way, that their value comes from their desirability in the eyes of men. This is one very effective way patriarchy keeps women in the chains of servitude. How are female-identifying people supposed to reach their potential when they dump all their energy and resources into looking like the filtered, photoshopped influencers they follow on social media or see on the covers of brainless beauty magazines?"

I'd expected to hear something about food, not oppression, but as always, talking with Mallory is surprising and illuminating. I can't help but wonder if all those fat models on her walls became offensive once she'd been in treatment for a while. They weren't your typical Hollywood types, but she still seemed pretty eager to get rid of them, as if even fat models can be harmful to a woman's self-image and personal growth.

I say, "So men are bad?"

"No, dork. *Patriarchy* is bad."

Okay. "But patriarchy is men?"

"Have you been doing your reading? Patriarchy is a societal model that *favors* men, particularly cis straight white able-bodied neurotypical ones."

I wish I had a notepad in my pocket. I've heard all of these terms before, I think, but I haven't given them much thought except for *white*, which of course I've been thinking about pretty regularly since reading Gloria Anzaldúa's book. "Okay," I say, "so the patriarchal *model* sucks, and it controls women with diet culture?"

Mallory gives me a gentle pat on the head. "Gold star, teacher's pet. Patriarchy controls you, too, just not to the same degree or in the same ways as women."

I kind of get what Mallory means, particularly where the white supremacist part is concerned. I'm thinking about that confusing feeling I used to get whenever I had to list "white" as my race when filling out an official form, a fucked-up circumstance predicated on the fact that America doesn't recognize my actual race. Something about checking that "white" box always felt kind of bad but also kind of good because most of the time I'd also leave off my middle name since those are optional. This way, whenever some stranger saw my forms, they'd think I was a white guy. Sometimes it felt like I could just *be* a white guy. But Evelyn never wanted me to be white. Kid Condor was never white. My head is kind of spinning into a shame spiral over this awful thing I used to do—I'm ashamed of *why* I used to do it—and I kind of want to punch something because it still pisses me off that any part of me might have believed the lie that being white is being better.

I gulp down my feels, blink them away as quickly as I can. I don't want Mallory to know that my thoughts have drifted to such a challenging place. I don't want her to see me the way Reed does: as someone who thinks everything is always all about him. This evening is decidedly about Mallory, not me, so I shake the racist bullshit off and refocus, even shifting my body so we're more perpendicular than parallel.

"Okay," I say. "So your mom is not really a villain—she's just being hella manipulated—but she *does* want to help you lose weight. Is that . . . ?" I take a breath, my body recognizing before I do that I should absolutely not ask what I'm about to ask. "Is there anything wrong with that?"

Mallory's growl of frustration comes with a neon exclamation point at the end. She sends up a cloud of orange dust as she storms back to the trail, heading not onward but back toward the base of the hill. "You're hopeless, dweeb! Why do I even try?"

What did I do wrong?

I sling my backpack over my shoulder and bolt to catch up. "Don't quit now! The best view of Tucson awaits you! Why are you angry?"

Mallory comes to an abrupt halt. She spins on her heel, lifts her arms, gesturing to the splendor of nature surrounding us. "This is not who I am! Do you know what a walk like this can do to the inside of my thighs? Do you know how much my joints hurt right now? I'm a fat *bitch*! Respect that!"

My shock gives Mallory another head start. On the move again, Mallory mutters, "And now you've made me say the word *bitch*. Do you know how long it's been since I've used that word? Goddamn it, Brett."

Finally, my feet activate. When I catch up, I gently grab Mallory's arm. "Wait, *please*. I just wanted you to get to the top to show you that you can achieve anything, that your size doesn't matter and it's okay—"

This is when Mallory literally throws ass, knocking me off my feet with just the power of her hip. I stumble, land in the dirt, narrowly missing the spines of an ocotillo.

"It *does* matter! That's the whole point of this fight, you jackass!"

Why are we fighting? What the hell is happening?

"*This* is my body! Look at it! Look!"

I cower, suddenly aware of just how much damage Mallory could do if she wanted to. Slowly, I lift my gaze to take her in.

"Look!"

"I'm *looking*! Jesus!"

"Now are you going to tell me how great it is at the top of the hill? Are you going to tell me that's where people like me belong in this world?"

I wince at every word. Whatever has gone wrong might mean I'm losing Mallory, and this possibility is too scary to endure. "I didn't mean to hurt you. I only thought . . . I was going to . . . I was thinking you'd feel really good and I'd feel really good, and then maybe we'd . . . I thought you liked me, and maybe if it felt right, I'd try to kiss you . . ."

"*What* the *fuck*?"

"After securing your consent, I mean! Only if you wanted—"

"Get a brain! I'm *gay*, dude! Your junk is cute and all—"

"Cute?"

"But I don't fuck with cis dudes, okay?"

Oh my God. Oh my God. Ohmygodohmygodohmygod.

My confusion and embarrassment quickly give way to anger. "Then why the hell have you been seducing me? I took my pants off for you!"

Mallory's chin drops. Is she as confused as I am? "You are so dense sometimes! You didn't take your pants off for me; you took them off for *you*. I wasn't seducing you. I was trying to *help* you."

Help me? I knew Mallory wanted me to have someone to talk to, but how was getting me down to my Superman skivvies a part of the plan?

"What the fuck, then? Because here I am, just trying to help *you* and—"

"I don't need your help! *You're* the hot mess in this friendship, not me, and you're too clueless to even see it. I'm grand, dude. I'm working on myself on the daily and crushing it in treatment. Fuck it. I don't need this shit."

I want to beg Mallory not to go. I want to tell her I'm sorry even if I don't know what I'm apologizing for, but this time when Mallory storms off, I think of what Ms. Finch said, that bit about hearing Mallory and respecting her feelings, no matter what they are. I stay right here in the dirt, my ass aching, body heaving. At least I can get this one thing right.

I reach for the M&M's in my backpack, rip through the paper with my teeth, and tip the pouch until the candy pours into my mouth. I chew. Chew some more, but nothing about this tastes right. Why doesn't it taste right?

I spit the glob out. I spit again, suck back some water, rinse it through my teeth and around my tongue. I spit once more. I toss the pouch into the brush. Dick move, I know. Yet another thing Mallory would berate me for. And it's here I finally notice the effects of the sunset. The sky is Insta-epic, something only Michelangelo could pull out of his box of paints. This sky is just what it was supposed to be.

So why am I so not?

Brett Harrison

Banksie

AP English

18 October

Idiom Essay Rough Draft—Attempt Number 3, Losers!

Don't Eat the Cake, Bro!

~~Uuuummm, where to begin? My new guardian asked me to~~
~~write about my mom, which I don't want to do, but I promised I'd~~
~~try, plus I have to write this damn idiom essay, so I'm going to~~
~~try to kill two birds with one stone. There's another idiom worth~~
~~hating. This is an essay about my mom and cake, not birds and~~
~~stones. Okay.~~

~~My mom is…Is what?~~

~~So I have this mom, right? Yes, Brett, you have THIS mom.~~
~~As opposed to some other mom?~~

~~FUUUUUUUUUCCCCCCKKKKKK~~

~~Fuck fuck fuck fuck fuck fuck fuck fuck~~

I haven't always had a mom.

~~Does that work? Yeah, I think that works. It means I can~~
~~put off talking about the new shitty stuff by talking about the~~
~~old shitty stuff so…~~

If you were to look at my childhood résumé, you'd see a
conspicuous three-year gap in the mom department. That's
right. Between the ages of three and six, I was motherless.
When people ask about the void, they're expecting a plausible
explanation (because who just doesn't have a mom for three

years?), but the story never seems vivid enough or real enough when I say it out loud, mostly because I only know the story through secondhand details. I was too young and too traumatized, I'm told, to properly remember what happened when my birth mother died. I was too disoriented to remember much of the years immediately after. Evelyn—that's my adoptive mom, my realest mom—she used to tell me this is probably a good thing, the not remembering. When I'd ask about my past, she'd get this ~~hella~~ [note to self: I have got to get over this love affair with my favorite modifier] sad look on her face, but that look never doused the burning torch of curiosity I carried within [nice metaphor, bro! Thanks, bro!]. I wanted the worst bits of my story in the way a little kid wants to watch a horror movie through his fingers. I was scared of my past, that much is for sure. If my bed-wetting and night terrors weren't proof enough, I also wouldn't go near the oven or a campfire or anything remotely hot until Evelyn started coaxing me deeper and deeper into the kitchen over a series of months, begging dramatically for my "expert advice" as she taught herself—and eventually me—to cook ever more elaborate Mexican dishes. Until then, I wouldn't even eat warm food, sticking almost exclusively to peanut butter and jelly sandwiches and Lucky Charms for a stretch of, I don't know, two years? I'd also start crying for no reason sometimes or throw these ~~fucked up~~ epic tantrums more characteristic of a kid in his terrible twos than a third grader.

Maybe I should have been running from my past, but instead I'd regularly beg until Evelyn would recite what she knew, the same canned version of events again and again—never any gore, no villains, no sensory details. I always hoped for one more insight that might bring the tale to life, but I only ever got the Cliffs Notes.

There was a fire, followed by three hazy years before Evelyn came along. There was the word "orphan," which is a really weird word to ascribe to a person in real life. Being labeled an orphan makes you feel like a character in some moldy leather-bound volume in the cobwebbed library of some craggy dude who reads by candlelight in his dressing gown. I don't think there was anything actually Dickensian about the whole affair, pretty sure I never had to beg for gruel or lube up to crawl into the tiny spaces of machinery in cotton mills for a ha'penny per week—which would have been a pretty ~~dope~~ affecting thing to put in a cover letter when applying for a summer internship—but I did have this sweet scar on my arm, the only detail that would fit into a movie set in Queen Victoria's smog-choked London. Otherwise, I was just another kid in the system who bounced around to three foster homes, places I only remember in dappled, impressionistic images, gauzy flashes of disjointed memory that come seemingly from nowhere whenever I smell a particular shampoo or cleaning product—Lysol makes my skin crawl; Dawn dish soap bums me out. I don't know why.

Maybe because the story was never really mine, the only version that feels real belongs to Kid Condor, my comic book protagonist. All the plot points are ~~way radder~~ better in his version. Plus, the villain is a muscle-bound, psychopathic demigod, not a spoonful of heroin. Kid's version of the story involves a whole planet blowing up, his parents—who were not drug addicts—sacrificing themselves to save him in Monos's final moments because they loved him so much. My version involves a trailer fire just outside Tubac started by a cigarette that fell from my mom's hand into a basket of dirty laundry by the couch. She and a boyfriend had gotten high ~~as fuck~~—a regular occurrence, I'm told—and passed out while I was playing with my Legos and eating Chef Boyardee dinosaurs right out of the can. They say I tried to pull my mom off the couch when the fire started, as if a toddler could drag a limp body to the door. How could anyone know such a thing? Did I tell them I did that? Despite my doubts, I cherish my scar because it's the only evidence I have that maybe I did try. Maybe I did behave heroically, as Kid would have. A report filed away in some coroner's office suggests my mom was already dead when her body burned. An overdose. The boyfriend wasn't as lucky.

I guess this is the part of the essay where I have to write about the things I DO remember, the things I can't just use as fodder for my fiction. I remember being alone in the dark of my hospital room. I remember tubes and beeping machines and a faint green glow. I remember the comforting faces of the conjoined twins, the two little girls on the cover of _Siamese Dream_, the Smashing Pumpkins CD I was found clutching when the people with paper shoes found me in the desert behind the blackened trailer. Of all the things I could have brought with me, I saved these two little girls in their nylon butterfly wings, their arms wrapped around each other.

And I remember being afraid. I remember crying and crying because of the unbearable pain. I remember asking for my mom every day. When was my mom going to come? Where was my mom? Why wasn't my mom coming to take me home?

The pain faded as I was treated for multiple conditions (some long-forgotten folder labeled with my name is sprinkled with terms like "malnutrition" and "failure to thrive"), but the fear never left me, not until Evelyn made me a son again. I guess that's the other way to look at the glaring hole in my résumé: These were the years I wasn't a son. It's weird to be a boy but not a son.

As I write this, I feel ~~like the biggest dick in the world~~ terrible because even though Evelyn made me a son again, I've never once called her "Mom," not when the adoption was finalized, not now. I wanted to, but every time the word stood poised at the tip of my tongue, I'd send it tumbling back to catch in my throat. It wasn't because Evelyn wasn't my real mom that I couldn't use the word, but because she WAS. Moms die. This much I knew. I loved Evelyn too much to jinx her, and I was too afraid of being an orphan again to risk jinxing myself. This is why, when I began drawing stories about Kid Condor, I gave him a dad instead. I didn't want him to lose anyone else. I guess the joke's on me, then, isn't it? Because never calling Evelyn the word couldn't save either of us from the shitty things to come. Ms. Finch has probably told you all about said shitty things. I wouldn't want her to, but it's probably her job. [Note to self: Am I writing with Banksie in mind as my reader or for a general audience? Also, work on your profanity, you shitbag.]

~~Okay,~~ So what does all this have to do with the fact that you can't eat your cake and have it, too? Well, I know Marcus (he's my new guardian, Reed's dad, you know) and Ms. Finch (whom you obviously know) and this therapist guy I haven't even met yet (some dude I'm going to see next week), they're all trying to help me because I'm kind of going through a hard time right now, and I've done a lot of stuff I'm not proud of, stuff I don't want to bring up in this essay but stuff that is really fucked-up, trust me. (You can read all about it on social media if you want, but I don't recommend fucking with social media. SAVE YOURSELF!) And I'm pretty sure the fucked-up stuff is ruining my life and costing me my friends, and I never had a surplus of those to begin with, and I know everyone just wants to help me feel better and stop doing the fucked-up stuff, but what they're really asking me to do is eat my cake and I don't want to lose my cake by eating it. Fuck. This makes no sense. What I mean is that my mom is the cake. Okay, that came out weird. What I mean is that telling the rest of the story about my mom is supposed to be the thing that helps me, it's what Marcus and Ms. Finch think I need, but if I tell you the rest, if I tell you the truth, I won't be able to keep Evelyn anymore. If I say the thing I can't say, the thing I've never once said, Evelyn will leave me for good, she'll leave forever. I know she will. It's like, sometimes it feels like, well, I mean, it's like Evelyn is already gone, you know? But I'm still holding on. What no one tells you about having your cake and never ever eating it is how exhausting it is to hold on. Marcus and Ms. Finch want me to let go, but I don't know if I can. I'm tired, so tired from holding on to my cake so goddamn tightly. Shit, this essay has gone way off the rails. I have a point, I think, I'm pretty sure I know what I'm trying to say, I know what I'm supposed to say, but I'm not articulating well, and I can't say it. I can't. Evelyn would tell me...Evelyn would say...What would Evelyn say? She'd tell me words like "stuff" and "thing" are the marks of a beginning writer. She'd say the reader's time is valuable and I owe him specificity and brevity. She'd say the essay is trying too hard to make the cake metaphor work when it really doesn't work and we'll look at it together when I get home from school. But I won't be coming home from school, will I? Not to her house, anyway. And she doesn't know about this essay, and I'm not going to tell her, because if I did, she'd say she's sorry that I'm hurting, and I don't want her to be sorry because that would feel so much worse than the zero I'll get when I turn in nothing for this assignment, because it's due tonight and these pages are definitely going in the trash.

CHAPTER THIRTY-SEVEN

Sometimes it's the simplest of delicacies that are the most memorable and precious. That's how I feel about one of my greatest signature inventions. I'm lying on my trampoline under the stars, balancing a bag of Malloritos—made by dumping a jar of marshmallow cream over a bag of Nacho Cheese Doritos—on my chest. I'm stuffing myself and watching *The Karate Kid* on my phone. My forehead pulses with hot flashes, almost feverish, though I'm not sure if it's because the humidity acts like a heating blanket or because I've just destroyed a family-sized bag of chips in one sitting.

It's hard not to think about Mallory while eating an invention that could be named after her. An image of her in her yellow thong comes unwelcome. I toss the bag to the dirt (the ants should enjoy the bits of marshmallow I couldn't scrape off). I sit up, tap the screen to pause my movie, and use my PopSocket to prop up my phone. With a couple awkward tugs, my T-shirt is off. I almost toss it to the patio, but take inspiration from Daniel LaRusso and tie the shirt around my head like the hachimaki he wears throughout the film.

I force myself to look down at my squishy body, which is decidedly not Daniel LaRusso–like. No one is here to see—even the neighbors are too far away to catch a peek—yet I still feel self-conscious as I pull my shorts and underwear off, both to cool off and to force myself to grow more comfortable in my skin. I wish Mallory were with me—full frontal and all. Somehow, when I'm with her I don't feel like there's anything wrong with my body. A lesbian? How could I not have seen that she had no interest in me in that way? How many rainbow accessories does a girl have to wear before I'll get it? Rainbows are gay, bro! How could I have screwed up so badly?

A familiar voice comes booming from far away in the stars. *Because you're a self-absorbed dick, Brett, a routine that's getting kind of old.*

I used to be comforted by the voice of Captain Condor, but these days he only ever points out my unworthiness to wear the purple and yellow of the Corps.

"Leave me alone," I mutter. "I feel awful enough."

This time a different, more sinister voice replies. *Isn't it about time to put your dick away and spew those Malloritos all over the toilet seat, fatty?*

Archer von Adonis, that fart box.

Adonis unleashes one of his epic villain cackles.

I close my eyes, will his voice away.

I want to give in to him, but I also really *don't* want to give in. I grit my teeth as I feel tears coming on.

Screw this. I am *not* crying about barfing right now. And I am *not* barfing.

I lie back down, grab my phone, and tap the play icon. I rub my temples.

Quickly, I'm drawn back into my favorite story.

Daniel has been hard at work painting Mr. Miyagi's house all day while Mr. Miyagi was casting lines without him. I love this part. Daniel blows up at Mr. Miyagi because he promised to teach him karate but instead has had him slaving away like a handyman, staining the fence and stripping the deck and, you know, waxing on and waxing off, until he's at real risk of carpal tunnel syndrome.

Daniel chases after Mr. Miyagi like, "What the hell, bro?" (I'm paraphrasing here.) And Mr. Miyagi is like, "You had to stay here to train in karate, bro." And Daniel is like, "Bro, this is bullshit! I'm not your servant! Why aren't you teaching me, bro?" And Mr. Miyagi is all, "Bro, I *am* teaching you." And Mr. Miyagi instructs Daniel to do all the property-maintenance moves he's taught him: paint the fence, sand the floor, paint the house, wax on, wax off. And suddenly Daniel is blocking every strike Mr. Miyagi makes like he was born a black belt or something. The scene is a masterclass in storytelling, the payoff one of the best—

Oh. Oh, *whoa*. Holy shit, whoa.

I shoot into a sitting position. My phone bounces on the trampoline mat, dropped from my grasp. In the movie of my mind, I'm seeing a montage: images of me and Mallory over the past weeks. I'm scraping inspirational pictures of fat women off her ceiling because she doesn't need them anymore. I'm upcycling half a closet's worth of superhero T-shirts into a dope blanket so I don't have to give them up. I'm opening up about my feelings. I'm making art that celebrates fat bodies.

Oh my God. Mallory is training me toward a black belt in being *fat*. She quit Overeaters Anonymous because she's no longer interested in being thin. She's interested in being who she is, and she wants me to do the same. Mallory is Mr. Miyagi-ing *me*. How did I miss this?

I navigate to my text messages, scroll to Mallory's name. I type wax on. I hit send.

Come on, come on. Please reply.

I remind myself that it's two a.m. and Mallory might be sleeping like every other normal person who has school at eight, but as I go back to the triumphant ending of *The Karate Kid*, as I watch Daniel fulfill his destiny and become a hero, crane-kicking some major ass, I can't help but long for the moment when a push notification might interrupt my film.

Back at the apartment, I finally fall asleep with my phone still in hand, no vibration heralding the words I'd give anything to see: *wax off*.

CHAPTER THIRTY-EIGHT

I don't know what I expected Dr. Bradford's office to look like. Okay, that's a lie. It was supposed to be paneled in rich mahogany, decorated with tribal masks and dusty curiosities collected during his youth as a safari guide in deepest Africa. It was supposed to feature a chaise longue upholstered in aubergine velvet upon which I would be hypnotized by a swinging pocket watch pulled from Dr. Bradford's pinstriped waistcoat.

I watch way too many movies.

"Call me Kenny," Dr. Bradford says. Instead of an ancient and studious Austrian weighed down by tweed, which would have delighted me, Dr. Bradford—Kenny, I guess—seems younger than Marcus, fit and handsome. How am I supposed to talk about my body with a guy like him? Reed comes to mind, and I feel a little worse because I know it's not Reed's fault that he's hot. I might be pissed about what he did, but I'd be lying if I said he didn't become a villain in my story partly because I'm envious. Reed didn't deserve what I did to him. And Mallory didn't deserve to be made to hike up Tumamoc just because I wanted to be her hero. I resist pulling my phone from my pocket for the millionth time to see if she's finally texted me back. She was right when she said I was the hot mess in our friendship. She's a total Mr. Miyagi of being in the body she's in, and the fact that I'm here is evidence enough that her teaching has been effective. I want this to go well. I want to succeed.

Kenny gestures to one of two leather armchairs positioned under a window featuring a view of Mount Lemmon. A fish tank populated by bright, darting Nemos and pair of lazy Dorys stands in one corner of the office. I like the fish tank. It lends the space a calming air. A practical laminate computer desk weighed down by several piles of messy paperwork encourages me, too. Maybe Kenny isn't as perfect as his looks suggest; maybe he's as disorganized and harried as anyone else. My favorite thing in the office is a glowing Pikachu clock that overlooks the fish tank.

Kenny's business card, which I finally shove into my pocket, tells me he specializes in sports psychology, a troubling detail. Is he like a coach or something? I hate those guys—always so loud and pissed off. I try to imagine Kenny standing on the sidelines, screaming at his clients to get their heads in the game. Fortunately, the image doesn't work. The most remarkable quality about Kenny is his mild-mannered air. If you swapped out his sweater vest and khakis for brown robes and sandals, he'd probably fit in quite well in a monastery.

I sit, glad that the chairs aren't directly facing each other. Kenny's tone is so even, his expression so reserved, that I'm kind of freaked out whenever I look at him. I want him to like me, but I can't tell how he feels by his body language or facial expressions. Is he judging everything I say and do? Does he see me for the loser I am? From my vantage point, the four university degrees hanging on the wall, each featuring Kenny's full name, Kenneth Louis Bradford Jr., tower over me, making me feel small. I try to imagine what it might feel like to see my full name on a degree someday—or several degrees if Evelyn gets her way. Would I finally feel confident? Proud? Would I care if people didn't know how to say *Isaias*?

These degrees suggest Kenny really knows what he's doing. I hope he does. I flash back to those first moments at Overeaters Anonymous. My body wanted me to run before my brain knew I should. I don't feel that way here. Kenny may be too good-looking for comfort, but at least he's male—and he fucks with Pokémon. We have that much in common.

Kenny sinks into the other chair and says, "What brings you in today?" I expect him to lean forward, pen poised to write down all the evidence of my dysfunction, but he's brought nothing from his desk but a mug of coffee, which he sets on a small table between our chairs.

Where to begin? I feel like John Cena in that episode of *Peacemaker* where he can't stop crying because he's such a fuckup and everyone hates him but he really, really didn't mean to be a fuckup and he really doesn't want to be alone and he never meant to screw himself so hard, but some really, really awful things happened that he absolutely did *not* respond to in a healthy way and he just made so many mistakes that he couldn't even track his path to this breakdown moment where he's crying on his bed, which of course is so, so funny in the show—I mean, give this man an Emmy already—but is definitely not funny at all when it happens to you in real life, when you're as *confused* as Peacemaker is in real life. In *my* real life, I feel all crushed and mixed-up over everything that's gone wrong: the food stuff, the drinking, the crying all the time, the shoplifting, the public humiliation, the hating my body, the losing my friends, and of course there's Evelyn, the one thing I can't imagine talking about.

I decide to say the most truthful thing I can think of. "I don't know."

Kenny creases his brow just enough to make me think he might be human. He says, "Experiences like these can be overwhelming. Does that resonate with you? Would you say you're overwhelmed?"

I nod. "Yeah, like, there's all this stuff that's going wrong and I don't know where to begin, and . . . and I'm freaked out to be here."

"That's okay. Therapy can be a scary step when you've never done it before. We have plenty of time. We don't have to cover everything today. Why don't you start by asking me questions? Whatever you like. This might be less frightening if you lead."

I did not see this coming.

"Okay." I glance at the books lined up on Kenny's bookcase. Stuff about cognitive behavioral therapy, stuff about ACT, whatever that is. A particularly wide spine on the top shelf reveals that the acronym stands for *acceptance and commitment therapy*. Many spines feature the words *sports psychology*. I figure this, the most unnerving aspect of Kenny's practice, is as good a place to start as any. "What's a sports psychologist?"

"I'm oversimplifying, but basically it's a psychologist who specializes in the effects of our thoughts and emotions on our performance in exercise and other sporting endeavors, including team sports. I treat a lot of athletes."

"I suck at sports."

Kenny shrugs. "I treat a lot of people who suck at sports."

I bust up, knocked off-kilter by Kenny's unexpected capacity for comedic timing.

He grins, obviously pleased with himself, which makes me feel 100 percent better. With one perfectly dry delivery, Kenny has become more of a person, not an automaton.

I don't see any books on the shelf about eating disorders, which is really where this line of questioning is going. I gather my courage. "I'm having some problems with food." I take a deep breath. "Like, I don't know, maybe I'm addicted, I guess?"

Kenny's eyes widen. "*Addicted*? Hmm. That *does* sound bad." He strokes his chin, nodding, thinking. And then he throws me a curveball so disorienting that I actually sit up straighter in my chair. "I wonder if a person can be addicted to something he needs to survive."

I'm blinking, blinking, shaking my head. "I mean . . . I . . ." I wrestle the stammer from my tongue. "But at Overeaters Anonymous they said I'd have to abstain from my trigger foods."

Kenny raises a brow. "Interesting advice. Did such advice feel good? Have you succeeded in abstaining?"

"Well . . . no, I guess. I mean, I haven't really tried. Abstinence seems like it would totally blow."

Kenny nods. "I'm pretty sure I wouldn't like it either."

It feels like I'm being woken from a vivid dream, coaxed by Kenny's steady voice toward a reality that is grounded and logical. Suddenly Kenny's question about addiction has become my own, and I can't help but think Kenny actually knows the answer.

"So, like, *is* food addiction real?"

Kenny shakes his head nearly imperceptibly, like he's afraid he might get caught sharing forbidden knowledge. He doesn't make me beg for a firm answer, though. "Some scientific studies *do* suggest foods, especially sugar, can be addictive, but none of those findings actually hold up to scrutiny because their scientific methodology is not sound or cannot provide conclusive results. So the short answer is no. Food addiction isn't real. There *are* plenty of circumstances that might make one *feel* he's addicted to food, though."

Holy shit.

I'm so thrown that I have to reach through the chaos in my mind to find the question I was originally planning to ask, which I ask anyway, even though it seems redundant based on the confidence Kenny brings to the subject matter. "So, like, do you specialize in food problems, too? Along with the sports stuff?"

"Eating disorders are common in athletes, so yes, I treat them."

Nothing in Kenny's tone suggests I've offended him, but surely I've offended him.

"I didn't mean . . . Shit, sorry." I bite my lip. I start scribbling on my thumb. "Sorry. Am I allowed to cuss? I have a pretty foul mouth, but I can rein it in if—"

"Cussing is fine. Your trepidation is to be expected. You've been facing this on your own for a long while, as I understand it. I assure you, treating disordered eating is within my areas of expertise. And I will never suggest you abstain from food. Ever."

"Okay, thanks. I mean, for understanding." My armpits are going swampy, but I push my anxiety down. Something Kenny said has caught my attention. It has me thinking about what Reed said during our fight, that some of the wrestlers he knows do fucked-up things to make weight. "You said lots of athletes have eating disorders. Are any of them men?"

"Is that important to you? That other men experience what you're experiencing?"

"Yeah. I mean . . . I feel like a freak."

"Eating disorders are common in men, athletes and otherwise. We can talk more sometime about orthorexia and muscle dysmorphia, if you like. And whether *freak* is a fact or merely a value judgment."

I have a feeling I'm going to learn a lot of new terms from Kenny. "Okay, that sounds all right, I think."

"Would you like to use some of our time to address your disordered eating?"

This seems like an odd thing to ask since Kenny knows this is exactly why I'm here, but I like that he's asked. I think of Ms. Finch and Mallory and Reed and Marcus and all my devoted fans on the internet—even

Robyn Fletcher—they all tell me what to do and what I should think and feel; they never ask me what I want to do.

"Yes," I say. "I'm having some other problems, too, I guess, but yeah, the eating problems might be the worst. I'd like to work on them."

"Good. It would have been rather awkward to have to tell your guardian he was paying for us to play *Legend of Zelda* for an hour every week."

I must look horrified at the mention of Marcus because Kenny quickly adds, "I'm only joking."

How's a guy to know with this dude?

"I won't tell your guardian anything without your permission. It's unethical for me to share anything with anyone unless you tell me specific details about a specific person you plan to murder."

I laugh.

Kenny doesn't.

"You're serious?"

"Are you planning to murder anyone?"

"No! Shit, man." I think it's going to take a hot minute to get used to Kenny's sense of humor. I'm not sure if he's messing with me like a buddy would or if he's legit as dry as he seems.

"Okay, good. So I think we're all systems go with treatment. In cases of disordered eating, I work with two colleagues whenever possible, a medical doctor and a dietician. They can work with you in conjunction with what we'll do here if you're up for that. Might you be willing to give that a try?"

Even though I saw this coming, I'm immediately overwhelmed by the idea of expanding my treatment—just getting to this chair in this office has been such a fraught journey—but I'm starting to like Kenny. I like how candid he is, and I like that he might be the first person I've met who hasn't pressured me to do anything or say anything I don't want to do or say. I nod; he's earned my trust. "Yeah, I'll try that."

"Good. Very good. Working with the three of us together will help you get to feeling better more quickly."

"Do you think . . . Do your patients usually learn to manage their eating disorders?"

"That's a complicated question. Sometimes yes and sometimes no. Recovery can look very different for different people, and success is predicated on countless factors. Ideally one would not have to manage his disorder after treatment because he would no longer *have* a disorder."

Wait, what? I didn't know overcoming an eating disorder was even *possible*. I thought at best I could become like those miserable ladies at Overeaters Anonymous, resisting my urges to binge and counting the days on a wall chart since my last Klondike Bar tragedy. "So, like, are you saying I might be able to *not* have an eating disorder anymore, ever again? I might not want to binge? Or throw up?"

Kenny smiles. "That's what I'm saying. Disordered eating is best left in one's past. It takes a great deal of work, but that outcome is possible."

"Holy shit."

"Indeed."

I lock my knees to avoid sliding from my chair. I'm excited, but I don't trust my excitement. Obviously, people fail at this—maybe they don't want it badly enough or maybe they don't try hard enough or maybe the disorder is too powerful. What if I'm one of the ones who fail? I don't want to fail. "What will I have to do? To get there, I mean?"

"I don't know for sure yet. The team will need to get to know you better, learn about your history and your relationship with food, along with other aspects of your life. You and I will talk about whatever you're struggling with—the thoughts and feelings, but especially the behaviors. I might teach you some coping tools to help with various aspects of your life. Perhaps the simplest answer is that you'll have to be brave and dedicated."

"Will it be hard?"

"Probably, yes."

This is when my emotions rise, a sudden storm that catches me by surprise. My eyes well. Damn it.

Kenny passes me a box of tissues. I place them in my lap in anticipation of the meltdown building between my temples.

"This is bringing up some emotions for you. What are you feeling?"

I shake my head. "I don't know. I just don't want it to be hard. Everything is always so hard for me. And I feel like kind of a failure at everything. Sorry." I gesture toward my face. "I'm like this a lot . . . but I don't want to be. I didn't mean to turn out this way—"

Kenny lifts his hand, a slight gesture that dams my flow of words but loosens my flow of tears. "Let's not talk for a minute. I want you to practice honoring your emotional experience. Don't try to explain your emotions away or judge them. Just sit with them."

I'm shaking my head, gritting my teeth. "I don't want to. I thought . . . *Fuck*. This was going well and I'm already ruining it."

"You're not. And you can do this. I believe in you."

With no lifeline but Kenny's tiny encouragement, I give in. I'm covering my eyes, almost clawing at my face, as if the inability to save it from this embarrassment is reason enough to toss it out and buy a new one. Behind my tears, I see myself like I am now, crying over and over again throughout these past unbearable months, so violently sometimes that I can barely breathe. I'm crying in Ms. Finch's office and in Marcus's arms last week. I'm crying in my bunk, so close to Reed but so far away from him. I'm crying in front of Mallory and I'm crying in the boys' room at school, on the bathroom floor at the apartment and at the top of Tumamoc Hill. I'm crying on my trampoline and crying in my old room at Evelyn's house. And then I'm crying in another room, the type with buttons and switches on the wall, a rolling table, a baby-pink pitcher of water, a curtain on a track in the ceiling obscuring a bed on wheels. This is the room I'm always in when I cry like this, the place I always go in my head. Through my tears, I see machines with digital displays perched on rolling posts. I see hanging bags of clear liquid and vases of flowers lined up on the windowsill, cards propped open beside them, cursive fonts, pastel colors. The smell of sugar and Bag Balm. I move through dim light toward the curtain, each step as if through wet cement. I touch the fabric, my fingers grasping the rough hem at its edge. I stand like this, too afraid to move, too afraid to breathe. One second, two. Then my hand relaxes, my fingers fall from the curtain. I can't. I can't, I can't. I turn away, find the darkest, blackest corner of the room and press my face into it. I sob.

At some point, I realize I'm still sitting in Kenny's office. There are spent tissues on my lap, on the floor at my feet. I'm too exhausted to be ashamed. How long have I been crying? I glance at Kenny's Pikachu clock. Our hour is almost up. I cried for forty minutes.

But Kenny just says, "That was pretty hard. I'm proud of you for sitting through it. What did that bring up for you?"

I scrub my face with my forearm and shake my head. "I can't tell you. I want to but I can't."

"Maybe try articulating the feelings themselves, not what's causing them. Better yet, let's start with just one thing—the one thing I want you to be brave enough to do today. Try to tell me just one feeling, the deepest feeling you're feeling right now."

So many emotions are battling inside me that it's hard to imagine choosing just one, but miraculously, the answer to Kenny's question is

245

immediately clear. "I'm afraid." Though I might have imagined I'd be relieved to be let off the hook so simply, my admission brings more admissions. "I'm afraid to talk about something really horrible, and I'm afraid if I can't talk about it, I won't ever get better. I'm afraid I'll be like this forever, and I'm afraid I can't bear to be like this forever, and what happens if I can't bear to be like this forever?"

Kenny says, "What if I told you I think you're strong enough to talk about whatever you're holding inside? That when you're ready, you will? You're just not ready today, and that's all right. Might you be willing to accept that outcome as a possibility?"

I don't know if I buy what Kenny is selling, but I want to so badly. I nod vigorously.

"Okay, good. Then when you're ready, you'll tell me and we'll talk about it, okay?"

"Okay."

I blow my nose for the dozenth time, drop my tissue into the small wastebasket that I'm *only now* realizing is right beside my chair.

Kenny, perfectly professional, like our exchange were the type you'd make with a bank teller, like I didn't just cover his floor in tissues, says, "So what's your schedule look like next Tuesday?"

CHAPTER THIRTY-NINE

Is it weird that I'm looking forward to next Tuesday in the way a little kid might a sleepover? My friendship garden, which was never terribly fertile, seems utterly barren now—evidenced by the fact that I've signed a year-long lease at the outcast picnic table where only the socially awkward kids sit, guys who can't even fit in with the theater thugs or mathletes or ganja gang. I pull my phone from my pocket once more. Nothing from Mallory. She doesn't have read receipts, so I can't tell if she's seen my message. Should I try again? I type, **Wax on.** I hit send and slip my phone back into my pocket.

As awful as all that crying in Kenny's office was, I kind of feel like he gets it and it's okay. I know he's not really a friend, and I have a feeling he's not going to put up with an ounce of my bullshit as a real friend might, but maybe he'll become the type of friend Ms. Finch is. My conversation with Kenny was surprising in all the best ways, and I don't feel so overwhelmed by what's to come.

I'm leaving the picnic tables halfway through lunch, on my way to tell Ms. Finch all about my successful appointment, when the beast herself, Robyn Fletcher, spies me from across the courtyard. *Damn.* Note to self: Don't tell Kenny about my very specific plans to kill the very specific person named Robyn Fletcher.

I brace myself as she waves, rises fluidly from her bench, and power walks toward me, somehow graceful despite her speed.

I take a breath, readying some excuse or insult, anything to send her scurrying back to her lair, but before I have a chance to take the first shot, I register the sling cradling her left arm. I get a better look at her face, the bruise above her eye. She actually glances down as she approaches, her posture cowed, as if she's not the most important person in the nation, nay, the world.

"Please don't run," she says.

This is a Robyn I've never seen before—her voice is thin, like she's trying not to cry—and I'm too disoriented to run even if such displays of athleticism came easily.

"Can we talk in private? Please?" It's here I notice she isn't wearing several of her own campaign buttons. Odd. Few billboards get more attention than Robyn's breasts.

"Uh. Yeah."

We make our way toward my secret spot behind the arts building, sit and prop our backs against the stucco façade.

No stranger to long silences, I let Robyn collect her thoughts. I pull a half-eaten packet of Corn Nuts from my pocket, pop a few into my mouth. I offer the package.

"Brett, you are so disgusting sometimes."

The words carry no real venom. I almost laugh, actually.

Finally, she says, "So our club—"

"The Robyn Fletcher for Class President Club. I'm familiar."

Robyn swallows in a labored way, like her mouth is full of peanut butter. "I never wanted to spin the club into votes. That's just the story

I told you because I was afraid if I told you the truth, the truth would become real. I won't be running for office this spring. I can't anymore."

It's lucky this wall is so solid because I could easily fall over at such a plot twist.

"Okay," I say carefully, unsure if I'm entering a minefield. "Why are you dropping out of the race? Isn't global domination your kink?"

Robyn pulls at the fuzz on her cardigan, dropping one pill at a time. "Have you ever made up a story to make yourself feel better about something unbearable?"

Perhaps Robyn is psychic on top of all her other talents, or perhaps she's merely speaking about the phenomenon in the everyday sense, like when you embellish an anecdote to make yourself look better or someone else look worse. I'm the most notorious storyteller I know, my embellishments rarely less than glaring plot revisions, but I try to play it cool. "Yeah, sure. What does Banksie call it? Controlling the narrative?"

"When I read what you wrote, I made up a story. In that story, you were someone who would be healed through helping others in similar pain. I was the good-hearted philanthropist who would facilitate this healing, and would therefore get to write about what I'd accomplished in several scholarship essays, leading to a memorable tenure in the Ivy League."

So far this is a predictable narrative—too familiar, too. Wasn't I supposed to be a hero for Mallory? I told myself I was prodding her up Tumamoc for her enjoyment, but it wasn't for her. It was for me. Maybe Robyn and I have more in common than I'd guessed.

She says, "And I would act as a sort of moderator of the club, sitting in at meetings and supporting its members."

Naturally.

"But my role in that story would have been a lie, because . . . I actually think I might have an eating disorder, too. My mom is scared of getting fat—terrified—and she's mean about *me* getting fat. She'll catch me eating anything made from grains, and she'll get this horrible look on her face, like I'm the scum on her shoe, and she'll be like, 'Robyn, you know that corn you're eating is what they use to fatten up cattle, right? They don't let cows become congresswomen, now do they?'"

"Savage."

"Right?"

"You don't look like a cow, by the way. Too much eye makeup."

She lands a fist dangerously high up my thigh, as if playing Whac-A-Mole. She thrusts an index finger toward my crotch. "Tread lightly or the next blow will be to whatever pathetic appendage you pass off as a dick."

I raise an eyebrow. *"Blow?"* I protect my junk with both hands, but Robyn doesn't strike again. Much to my amazement, she releases a small, melodic laugh. I didn't know Robyn had the capacity for jocular banter, but maybe I should have. Such a fine line between ribbing and roasting.

Her expression grows serious again. "I *know* I don't look like a cow. But that's the thing. I'm so afraid that one day I might look like one. I measure and weigh myself multiple times a day, and I don't eat anything but the chicken breast and green vegetables my mom makes for me, which I also have to measure. My teeth ache nonstop because I sleep in whitening strips every night." Robyn starts crying, and I find it disorienting that I'm not the one crying for once. She says, "I got a B on a quiz the other day. I don't get Bs. I'm Robyn Fletcher, you know? Nobody wants to hear me talk about this stuff. I'm supposed to be perfect. I'm the person everyone wants to be."

Well . . .

"But I don't want to be me—not like this." Robyn wipes her cheeks.

"And I wanted to start this club because I thought maybe it could help me. If I was just there and I could listen. When everyone was posting about their own experiences with food, I was so jealous—"

"Envious."

Robyn impales me with a glare.

"Sorry, it's one of the more annoying things about me, I know."

"I was *envious* because all I wanted to do was dump this burden on everyone else so I wouldn't have to carry it anymore."

"And now? Why are you fessing up? You got what you wanted. The club is a go."

"Because I passed out and fell in the shower." She lifts her arm. "When I got home from the urgent care, I read your words again, and I realized I've been a coward. Maybe they don't let cows be congress-women, but they don't care much for cowards, either."

I never thought I'd say it, but something akin to compassion stirs in my chest. I remind myself to be honest but kind. I want to be worthy of Ms. Finch's confidence in me. "I'm sorry this is happening to you. Genuinely, I wouldn't wish it on my worst . . . well, I wouldn't wish it on you."

Despite her tears, Robyn laughs again. "Fuck you."

Turns out honest and kind can also involve a healthy dose of nut stomping.

I say, "But when I said I was no role model, I actually meant it. I'm a kid who's *bulimic*, and I've really messed up my life with this stuff." I can't believe I owned that just-right word so readily.

Robyn guides a lock of hair behind her ear. "I didn't know you were purging."

"You weren't supposed to know any of it. You're not the only one who couldn't talk about their problems."

"So you didn't post that confession?"

"The journal fell into someone else's hands, that's all. But now here we are. And we're both talking to someone."

If there's an ounce of anger or blame left at Reed's feet, it evaporates now. Maybe I was humiliated because what I was doing was humiliating, not because Reed let the world in on my secret.

Robyn says, "I'm afraid people might find out if I can't get this under control. Do you think maybe we could talk about it once in a while?"

In a million versions of this narrative, I could not have seen it coming, but I reach out and take Robyn's hand. "People might see us together. I might be as damaging to your reputation as getting fat, you know. I'm not willing to meet in secret like this."

Robyn's tears darken her shirt. "God, I'm so, so sorry for the hell I put you through. I'd look at you—at the weight you were gaining—and I'd see myself, which doesn't even make sense because my mom has had to take in every one of my skirts this year; they're all too loose for me now. I'd be really scared, and I'd hate you for bringing out that fear. I'm sorry I've been such a brat." Robyn's tears choke her words, and I let them. I think about what Kenny made me do yesterday. There may come a time when I tell Robyn about treatment and encourage her down a similar path, but maybe the best thing I can do for her today is let her feel the shitty kind of way she needs to feel.

When she comes up for air, she says, "I wouldn't be ashamed to be seen with you, actually. I mean it. Everyone thinks you're adorable, you know. They really do think you're a hero, even if you don't feel like one. Your comic books aren't that cringe, either. The food constellations are kind of sus, but, I mean, I get it."

It's hard to buy that my social rating isn't as abysmal as I imagine, but maybe my self-esteem has taken too many hits to see clearly anymore. I think about all those unread DMs. Maybe it's time to read them.

I can't believe I'm saying this, but here goes. "I'm chill with hanging sometimes—even if hanging with you might hurt my street cred." I've earned another whack, fortunately not to the dick, which makes us both laugh. "But the club has to go." I'm thinking about Kenny, how safe I feel in his hands. He knows what he's doing, and judging by how far Mallory has come with her treatment team, I think knowing what you're doing might matter. "We're not professionals, and we don't have the answers that can help anyone, but there *is* someone who comes to mind who might be willing to be a friend and a sympathetic ear, just not in a weekly-club-full-of-messed-up-kids kind of way. Might you want to meet her if she's willing?" *If she ever texts me back, that is.*

Robyn's smile—so often fake—rings entirely genuine. She runs her fingers through her hair, already putting herself back together so she'll be ready to present perfection for the rest of the school day. "Sign me up."

"And her name is Mallory *Clark*. Nothing else."

Robyn's eyes light up with recognition. Her smile turns sheepish, and she nods. "Nothing else."

I reach for my phone, release a deep sigh of relief as its screen lights up. Push notification. Six minutes ago, as if I'd finally earned it by doing a little good in the world. Uuuuuugggggghhhhh. Wax off, already. God.

CHAPTER FORTY

Mallory's Fat American prints are an imposing presence in the deserted student gallery. Each print floats a few inches from the deep navy walls as if by enchantment, cross lit in the otherwise-dim space, bringing the vibrancy of the cheese dust to neon life. It's hard to believe these are the same prints I saw a couple weeks ago on Mallory's patio. Mallory said installation elevates any work, and she wasn't kidding. Besides that, each print—featuring interesting angles of Mallory's body, all the ways you might lie in bed, say—is embellished with beadwork sewn right into the paper. Long, thin beads in bright red and navy blue, arranged in various star and stripe configurations unique to each print. A few prints even feature thick lengths of red beads hanging freely from the paper.

I step closer. No, these aren't beads. They're dyed macaroni noodles, the very noodles, I'm guessing, we saved when we procured the cheese powder.

Mallory sits in her signature style on the polished concrete floor before her prints, gazing upon them like a proud mother. Come Friday, she'll be the star of her first reception, and maybe everyone will see the inner brightness she's let me in on. Maybe she'll never be that girl in Earth sciences again—not for me, not for anyone.

Mallory's gaze doesn't leave her work as my footsteps approach, but she does speak. "You may commence your groveling now."

This is better than the physical violence I might have anticipated.

I sink to the floor to sit beside her, lean back and prop myself on my arms, soaking in Mallory's triumph. "I'm so proud of you."

"I don't need you to be proud of me." Mallory's delivery is matter-of-fact, not cruel, but her words still sting. Her voice softens. "But thank you."

We let the silence expand. It almost echoes in the gallery, which is not cavernous but seems increasingly broad and deep in this light. I can almost feel Mallory drifting into the darkness, and I don't want to risk losing her again. I force myself to speak.

"You're the Miyagi to my Daniel LaRusso, right? Not the love interest?"

"I wondered when you'd see it . . . if you'd see it."

"It would have helped to know you're gay."

"It would have helped if you weren't so dense."

I laugh. I can't deny it. I gather my courage and say, "I throw up my food sometimes."

"I know."

Of course she knows.

I say, "I started treatment on Tuesday."

Here's the violence I was waiting for. Mallory slaps me on the back, grips and rattles my shoulder. "Fuck yeah, nerd!" She raises her arm again, but this time only for a high five. I oblige. The crash of our palms reverberates. The sting feels awesome.

We settle back into our lazy postures.

I say, "I'm both anxious and excited. I don't know how to feel."

"I felt the same way at first, but my therapist told me something that helped me be patient. She was like, 'It can be hard to find your footing in uncharted territory. Just take it one step at a time.'"

"Okay, why is *that* not on a poster in the counseling office?"

Mallory shrugs. "Would it show a tragic lack of self-awareness if I told you I was proud of you?"

I shake my head. "Nah, I want you to be proud of me . . . because you're my Mr. Miyagi . . . and . . . because you're my friend."

I'm too embarrassed to confirm if Mallory is smiling, but I can feel her smile. "It means a lot that you're proud of me, too. I do love you, you know."

My body tenses. I'm holding my breath.

"And I mean that in the gayest way possible, so don't start getting a bunch of grand romantic ideas again, you jackass."

When our laughs fade, I say, "I love you, too, Mallory."

She gives my knee a squeeze. "Batter Boys for cupcakes, Daniel-San?"

"Oh my, yes. It'll give us a chance to talk about *this*." I pull a dog-eared copy of *A Room of One's Own* from my backpack. It occurred to me that if my Mr. Miyagi has a Mr. Miyagi of her own, I should start there in my reading assignments. I scored the paperback at Bookman's on the way home from my therapy appointment.

I've earned my favorite kind of Mallory smile, unabashed and radiant.

"I've only finished the first two chapters, so no book report yet, but I do have a list of talking points."

"You know something, nerd? I think there's hope for you yet."

CHAPTER FORTY-ONE

As the bell rings and my classmates file out of Banksie's classroom, I linger, pretending I need another moment to gather my materials. Ruby Orange, who's packing up beside me, spins on her heel and slaps a *Fat American* flyer down on my desk. She kneels and flips what's left of her hair from her eyes. Her smile is warm, even if it comes from behind several bolts and rings of facial hardware. She leans in close enough that I can smell the Pez she's forever crunching on (no dispensers, ever). Her tone is conspiratorial. "So, like, you're friends with Mallory Clark, right?"

Ruby has always been chillax with me, but it's hard not to be at least a little terrified of a girl who barks at her enemies in the hallways. Does Ruby merely play at being rabid or is she *actually* rabid? The world may never know.

"I sure am."

"Do you think you could introduce us at her reception tomorrow? I've been crushing on her for months but am too shy to say anything."

Ruby? *Shy?*

"I'd be honored to facilitate such introductions."

"Bitchin'. Thanks a ton, Brett. You're one of the good ones."

As she turns to leave, Ruby glances over her shoulder, a demented twinkle in her eye. She whispers, "I'll tell Satan to spare you, my child."

"Um . . . thank you?"

She winks, then pushes through the door. The thought of two personalities like Ruby and Mallory possibly ending up together . . . I shake my head and smile. I do love an adventure.

As the door latch slides home, Banksie looks up from his desk and gives me his affable grin, the seemingly oblivious but not *actually* oblivious smile he uses when *he* knows that *I* know that *he* knows I've screwed up. "Are we finally going to chat about what I think we're going to chat about?"

My face grows warm. For a moment, I consider bolting, but I'm on a roll with this being-brave business. I can't avoid my mistakes and failings forever. I nod.

"You're not the type to skip out on an assignment, Brett. Your essay was due nearly a week ago. I was looking forward to another serving of your killer voice. What gives?"

The compliment does nothing to empty the butterflies from my belly. Opening up to Banksie feels like admitting I'm not worthy of his admiration. I don't want to give him reason to think less of me. But my vulnerability has proved quite fruitful over the past few days. My hiding, on the other hand, has caused so much harm. I don't want to hide anymore. I channel my inner Captain Condor.

"So, um, I'm kind of struggling with some stuff right now . . . like, pretty bad stuff, it would seem." I plant my gaze on Banksie's wall of poets, all these people whose words have given him strength. "I think I might . . ." I shake my head. "Not *might*. I *know* I have an eating disorder. Binge disorder, to be precise. Or, like, bulimia? Both? I haven't figured it all out yet." I release a long breath. I force myself to look

Banksie in the eye. His expression is like that of a parent when his kid trips and falls at the playground, that moment of restrained concern before the kid either starts wailing or confirms he's fine by jumping up to go play.

Banksie moves from behind his desk, props himself on the student desk in front of mine. "Thank you for trusting me, Brett. I'm so sorry you're going through that."

I don't want Banksie to think he should call in the psychological SWAT team, so I raise my palms to bar any misunderstanding. "I've started therapy—treatment, I guess. I should be all right. Eventually."

"I'm relieved to hear that, though you don't sound convinced."

I'm not convinced, am I? Kenny's voice springs to mind. *Disordered eating is best left in one's past.* This outcome feels like a prize on a high shelf, too far away to see if my name is engraved on the trophy. "Well, I know I'm on the right path, at least. It's just . . . my whole life has become this massive mess to clean up. I don't know if I'll ever be able to forgive myself for fucking up so hard." I catch my curse word and grimace. "Sorry."

Banksie shrugs and says something Evelyn would appreciate. "Sometimes *fuck* is the only word that will do." He affects a stern tone. "Just not in class, homeboy."

I give him a sheepish smile. "Anyway, I got pretty stuck on this essay, obviously, but that's nowhere near the worst of it. I've really hurt people." I've hurt the *most important* person, actually. Reed completely ignored my existence in class today. It's bolstering to be attending peace accords with Robyn and an incredible relief to have Mallory back in my life, but what happens if I can't make things right with Reed?

Banksie gestures to his pyramid, to the friendly-looking grandpa dude at the very top. "Do you know much about Desmond Tutu?"

"Only that if he means more to you than Hova, he must be a pretty amazing guy."

"He was head of the Truth and Reconciliation Commission in South Africa after the fall of apartheid. You know about apartheid?"

I literally remember *singing* about Nelson Mandela in elementary school, but Banksie doesn't need to know as much. He might ask to duet with me. "I'm familiar."

"So after all those years of intense trauma and oppression, South Africa had to find a way to heal, the indigenous population and the white Afrikaners, not to mention everyone else, working together toward a better, more just future."

"Okay."

"And my pal Desmond Tutu there—" He points toward the portrait. "He led the commission that allowed those who'd committed human rights violations to own up to their mistakes and evil deeds. He allowed them to recite their wrongs and to ask for and receive forgiveness. Can you imagine that? Instead of throwing these people in prison—these people who committed unbearable atrocities—he gave them a chance to change?"

I raise my brow.

"And do you know why?"

Honestly, no. Captain Condor would have dumped them in the dreaded Ner'l'chal Prison on Cerolius-5 and thrown away the key.

"Because Tutu and the commission believed that these violators *could* change. They understood the incredible transformative power of forgiveness. Only through reconciliation could the nation become whole."

I think I understand what Banksie is getting at. If those who had done such terrible things could be forgiven, if they could change for the better, surely I can, too. But how do you seek forgiveness from someone who has no interest in hearing an apology? "What if Reed's not as chill as Desmond Tutu?"

A look of recognition passes over Banksie's face. I've just told him more than I meant to. "Reed is your family. I don't know what's going on between you, but I'm guessing you've got a pretty good shot at mending things if you're ready to own up to your mistakes and put in the work to change. And even if Reed doesn't forgive you, you have the power to forgive yourself. You may always feel remorse, but you don't have to stay weighed down by guilt."

I'm the wording-est guy I know, and even I'm struggling here. Remorse? Guilt? Aren't these synonymous? My expression begs for more.

"Your guilt is making you feel like you're a bad person, right? That you might not be capable or worthy of change? But forgiveness turns your guilt into remorse. Remorse is more like, *If I knew then what I know now, I'd have done better. I would have made a different choice.* The difference is subtle, but remorse acknowledges that we have the capacity to change, to become better, more compassionate, empathetic people—*and* to overcome our harmful habits. I myself carry a great deal of remorse, but I don't carry *any* guilt."

I'm gazing at that trophy on the high shelf again. I can almost see the letters of my name forming on its plate. I'm filling with a warmth I can't quite identify. I think it might be hope. I shake my head. "Damn, dude. You're kind of blowing my mind right now."

Banksie affects his rapper voice and pumps a fist in the air. "Ahhhh, yeeahhhh. Dat's wha'cha boy is known for, my homie." He settles back into his studious teacher posture. "Well, that and granting extensions to the needy."

"For real?"

He nods. "You've earned it. And you got this. May the Tutu be with you." Banksie extends his fist. "Now bump this fist and get outta here, homeboy. You got an essay to write—and some reconciliation to facilitation, ya'm'sayin'?"

CHAPTER FORTY-TWO

Since the school year began, I've spent too much of fifth period in Ms. Finch's office instead of here in my journalism cubicle, but maybe that's about to change.

Though pretending to format yearbook pages, I'm actually working up a treatment for the next Kid Condor issue, dwelling on my conversation with Banksie, killing the afternoon until school lets out and I can pay Dean Ricamora a visit. He doesn't know it yet, but we have negotiations to navigate.

In the meantime, I'm struggling to figure out how to throw Captain Condor and Archer von Adonis together as teammates instead of adversaries. I need Captain to recognize that he owes Adonis an apology. I need him to ask Adonis for forgiveness. The two may never be friends, but what might happen if, for once, they weren't enemies? Basically, I need to rip off *X2: X-Men United*. It's time to write an even bigger big-bad than Adonis, and, just like in *X2*, that big-bad is going to be systemic.

Now that the beautiful and powerful Therma is going to be a super fat (still Black like Thandie but with the shape and sarcasm of my favorite super-fat inspiration), I need to get a better understanding of what patriarchy and white supremacy have to do with the shapes and sizes of our bodies. Maybe I can run all this by Banksie. Based on the talk we had after class, I'm thinking he'll have hella insights about the racist roots of fatphobia and how someone like Kid Condor can be a good ally. Of course I need to pick Thandie's brain as well—*if* I ever get the courage to speak to her again. The options suddenly seem endless—and dizzyingly overlapping.

I jolt, literally jump out of my chair, when I realize there's a chin hovering a centimeter above my shoulder. "Ajay, Jesus! I thought I was in for a lunch detention, for sure."

Ajay Mukherjee's lanky frame bobs with his laughs. "Yooooooooo! I was hoping you'd piss yourself so we could roast you mercilessly until the day you die, but the crippling anxiety you'll carry into adulthood is reward enough."

He tries to flee, but I'm faster. I secure him in a headlock and commence the fake punching that's become as routine as replacing the pot of coffee left over from fourth period.

After a committed performance featuring bulging eyes and a lolling tongue, Ajay says, "I like what I see, my man." He gestures to my computer monitor. "Storytelling's maturing." He pulls me close for an epic noogie. He plays at tearing up. "Our little guy is growing up."

I shove him off, but my grin is unbridled.

Reminded of what he wrote about my first issue, I blurt, "Did you really mean those things you said? What you wrote about issue one?"

Ajay looks perplexed. "Of course I did. Do I look like a bullshitter to you?"

I shake my head. "It's just . . . I guess for a minute there I thought maybe Reed made a deal with you or something—you know, to write something nice."

"Our little guy still has so much to learn." He sounds like a dad watching his son shave for the first time. "There's this thing called journalistic integrity. I wrote what I did because it was *true*."

Ajay turns toward the break room, limbs ready to spring into a trot, but I stop him with a hand on the shoulder. "Hey, uh, so any chance you're a *Fortnite* man?"

"Am I *even* a man, you mean?"

"Well, I was thinking of putting together a game night pretty soon. Want to come?"

"Wouldn't miss it for the world, bud."

As Ajay trots off toward the break room, he calls out, loud enough for all to hear, "Seriously looking forward to issue three, my man! Get that hot shit in my hands ay-sap!"

CHAPTER FORTY-THREE

I have exactly seven minutes," says Dean Ricamora, "so make it quick." He pushes his rectangular glasses up on his nose, motions for me to follow, and brushes past his secretary's desk into his wreck of an office. Ricamora is kind of old—like forty, maybe—and I wonder if he still has a mom to scold him for not cleaning up after himself. He tucks a rogue edge of his polo shirt into his jeans, defying in some small way his typical disheveled state.

I drop my backpack on the floor and take a seat across from him. I'm not used to talking to Ricamora—I don't know him at all, really, certainly not like Reed does. There's no easy rapport or good-natured ribbing about the size of his keychain, and I'm trusting in the innate goodness of his humanity to see this conversation through to a satisfactory result.

I say, "I'll cut to the chase. I assume you know there was another student with Reed Sheldon when he broke into the library several weeks ago, and I assume you know, because you know Reed, that the student was me."

Ricamora nods. "The security footage showed Reed's license plate. Assumptions were made about his accomplice, of course, but Reed refused to confirm."

"I see."

Ricamora leans back in his chair, regarding me thoughtfully. "Mr. Harrison, why are you here?"

"Because Reed doesn't deserve what happened to him—being kicked off the team, I mean. If anyone deserves punishment, it's me. Reed was only acting on my behalf, being a good buddy. I've been going through a rough time for a while now, which I imagine you know all about. Everything he did. He shouldn't have done it." My words catch in my throat. I'm talking about our covert comic-booking mission—I know this—yet I'm talking about *more* than our covert comic-booking mission. I swallow the lump in my throat and measure my words. "Reed was wrong, but . . . he was trying to make things better for me. We were just blowing off steam. We didn't mean any harm, just having fun."

"Breaking and entering could have landed you in jail, you realize?"

"I know. It was juvenile delinquency at its finest, and I'm not proud of it."

"And our new guard broke his nose trying to chase you down. Did you know that?"

"Holy—!" I catch myself before the second part of the exclamation comes out. Randy Savage broke his nose?

"Fence posts pack a punch."

I guess that's it, then. My hope that I could get Reed back on the team is draining into the carpet tiles beneath my feet. I should count myself lucky that I'm not visiting him in prison.

Ricamora lifts the receiver of the phone on his desk. "Dave, yeah. You got a sec? Thanks. Yeah, my office." He cradles the receiver and says, "Okay, I'm giving you five extra minutes."

What's happening, exactly?

In seconds, Randy Savage appears. A thick strip of tape holds a plastic brace over his nose. He looks to me, then to Ricamora. He leans casually against the doorframe and crosses his monstrously swole arms over his chest. With the nose injury, he's even more imposing. If only Ajay had tagged along. He just might get to see me piss myself.

Ricamora says, "Someone has come to confess to the library break-in. Our accomplice."

Randy Savage—Dave, I guess—lifts his brow. "That's surprising. You turning over a new leaf, son?"

I can't believe he just used the word *son*. Imagine it with the same gravelly inflection you'd hear from the real Randy Savage. *Goddamn.* This Dave guy is cool as *fuck*.

"I'm merely begging you to reconsider Reed's punishment. He's worked so hard to be on that team and he's really talented, and he needs it, you know? It's good for him. He's trying to be happy. I know you don't know him like I do, but he's been through some tough things, too, and he deserves to be happy."

Ricamora and Dave share a glance, seeming to have an entire conversation in one barely perceptible nod.

Dave says, "I was sixteen once."

Wait, so . . . ?

Ricamora turns his attention back to me. "Three days in-school suspension each."

My face brightens too soon.

"*Not* to be served at the same time."

Damn.

"And Reed can rejoin the team if Coach Houston will let him, which he will."

I jump out of my chair and shake my fists in the air in triumph.

"Ohhhh yeeaaahhhh!" I spin toward Dave and say, "Would you mind . . . you know?"

He looks at me like I've spoken an alien tongue.

"Would you say 'oh yeah' for me?"

"Oh yeah?"

"You know how I mean, like . . ."

Dave fakes confusion for half a second more, and then he gives me what I want. "Ohhhh yeeeeaaaahhhhhh!"

We both mime tearing into a Slim Jim at the same time.

I say, "Almost had me there. Almost convinced me you didn't know what I meant."

"Please. Savage is from *my* time, kid. I've been pulling that voice my whole life. Stop by security sometime and I'll show you my Halloween pics. My husband looks just like Hulk Hogan, so we make quite a pair."

As Dave walks me out of the office, he adds, "And bring your buddy Reed. I have a feeling I'm going to get to know him one way or another."

CHAPTER FORTY-FOUR

I'm working up a sweat in the dark, trying not to think about idioms as I bounce beneath the Great Cool Ranch Dorito in the Sky. The Pumpkins are boring holes into my brain from my headphones, and I'm thumping away at the air with my favorite set of drumsticks. The breeze is actually sort of cool tonight, fall finally claiming a foothold, and I feel like I can breathe for the first time in weeks. Mallory's reception was a glowing success. It was awesome hearing her speak to Ajay Mukherjee about body liberation and Health at Every Size, concepts I've never heard of but am pretty sure I'm about to become expert in. His article in the school paper could go a long way in making sure invisible Earth sciences Mallory is a persona of the past.

If only it could help with my idiom essay. It's an hour past my new deadline. I felt so empowered, so capable after talking with Banksie. But now the familiar feeling of defeat is telling me I should grab that bottle of vodka spying me from the patio steps where Mallory left it the night she visited. I'm resisting, but I'm beginning to wonder why. I want to change in the ways Banksie described. I want to do better. But doing the same is easier.

Most of the time, extreme trampoline air-drumming clears my

mind, but tonight my brain swirls with having and not having and still having, all at once. I jump harder, thrashing the air with my sticks. How is it that I can't wrap my brain around the metaphor of the idiom? It just feels like there's something missing, like I'm so close to getting this essay right, like I already *know* how to get this essay right, but I just can't see . . . Suddenly the heavily highlighted pages of my Gloria Anzaldúa paperback flash through my mind, her words blurring as the pages fly by, flipped by an invisible thumb. The answer is *in there*, in something she said; I'm sure of it. What, though?

I resolve to crack the book when I get back to the apartment, as if it matters now. Surely, summer school looms in my fu—

Snap.

Fuck!

I fall to the mat, my leg knocked out from under me as if by a gunshot . . . or an archer's arrow. I grab my calf and roll in pain, blood seeping through my fingers. A broken trampoline spring rolls beside me, its jagged edge wet with blood. I lift my hand for a look. The sight makes me woozy. Blood pulses from a tiny hole in my calf, and my leg is imprinted with the red spiral pattern of the spring. I look to the western sky and scream, "Adonis, you jack-off! And here I was trying to help you in issue three!" I clutch my cramping leg.

The neighbor's dog loses its mind. A light comes on across the street. I scream, "I will have my revenge!" I roll to my knees, muttering. "Punk move. Shooting me from behind."

Slowly, I crawl to the edge of the trampoline, slither to the ground, and hobble toward the kitchen, trailing blood. I leave a slightly larger pool on the patio steps, where I pause to grab the bottle of vodka. Fuck it, you know?

In the kitchen, I yank on the handle of one drawer after another.

Surely there's something here to stanch the blood. Why are the drawers so empty? Why are there no paper towels? I yank on the final drawer; it sticks halfway open. Maybe . . . I reach in, probe with my fingers. Yes. My hand emerges clutching an oven mitt that must have been caught between the drawers. I put my back against a bank of cabinetry and slide to the floor.

It's perhaps an hour before Reed finds me here, wearing the oven mitt pressed to my leg, plenty of time for the remainder of the vodka to warm my insides and blur my brain. The empty bottle sits beside me. I blink several times to be sure he's real. What's he doing here?

Reed strokes his jaw. "Bro . . ." The moonlight highlights his expression. I wish he wouldn't stare at me like this. Like a disappointed dad. He plops down beside me, looking like he just stepped out of an ancient PacSun ad. Who wears a beanie with a tank top and board shorts? The things he gets away with. He says, "You drunk?"

I shake my head.

"You too drunk to know you're drunk?"

"It's for my leg." I lift the oven mitt from my wound. The bleeding has dried to a trickle, but my whole calf looks like a war zone.

Reed grimaces. "What happened?"

"Adonis, that piece of—"

He raises a hand. "No, I mean what *actually* happened?"

"Sorry." It's only now occurring to me that drinking encourages my penchant for high fantasy. "The trampoline. I came to extreme trampoline air-drum for a while. A spring snapped. How did you know I was here?"

"You're always here. I'm not stupid, you know. I know you sneak out at night. I followed you once. How do you even get in? I thought the realtor changed the locks."

"Does this mean you know about the drunk drive-thru'ing, too?"

"Drunk? I didn't realize you were drinking and driving. Come on, mang. You can't do this shit."

"I take an Uber."

"Thank Christ. You saw those videos Officer Amy made us watch in driver's ed." Officer Amy seemed to relish her visit to our class last semester, a sadistic grin on her face as she clicked through her PowerPoint, one picture after another of tragic, dead kids in their finest prom wear.

"I only drink sometimes. Only when . . ." I'm blinking, blinking. "Only when I come here."

"The door was unlocked. How'd you get a key?"

"My old bedroom—the lock on the window doesn't catch. I found an extra set of keys just sitting on the kitchen counter. I took them."

"And the booze? That's not Dad's brand."

"Hidden under the air vent in my bedroom before the move out."

"Damn, bro. Stealth."

I smile despite myself.

"Why, though? Why do you come here all the time? Evelyn . . . she's . . ."

At her name, I crumble. I'm nodding my head, weeping into my hands. Reed drapes an arm over my shoulder. I realize I haven't heard Evelyn's voice even once tonight. When was the last time I saw her? Felt her? I'm looking around—everything blurry through my tears—and I'm seeing how empty the house is, how bland and stark and devoid of life, not even a chair to sit on. I'm seeing the truth as if for the first time. Evelyn's voice finally comes, yet she's saying Ms. Finch's words.

Face reality, Brett; don't hide behind your fictions.

But what if reality is worse than fiction?

Then face it bravely.

I sniff and wipe at my eyes. I choke on my words. "I miss her so much."

"I know."

"Why did she have to go?" I'm gritting my teeth, rocking in place, the sobs almost violent. "I still need her."

Reed massages my shoulder. "She didn't mean to. She'd have stayed if she could. She was in so much pain, but she wanted to stay for you. That's how much she loved you. And . . . and I love you, too, and my dad loves you, so you have to stop hurting yourself. Please. Please stop. For me. I don't want *you* to go."

Now even Reed's crying. He looks nothing like a PacSun model in this moment, nothing like Archer von Adonis, either. In fact, he looks a lot like me—just a boy who's scared more often than he wants to admit.

Evelyn says, *Hasn't he always been just like you? Brett and Reed, two peas in a pod. There's an idiom for you.*

Reed rubs a hand over his face, wipes his eyes with his tank top. "Damn, dude. Don't make me cry like this again, okay? Seriously, you're fucking with my street cred."

I release a wan laugh. I lay the bottle on its side and roll it across the kitchen. It comes to a stop, wedged beneath the far cabinets. I think of Ms. Finch's poster, the one featuring the nebula, and I wonder if some part of me is being born. Maybe the implosion that has to happen isn't so much about destroying myself as it is about being willing to feel the pain I feel right now.

I lean back, toss the sticky oven mitt toward the sink, and let my hands fall into my lap. My leg hurts, but it's no longer making a crime scene of the kitchen. "I guess I've really made a wreck of myself."

"Nothing is as bad as it seems right now, I promise you that—well, except for the fact that you totally decided to shoot your shot with a lesbian." The only thing more resonant than Reed's laugh is my own. He's earned himself a fake-out punch to the skull—well, mostly fake. The vodka in me makes it hard to hold my fist firm and my aim is shit. I graze his tragic beanie. He groans and grabs his temple, rolling his head as if cartoon birds were flying circles around it. "She seems super rad, by the way. I can't wait for us all to hang soon. If you're willing to hang with me and Thandie, that is. I saw the drawings in your journal. I'd never have gone for her if I'd known . . ."

I wave his apology away.

"*I'm* sorry. Women aren't possessions. She made a choice, and it was a good one. I'd jump your bones in a heartbeat if I swung that way."

"Awww." He gives my cheek a gentle stroke with the back of his fingers. "I'd bang you so good, bruh."

We're laughing again.

"This is why I need you to take care of yourself," Reed continues. "How are we supposed to stay up all night braiding each other's hair and talking about our girl problems if you're too drunk or sick to have girl problems?"

"As if *you* have girl problems." The words sound bitter, but I don't mean them to. I surprise myself with the selflessness of my next question. "Have you, you know, gone there with Thandie yet?" In the very recent past such a question and the possible answer might have caused me pain, but I'm proud to realize I genuinely want to know. I don't want Reed to hide his life from me, and more than anything I want him to be happy.

Reed colors. He breaks eye contact and sucks a breath through his teeth, releases a small groan as he rubs the back of his neck. Is he afraid to tell me the truth? Finally he speaks. "We tried . . . I mean, *she* tried, but, I don't know, like, I kind of froze up. Thandie was chill about it, but I don't know. Maybe I'm just not ready?" He lets his arms fall into his lap. "Is that weird?"

I think of my conversation with Ms. Finch about this sort of stuff. I might just have what it takes to be Reed's MVP right now. "It's not weird at all."

Judging by the arrangement of his brow, Reed obviously doesn't believe me.

"It's *not*. When it's right, you'll know. When you're ready, you'll know. And if Thandie is the right girl, she'll be cool waiting and won't pressure you. She'll listen to the messages you send her, not just the things you say but the messages conveyed by your body."

Reed's incredulity morphs into a grin. "When did you become the love guru?"

"You'd be surprised what you can learn from crushing on a lesbian."

When our laughs fade, I say, "Do you think I'll ever have a girl to have problems with?"

"I *know* you will—when you're healthy again."

I release a pent-up breath. "Every time I go drunk drive-thru'ing, I want to take it back, but I don't know how to undo it all."

"You're better at undoing than you give yourself credit for. After all, you undid what happened to me."

That's why Reed sought me out tonight.

"Guess who's back on the team, motherfucker!"

I bowl him over with a hug.

He rolls and pins me, slaps me across the face several times, then offers his hand to pull me to my feet. Despite the numbing power of the vodka and warm fuzzies floating through my system, I still perform an awkward hop the moment I put pressure on my injured leg, a reminder of just how rare it is to escape the effects of the bad things that happen to us.

I say, "Wouldn't it be dope if life had a rewind button? The undoing would be so simple then."

Reed's expression grows curious, then his face opens into the type of grin that says he's got trouble on the brain. "Come on. I've got an idea."

I limp as we make our way from the house and into the still night. The Great Cool Ranch Dorito straddles the sky, steadfast as always. I feel good under Captain Condor's wings. "Where are we going?" I move toward Reed's pickup, parked behind my sedan on the street's narrow shoulder.

He shakes his head. "Toss me your keys. We gotta take your car."

I fish my keys from my pocket, pass them his way, then awkwardly wade into the passenger side. The floor filled up with fast food trash in record time after my shameful attempt to march Mallory up Tumamoc Hill.

Reed turns the engine and guns it, tearing off with a squeal of rubber as if this were a muscle car rather than a practical starter sedan. He beeps the horn and howls out his open window, only slowing to a safe speed when he's reached the end of the street. We head south, toward the city proper, turning onto Campbell Avenue. He gives nothing away, and I don't press for details. I just enjoy being here with him, the wind in my hair and the tunes loud enough to drown out our terrible singing.

We're almost to Prince when he turns into the strip mall with my Wendy's in it. Wendy's is already closed—there's no danger of walking away with several thousand nuggs and a Frosty—but I'm uncomfortable anyway. What are we doing here?

Reed pulls the car up beside the exit of the drive-thru, does a three-point turn, shifts into reverse, and drives *backward*—a little too recklessly—into the narrow lane.

"What the hell?"

"We're hitting the rewind button."

He slams on the brake when we reach the window, shifts into neutral and pulls the parking brake. He cranks the music to full blast. "Find me some Wendy's shit. Quick."

"What?"

He snatches a greasy chicken-tenders box from the center console and grabs me by the shoulders, dropping crumbs over my shirt. "I need you on your A game, champ! Beast mode! Beast mode! Level one hundred!"

Damn it all, I give it to him. "Beast mode as fuck, motherfucker!"

"Hell yeah! You ready to be the most pissed-off Karen who ever demanded to speak to the manager?"

"Fuck yeah, I am!" Wait, what?

"That's right, you monster!" He claps me over the ears and screams, "Now get out that window and return this food binge!"

He pulls himself up and out until he's sitting on the open window, torso in the night air, legs in the car. I follow suit, exhilarated by the absurdity of it all. He pumps his fist and screams at the top of his voice, and then he's lobbing my trash at the darkened drive-thru window. "You call these chicken tenders, you shitbags?" He reaches for his next projectile before the box even hits the glass. "They're just nuggs you made bigger and longer to trick us! Charging five bucks for this? Fuck you!"

I'm laughing hysterically, almost falling from my perch. I grab a large fountain cup and a handful of ketchup packets, raining fury down on the window. "Charging extra for more honey mustard? Suck a dick, Dave Thomas!"

Reed sways. "Haha! Yes! Flex on 'em, white lady! They'll never take advantage of you again. Never!" He slides back into his seat for more ammunition, tossing the stuff from other restaurants out of his way.

We stay like this for several minutes, throwing trash and screaming obscenities to the beat of our favorite hair metal, and somewhere in the din I realize I don't want to cry about anything for a change. I feel alive, more human than I've felt since I had to watch them lower Evelyn into the ground. Before I had to go back to the house, still in my new suit, to pack up my things until it looked like I'd never lived there at all.

I'm rummaging around in my garbage but can't find any more images of the familiar redheaded girl. "Dude, I think we're out of Wendy's stuff."

Reed's chest heaves, as if he's emerging victorious from one of his wrestling matches. "Good. Good fight there, kid. You got heart."

We settle back into the car and he reverses some more until we're at the menu box where you place your order. He leans out the window. His voice so polite it could almost be described as British, he says, "Nothing for us, thank you very much."

And then we're squealing out of the drive-thru, pulling back onto Campbell, headed, I'm certain, for the McDonald's a block away, the two of us more powerful than even Captain Condor tonight.

CHAPTER FORTY-FIVE

It's rare that Reed and I pack so many pals into the apartment at once, but this evening's celebration—a fiesta for the dead—requires as many living souls as possible. A glance around reveals boisterous groupings I could never have imagined a few weeks ago. At the kitchen table, Mallory shows Reed and Ruby Orange how to wield cutting gouges to make skeleton linocuts in the style of this famous Mexican printmaker she taught us about, a guy named José Guadalupe Posada. Evidently, his woodcuts were the original inspiration for the calavera masks Thandie is painting on Robyn Fletcher and Ajay Mukherjee from her perch on the couch, her impressive cache of makeup and face paint strewn across the coffee table. Marcus—his face already decorated with hollowed eyes, grinning teeth, and colorful flowers—pours me a glass of homemade agua fresca, which has been chilling in the fridge for several hours. I receive it gratefully.

We clink glasses as he stands beside me in the cramped kitchen, hovering over the pot where Evelyn's signature chile colorado simmers. Evelyn was always the neatnik in our cooking endeavors, but one look at the counter—strewn with dirty utensils, measuring equipment, and splatters of sauce—tells me I might have to fill that role in my new super-chefs duo. At least Marcus knows his way around a kitchen. I have a feeling we're going to learn a lot from each other. He was especially gratified to be invited to this evening's festivities. "I can vacate. You kids can have the place to yourselves." I shut that noise down immediately. "Día de los Muertos is about family. You're my family now, right?" He pulled me into a bear hug. "You bet I am, bud." He was even more excited when I told him what was on the menu, Evelyn's favorite Mexican dish, prepared from a recipe she got from who knows where and marked up by hand, recording her own inspired modifications. "Sounds fantastic! And I never met a piece of beef I couldn't cook to perfection. Trust me, kid. You might as well show up in flip-flops 'cause I'm about to knock your socks off."

Today is November 1, the Day of the Dead, and for the first time in all the years I've celebrated it, Evelyn isn't by my side. Well, not physically, anyway. Día de los Muertos is the one time each year when the border between this world and the next disappears. For these few precious hours, I won't have to merely imagine Evelyn's presence. She'll really be here. And my birth mother will, too. At least in spirit. They're the guests of honor, after all. I glance at the framed pictures on the ofrenda, the altar we've set up beneath a window and surrounded by candles, paper marigolds, and Evelyn's favorite fruits. I see myself in Evelyn's arms when I was six years old, still small for my age, my legs dangling off her hip despite her short height. I see Evelyn laughing from a hospital bed sometime last year, her cheeks pale but her eyes alight—I snapped the picture just after telling her a stupid grammar joke I'd learned from Banksie: *Knock, knock. Who's there? To. To who? To whom!* I don't see any photographs of my birth mother—those were lost long before Evelyn came into my life—but I do see the framed crayon drawings I made of her the very first time Evelyn and I celebrated Día de los Muertos. Her hair is yellow as sunshine and she sports a pair of fairy wings just like the girls on the cover of *Siamese Dream*. I wonder about my birth father. I hope he's alive somewhere out there. Maybe in Mexico. Maybe here in the borderlands. I hope wherever he is, he's living the best life he can. I hope he's happy.

This weekend, my friends and I will walk in the All Souls Procession with much of the rest of Tucson, over 150,000 people. We'll watch as the ceremonial urn is lit, sending a city's worth of well-wishes and prayers to the dead. But none of that happens tonight. Tonight is just about us, *my people*, this eclectic mix of buds and bros and girlfriends and girls-who-are-friends and one awesome dork of a dad.

Marcus holds his stirring spoon out to me for a taste.

The rich, spicy tang of our chile sauce sits perfectly on my tongue—hints of garlic and cumin. I give him a nod. We're ready.

"Let's eat!" he declares.

While the others clear the table and gather chairs from every corner of the apartment, Robyn helps me set out the food on the peninsula. Heaping dishes of rice, warm tortillas, and colorful garnishes of chopped radish and cilantro—an impressive spread. I pull plates from the cabinets. If we serve ourselves from the peninsula, there just might be enough space for all of us to squeeze around the table.

As I pass Robyn the silverware, she stops me with a hand on my arm. From behind her calavera makeup, she looks panicked. She whispers, "Is it okay if I don't eat? Will it be weird? I thought I could do it, but I don't know. I'm not sure if I can. Not in front of everyone."

I'm not sure what to say. How do I help her? She's ready to open up to Mallory, but this is only our first group hang. I won't out Robyn to the group—or at all. The only one who's going to reveal her struggle is her, and only when she's ready.

I take a beat to think, then I say, "Do you *want* to eat, though? Does the food appeal?" I slap on my best car-salesman smile, which must be pretty creepy with my spiderweb-themed face paint. I scoop my hands above the pot of stew, gently wafting the enticing smell her way.

She nods. "I just feel . . . I don't know . . . afraid of being judged, maybe? Does that make sense? I never eat stuff like this." Despite the black makeup casting shadows over her eyes, I can tell Robyn is close to tears. "I should go. Every time I look at Ruby she growls at me. I don't belong here. I'll slip out quietly . . ."

I shake my head. "Like hell you will. You belong here because *I* want you here." Admittedly, it *was* an awkward moment when Ruby arrived to find Robyn chatting with Thandie about a possible fundraising collaboration (hopefully Thandie's pure motives will rub off on Robyn now that she doesn't have an election to win). Ruby gave me a look like we'd stumbled into a wholly different world of the multiverse, but I just mouthed, *Be chill*. Ruby shrugged, made a beeline for Mallory, and commenced some pretty hardcore flirting, which seemed about as good a start to the night as I could hope for.

"Please stay," I say. "How can Ruby see another side of you if you don't stick around long enough to show her?"

Robyn releases a sigh, glances longingly toward the door.

"And I do get how you feel. I *do*. I have to psych myself up for this stuff, too." My light bulb moment finally arrives. "How about we make a deal? You'll put the food on your plate that you *think* you want, and then sit across from me. If you're struggling to take a bite, tap my foot and I'll say something hilarious or stupid or whatever so everyone's attention will be on me rather than you. And if *I* feel weird about taking a bite, I'll tap your foot and you can create a diversion for me."

"Is this your perverted attempt to play footsie under the table, you little horny toad?"

"Depends. Is it working?"

Robyn's laugh—not nearly as evil as I once thought—tells me she just might make it through dinner.

And she does.

After many jovial moments—including a hilarious story from Ajay about the time he accidentally ripped a fart while making out with his sophomore crush—the dishes are cleared and both Robyn and I have some thoroughly rad food in our bellies. I wonder if I ate more than I should. *She* probably wonders if she ate more than she should, too, even though her meal was minuscule. I'm determined not to dwell on the uncertainty. I force the ever-present thoughts of purging from my mind. There's no way I'm going to ruin this night with that bullshit. I don't want to ruin any more nights at all if I can help it. Not ever. Robyn and I killed it at dinner. I'm giving us each a gold star, and that's the end of it.

While the others go back to their face painting and printmaking, Mallory joins me at the sink. "So . . . Little Miss Student Government. Care to explain?" She pulls the dishrag from my shoulder and begins wiping down the plates stacked in the dish rack.

"It's not what you think."

"God, I hope not."

"She's not as bad as she seems. Or maybe she is. The jury's still out. Whatever. I'm kind of trying to rehabilitate her. She's got a long way to go, but I believe in her potential. One day she's gonna be a hella dope person."

Mallory laughs. "All right. I guess if *you're* not hopeless, neither is she."

I pass her a squeaky-clean glass and plunge my hands back into the suds.

"But if she continues to shit on your comic books, I *will* be forced to pull a Reed and put her other arm in a sling."

"No more ass-kicking—from anyone. Besides, I don't care if people make fun of my comics. They matter to me, and I love them, and I'm proud of them. I think I'll even put my name on the cover of the next issue."

I steel myself for the obligatory punch to the arm. Mallory doesn't disappoint. "Fantastic news." She cocks her head. "And yet . . . you've got this weird look on your face—and not just because you smeared your makeup. What is it?"

"Well, I'm kind of thinking of using my full name."

Mallory nods. "Makes sense. Brett Harrison isn't as bland as John Smith, but pretty close. Best to set yourself apart."

"It's just that my middle name, it's kind of hard for English speakers to pronounce. They mangle it all the time."

"Let's hear it."

"Isaias. It was my birth father's name—*is* my birth father's name? I don't really know anything about him besides what's listed on my birth certificate. The authorities couldn't find him after I was orphaned. I don't know if he's out there somewhere. All I know is that we share a name, Isaias."

"Spell it."

I recite the little jumble of vowels and *S*'s.

Mallory nods. "Yeah, I probably wouldn't have known how to say that, but so what? If people don't know how to pronounce it, you'll teach them—patiently, just like me when I teach you about basically everything, you big dork." Mallory roughs my hair.

"Thank you, Mr. Miyagi." I like what Mallory has to say. It feels right to use my full name on my comics—like a declaration that I'll always show up as *all* of me, just like Gloria Anzaldúa would. My middle name might be hard for Anglos to say, but it *is* mine. Plus, it's all I have of my birth father. I think of Kid Condor, who has his dad's brechenium gauntlet, a tool that gives him incredible power. Maybe this *name*—Isaias— gives me power, too. For the first time since I was seven years old, it sounds pretty cool.

When the dishes are stacked in the cabinets, I pull everyone together once again to decorate the sugar skulls Reed and I molded yesterday. They've had plenty of time to dry overnight, so they're ready to be covered in designs that rival those on our faces. I place a tray of food coloring, paintbrushes, toothpicks, and Sharpies on the table.

Ajay immediately licks his sugar skull, earning a look of disgust from Ruby. "That's like licking a dead body, you sicko."

Ajay grins. "So we're not eating these?"

To prevent Ajay's untimely death by glare, I intervene with the history of calveras de azúcar, which are decidedly not food but representations of those we've lost. "If you're making one for a specific loved one, be sure to write their name somewhere on the skull. When we're done, we'll place them on the ofrenda as an offering to the dead."

Ajay polishes his skull on his shirt and kisses the cheek gently. "Sorry, Grandma. My bad."

Taking pity, Ruby pulls a pack of Pez from her pocket and dangles it in front of him. His eyes light up, but she pulls it away when he tries to pluck it from her hand. She wags a finger in his face. "Behave now . . ."

"What gossip have you been listening to? I'm a very good boy."

"Sit . . . Stay . . ." Finally she tosses the pack his way. He tears in gratefully.

As we paint intricate designs on our skulls, I lose myself in the familiarity of the work. I use warm colors, summer colors, which is how I'll always remember Evelyn—a little sunburned, a lot bright. I can't see Evelyn in the room. I don't hear her voice. But I *do* feel her with me as I carefully write her name on the first skull I've ever made for her. I feel my birth mother, too. On her skull, I spell out *Annie*. I bet the two have a lot of stories to tell each other.

When every skull is loaded with festive patterns, we move to the living room to place our sugar skulls on the ofrenda one by one, nestling them among the other colorful offerings. When it's her turn, Thandie says a prayer for the great-aunt who died before she was born. Marcus tells his grandfather that he still thinks of him whenever he mixes ice cream into his coffee.

I hang back as Mallory, then Ruby, then Ajay take their turns. I'm telling myself I'm being polite, allowing my guests to go first. The truth is, I'm avoiding, postponing as long as I can. I don't *have* to say anything to Evelyn—I don't have to show my feeling in front of all these people—but I *want* to. I want to find my voice for her, and for myself. And I want to do this with my friends. I don't want to talk to Evelyn alone anymore.

When Reed and Robyn have gone and it's finally my turn, I step forward hesitantly.

Marcus grips my shoulder. "You okay, buddy?"

"Yes. Yeah. I can do this."

Marcus retreats, and I place Annie's sugar skull beside my childhood portrait of her. "Thank you," I simply say. And then I place Evelyn's sugar skull in the center of the ofrenda. My tears hit before I even open my mouth, but I don't let them silence me. I stare at the photographs of Evelyn and force myself to speak.

"So I've been thinking a lot about Captain Condor lately, where he came from and what he means to me. We talked a lot about his mythology while you were alive, and of course the details have evolved over the years. But there's one thing I never told you. I want you to hear it now." I release a shuddering breath and wipe my eyes. I swallow hard and force myself to keep talking. "The condor holds special significance to several tribes in the Americas, not just to the Inca. There are a few tribes in California that caught my attention when I was conducting research because they think of the condor as a finder. The Yokuts and the Western Mono, for instance. Condor feathers can help them track down lost objects. Back in the day, the shaman of the Chumash could even find lost *people* when he wore his cloak of condor feathers. When Captain Condor found Kid, he gave him a home and made him feel safe and loved. Kid was lost but then he wasn't anymore. Do you understand what I'm trying to say?"

Robyn sniffles noisily, and I realize I'm not the only one crying. "Sorry," she says. "Don't tell anyone I can actually feel things."

Mallory, whose eyes are also red, mimes zipping her painted calavera teeth. "Your secret's safe with us."

I turn back to the photos of Evelyn. "I was a lost boy, but then you found me. I am *your* Kid, and you are my Captain." I sink to my knees and manage a few more words before the sobs take me. "Thank you, Mom. *Thank you* for finding me."

I hang my head, knowing this is supposed to be a celebration, knowing I'm nowhere near ready to celebrate without the pain—and knowing that's okay. I feel a presence at my side, not Evelyn but Reed. He extends his hand to pull me to my feet. He opens his arms. "Bring it in, king. Your boy's cold and he needs a cuddle."

I let my brother wrap his arms around me. I rest my head on his shoulder. In seconds, the entire squad surrounds us, arms interlocked around backs or shoulders. Reed screams, "Cuddle puddle!" And suddenly we're on the floor, thoroughly tangled up in a swarm of limbs and warmly beating hearts.

Eight voices meld into one. "Cuddle puddle! Cuddle puddle! Cuddle puddle!"

And through my tears, I laugh.

Brett Isaias Harrison

Banksie

AP English

2 November

Idiom Essay Final Draft—Finally

If You Love Your Cake, Let It Go

This essay is not about food, but I didn't know that at first. I tossed out a few attempts to build an essay on my idiom—*You can't eat your cake and have it, too*—because my relationship with food was all over the pages, either overtly or in the subtext. The drafts were missing the mark, that much was clear, but if I'm being honest, I actually gave up on them because their content left me ashamed. I'm going to admit something I've only ever said out loud to my new therapist: My relationship with food shames me.

Shame is a topic that comes up a lot with my therapist—I don't like to be ashamed and I don't like to talk about anything that makes me feel that way. But in our most recent session, my therapist pulled a Mr. Rogers on me, quoting the legendary television personality. "Anything human is mentionable, and anything that is mentionable can be more manageable." What he was getting at is that things like fear and shame, these feelings I don't like to feel, can be alleviated by talking about their causes. Being honest and open doesn't just make one's problems go away, but it does help a person manage them. My problems, whose names I might never stop feeling ashamed of, are binge eating disorder and bulimia nervosa.

I write about these shameful and scary things because they help put my thinking about my idiom into context. From the day this essay was assigned, I've been thinking about my idiom through the lens of food and eating and consumption. This interpretation, this narrative about eating, makes sense from someone like me. When your relationship with food is disordered, it's hard to find the space in your brain for anything else.

But here's what I've finally figured out, independent of my therapist and Mr. Rogers, God bless his long-dead soul: My idiom has nothing to do with food. My mother taught me that the point of metaphoric language is to make the intangible concrete, so in my idiom, the cake is not really cake. It's a symbol. The simplest interpretation of my idiom, therefore, is that you can't have something that's already gone. Trying to have what is already gone—holding on to what is no longer yours—can only hurt you, can only bring misery and pain. Here's another admission: I've been holding on to someone I love, someone who died nine months ago, and ever since I have been in incredible pain. I'm holding on to my mother, and this holding on hurts so much more than the grief my therapist tells me I need to process if I'm to heal from her death and overcome my disordered eating.

I read this story in Mrs. Annalisa's class last year about the Greek demigod Achilles and his trusty sidekick-slash-boyfriend, Patroclus. After they're killed in battle (don't blame the spoiler on me; you've had a few millennia to get caught up on pop culture), Patroclus doesn't get buried properly. He's left wandering Troy as a ghost, tethered to his body, unable to descend into the underworld to find his best buddy and love of his life. Patroclus is in limbo, arrested in his place of deepest pain, stuck between the life he once had with Achilles and the life he might have after death.

This is the state I've been living in these past months. I've been wandering my own Troy as a ghost, reliving my life as it was when my mom was still alive, relying on my imagination to fill the void left when she died. I can't have her back, and I can't join her—not yet at least; there's far too much life left to live. My behaviors, I've come to understand, weren't just hurting me but endangering my life. To save myself, I've had to let my mom go. To reference a mythology much closer to my heart, that of the Inca, I've had to get out of the way so the mighty condor can carry her from Kay Pacha, the earthly realm, to Hanan Pacha, the realm of the gods. I've had to buy into the idea that I can't hold her down; I need to let her fly. When I opened up to my therapist about all this, he said there's a term for the work I have to do around my mom's death: radical acceptance.

And yet, what if I'm still thinking too simply about the nature of my idiom? My mom taught me that we should always write to the complexity of any situation, not to the simplicity of it. I need to peel back another layer of meaning. An anecdote will help me illustrate my point.

When I was very small, I was delayed and didn't begin learning to read until I was six. I was a quick study, and to help me along, my mom would play this game to develop my diction. Sitting beside me on the couch or behind me on my bed, she'd trace letters on my back or on the palm of my hand, the bottom of my foot or the pad of my thumb. She'd spell while I strained to sound out the words—*rueful, adept, unabashed*—plenty of words that would sound absurd coming from an eight-year-old's mouth.

Rueful. Now, what does that mean, Brett? Do you remember?

Sad.

More specific.

Sad, but, like, so sad that you almost have to smile.

Part of speech?

It tells us about a noun so . . . adjective.

Good.

One word I learned in this game was *deboss,* which means to imprint into a surface.

Every time I work on my comic book series, *Kid Condor: Cadet First Class of the Constellation Corps,* or any time I'm struggling in my day-to-day life, I hear my mom's voice giving me advice as she always did in life, like she's the cartoon angel sitting on my shoulder. Better still, when I show Reed love, when I show my new squad love, I know my mom is still with me. I only know what love is because she loved me, and that love left a debossed impression of her on my life. This is how I *can* eat my cake and have it, too. Yes, my mom is physically gone, but what she instilled in me will be with me forever. In letting my cake go, I've found my cake will never truly be gone.

Of course this ambivalence may seem hard to

reconcile—and it is—but I'm a mestizo, and few are as well equipped as mestizos to wrestle with, juggle, and ultimately honor multiple perspectives. Gloria Anzaldúa says mestizos are awesome divergent thinkers because straddling cultures pushes us to create new, complex ways of seeing ourselves and the world. She calls this state of mind a "new consciousness," and it might be our most incredible superpower.

Recently, I felt like the unluckiest kid in the world. Everything was going wrong, and I was overcome by fear and shame. Today I'm grieving, and that grief hurts terribly, but there's too much love in my life for me to believe this grief is too much to bear. I bear it with my friends and my new dad, and with the memories of my mom, a superhero of a woman who may have been mine for only ten years, but will remain debossed on my heart as long as I live.

CHAPTER FORTY-SIX

Just as the brilliantly speckled sky in the east fades to dull gray, Reed and I flop onto our backs on my trampoline and gaze up at the Condor boys. Our chests rise and fall with the deep, satisfying breaths of those who truly respect the ancient art of extreme trampoline airdrumming. Reed has joined me for my final trip to my old house, and I wouldn't want to say goodbye to this place with anyone else. I'm so glad he's by my side.

We enjoy the silence as the stars begin to disappear, as if an artist were at work, only backward, leaving an ever-starker canvas above us. When my breath reaches its natural pace, I say, "Do you think maybe if I work hard enough—like, if I really, really try—I can beat this food thing?" Kenny and my team have me working on the principles of this kick-ass practice called Intuitive Eating, basically reacquainting my mind with my stomach and even my spirit so I can experience something my dietician excitedly refers to as *food freedom*, but some days the work is really confusing; some days it's really hard. I especially hate the diary app Kenny has me logging every night before bed. I track my problem behaviors and self-care behaviors, my emotions and my hunger and my fullness and food, food, food, food, food.

Reed hooks one arm behind his head. I'm glad he doesn't immediately tell me what I want to hear. I've been working on being honest and asking for support when I need it, and he's been working on letting me feel like shit when I need to feel like shit—which is often. I've come to think of treatment like pushing a massive boulder up Tumamoc Hill, which is to say, relentless and exhausting. But if I stay the course, I just might make it to the top; the boulder will roll down the other side of the hill and finally I'll be free of its weight. Until then, I'm moving in fits and starts, backsliding on occasion. Sometimes I'm so tired that I need to rest. I'll turn and prop my back against the boulder, dig my heels in—hitting a plateau, Kenny calls it. These times scare me. I fear if I take even a moment to collect my strength, if I'm not progressing, the boulder might break free and I'll have to start my climb all over again. Kenny helped me see that my plateaus aren't something to be afraid of, though. With my back to the boulder, I've got a glorious view of how far I've come.

Finally, Reed says, "Honestly, I don't know. But I do know some other things. I know you're a killer artist and that I'm going to make you take me to Comic-Con someday when you have your own booth. Screw it. When you have your own *hall*. I know you're a good bro with a big heart—bigger than your appetite."

I laugh, kind of stoked that I *can* laugh about such things.

"And you don't mind? Being friends with a train wreck?"

Reed points up. "You see the star on the western side of your Dorito, the brightest one?"

"Yeah. Kid Condor's propulsion pack." This particular star is part of both the Kid and Captain constellations, the point where the two overlap.

"I learned some shit in astronomy that I think you need to hear."

Reed knows I took Earth sciences instead of astronomy for a reason. He knows I didn't want Mr. Katz filling my head with all sorts of alternative facts about the cosmos—the constellations as they're recognized in America, say, or how planets *actually* form, which, evidently, has nothing to do with Captain Condor flying so fast around an asteroid belt that the asteroids and space dust all fuse together to make Universópolis, the home planet of the Constellation Corps.

Might hearing whatever Reed has to say cost me my fiction? A story I've used my whole life to avoid facing the truth of my own mythology? I think of everything I've learned. I think about this part in *A Room of One's Own* where Virginia Woolf writes about how fiction often contains more truth than reality. My truths have been all over my stories all along; I've just been hiding them from myself. If I'm ready to face reality bravely, I might even be ready for a more mature version of the Condor boys' universe.

"Okay," I say. "I'm listening."

Reed makes a dramatic show of clearing his throat. "Well, the Dorito's real name is the Summer Triangle, and that star—Kid Condor's pack, I mean—is named Vega."

I wince at this offensive information, but I don't interrupt.

"Vega is kind of a big deal. It even used to be the North Star thousands of years ago before Earth wobbled on its axis."

Now there's a detail I love. "Cool."

"Yeah, thought you'd like that. Vega's one hell of a hot mess, though. It spins fast as hell—like superfast—and this makes the equator way cooler than the poles."

"So . . ."

297

"So shut your face. If Vega spun any faster, it would self-destruct, but it doesn't. It just chills up there for millennia being rad! Boom! You just got schooled, son!" Reed falls silent with a satisfied sigh, letting his science lesson sink in.

Maybe I'm not the best student. "What does this have to do with our friendship, exactly?"

"Which character are you in your stories?"

"Kid Condor, obviously."

"Obviously. Kid Condor's the shit. He might be damaged, and a tragic and brave orphan and all that, but he's strong, and he's a good guy, and he's a loyal sidekick to Captain. If Vega—if Kid Condor—can endure the kinds of stress and pressure of such a crazy rotation, if he can keep it together even if everything around him is falling apart, if his proton pack—"

"Propulsion."

"If his propulsion pack can handle the insane RPMs of being him, *you* can, too."

Reed surprises us both by reaching for my hand. He gives my fingers a squeeze. I expect him to snatch his hand away before the awkwardness of the moment can redden our faces, but he doesn't. "Never forget that anyone would be lucky to be friends with a guy like Kid Condor, no matter how many obstacles you write for him to overcome. And anyone would be lucky to be friends with you, no matter what you eat or what you look like. You got that?"

I kind of want to cry, but this time, for once, in a really good way. I say, "Yeah. Yeah, I read you loud and clear, buddy. Thanks . . . thank you."

We watch the stars slowly fade with the dawn until all that remains are the three points of the Summer Triangle, its Dorito dust licked clean by the rising sun. When even the points wink out for another glorious day, we creep to my car, leaving my house keys where I found them on the counter all those months ago, not exhausted as one might expect, but energized, not hungry, but satisfied.

RESOURCES

I f you're struggling in your relationship with food and/or your body, please reach out to a medical or mental health professional, or merely to an adult you trust (even if you *are* an adult!). In school and college settings, teachers, professors, and counselors can connect you with support services to set you on a path toward peace and healing. I also wholeheartedly recommend checking out the following incredible resources, many of which significantly contributed to my own healing from disordered eating and diet culture. These resources are *not* a substitute for professional help but rather tools in one's consciousness-raising journey. Even those who do not suffer from disordered eating or body dysmorphia can benefit from a value system that rejects diet and wellness culture. The first step to developing any value system is thinking critically. These resources will help you do just that.

— Josh

Books

Intuitive Eating, 4th Edition: A Revolutionary Anti-Diet Approach
by Evelyn Tribole, MS, RDN, CEDRD-S, and Elyse Resch, MS,
RDN, CEDRD-S, FAND

*The Intuitive Eating Workbook for Teens: A Non-Diet, Body Positive
Approach to Building a Healthy Relationship with Food*
by Elyse Resch, MS, RDN

Being You: The Body Image Book for Boys
by Charlotte Markey, Daniel Hart, and Douglas N. Zacher

Health at Every Size: The Surprising Truth about Your Weight
by Lindo Bacon, PhD

*Anti-Diet: Reclaim Your Time, Money, Well-Being, and Happiness
Through Intuitive Eating*
by Christy Harrison, MPH, RD

*The Wellness Trap: Break Free from Diet Culture, Disinformation, and
Dubious Diagnoses and Find Your True Well-Being*
by Christy Harrison, MPH, RD

Reclaiming Body Trust: A Path to Healing & Liberation
by Hilary Kinavey, MS, LPC, and Dana Sturtevant, MS, RD

Articles

"My Journey Toward Radical Body Positivity" by Matt McGorry:
humanparts.medium.com/my-journey-toward-radical-body-
positivity-3412796df8ff

Podcasts

Rethinking Wellness
    Hosted by Christy Harrison, MPH, RD, CEDS

Food Psych
    Hosted by Christy Harrison, MPH, RD, CEDS

Men Unscripted
    Hosted by Aaron Flores, RDN

Dieticians Unplugged
    Hosted by Aaron Flores, RDN, and Glenys Oyston, RDN

Websites

Reach Out's Body Image Page: au.reachout.com/challenges-and-
coping/body-image

Association for Size Diversity and Health: asdah.org

National Eating Disorders Association: nationaleatingdisorders.org

Center for Body Trust: centerforbodytrust.com

Other Resources

The Intuitive Eating Card Deck: 50 Bite-Sized Ways to
Make Peace with Food
    by Elyse Resch, MS, RDN, and Evelyn Tribole, MS, RDN

The Making Peace with Food Card Deck: 59 Anti-Diet Strategies
to End Chronic Dieting and Find Joy in Eating
    by Christy Harrison, MPH, RD, CEDS, and Judith Matz, LCSW,
    ACSW

The Body Positivity Card Deck: 53 Strategies for Body Acceptance,
Appreciation and Respect
    by Judith Matz, LCSW, ACSW, and Amy Pershing, LMSW, ACSW,
    CCTP-11

Intuitive Eating for Every Day: 365 Daily Practices & Inspirations
to Rediscover the Pleasures of Eating
    by Evelyn Tribole, MS, RDN, CEDRD-S

The Intuitive Eating Journal: Principles for Nourishing
a Healthy Relationship with Food
    by Elyse Resch, MS, RDN

ACKNOWLEDGMENTS

W hen people find out you're drafting a novel, the first question they ask is what your book is about. Generally, you want to get in and out of this question as quickly as possible because writing books is overwhelming and confusing and half the time you have no idea what you're doing. You feel compelled to articulate all that the book is—or all that it *might be; could be; will someday be, I swear*—but doing so is daunting. Because I'm a classic avoider, I developed several responses to this question, each designed to make the inquisitive uncomfortable and therefore end the conversation before it began.

It's a fun book about grief.

It's about disordered eating in boys.

It's about taking down diet culture.

It's about fat people.

It's, you know, feminist.

All of these responses were true, but they weren't the just-right answer, at least not to me. Now that the book can speak for itself, I need only provide the simplest synopsis: *The Great Cool Ranch Dorito in the Sky* is a book about *love*. Just love, that's all. So if you'll indulge me, I'd like to write a few more paragraphs expressing my love for everyone who made this book about love possible.

Unending gratitude to my writing mentor at the University of Nevada, Reno, Christopher Coake. Your generous guidance and patience during my most difficult growing pains contributed greatly to this book and to my belief that I was worthy of writing it. Many thanks, as well, to all the faculty I worked with as I drafted this novel, including Micah Stack, David Durham, and Sarah Hulse, and to the many classmates who contributed valuable insights and plenty of laughs. Big thanks, too, to my mentors in the art department: Eunkang Koh, Samantha Buchanan, AB Gorham, Brett Van Hoesen, and Inge Bruggeman. Your influence over my artist's practice, including my writing, was immeasurable. To Jodie Helman, thank you for working so hard to keep me employed in the leanest year of my life as I polished, queried, and sold this book. I miss all our departmental gossip—what happens in the Art Office stays in the Art Office!

Extra-special thanks to my incredible treatment team, without whom this book could not exist: Dr. Cheryl Hug-English (the most aptly named doctor on the planet, probably); Dr. Yani Dickens; Dr. Joey Walloch; Dr. J. P. Crum; Maureen Molini, RD; Renee Bauer, RDN; and Ashley Darbey, LADC. It's no exaggeration to say that your efforts saved my life. My gratitude is boundless.

To my brilliant, rock-steady agent, David Dunton, thank you for seeing something unique in my voice and fresh in my storytelling, and for believing this was a "swing-for-the-fences" kind of book. It's rare to find an editorial eye as precise and mindful as yours; I am so lucky to have you on my side. Much gratitude, as well, to the team at Harvey Klinger, Inc., who continue to toil on my behalf.

To my deeply insightful editor, Jess Harold, thank you for treating my characters—and my identity—with such care and enthusiasm. I'm moved by what you were able to coax out of me simply by asking the right questions, and I'm thrilled to work with an editor carving out space for marginalized identities and fearless stories in the publishing industry. Thank you for keeping me bold.

To everyone at Henry Holt Books for Young Readers and Macmillan, thank you for championing this book and working so hard to get it into the hands of readers who deserve challenging stories that reflect their challenging lives. The fact that you published this book at all is proof that you value the humanity, intelligence, strength, and capacity of young people. I'm grateful to have found a home where my values are shared. Extra-special thanks to editorial intern Caylee Gardner, who had first eyes on this book and contributed to its acquisition; book designer Julia Bianchi, who beautifully illustrated the fun in my "fun book about grief"; copy editor Jackie Dever, whose incredible skill and sensitivity *cannot* be overstated; production editor Kristen Stedman, who put up with a *lot* of strike-throughs and other typesetting tomfoolery; proofreaders Emily Stone and Jessica White, who carefully attended to every detail and taught me what a hair space is; production manager Jie Yang, whose efforts kept this book on time and on budget; senior managing editor Alexei Esikoff, who oversees Henry Holt Books for Young Readers; department head David Briggs, who makes the process of putting books into the world look easy; senior editor Dana Chidiac, who generously assisted at a crucial juncture; publicity director Kelsey Marrujo, whose efforts ensured readers like you would find out about this book's existence; and many others.

To authenticity reader Christian Vega and expert reader Allison Jupiter, LCSW-R, thank you for boosting my confidence during the final stages of drafting this book. My intention has always been to tell a difficult story with honesty and care, and your valuable expertise contributed greatly to that end.

Deepest gratitude to the Nevada Arts Council and the National Endowment for the Arts for being the first financial supporters of my writing and visual art.

Much love to my found family, both past and present: Audrey and Trevor Clark, Joel Allée, Leala Lierman, Jen Allen, Tricia Laske, Curtis and Sarah Newbury, Zena Foss, Tara Moylan and Darby Baligad. Special bonus adoration to Trishia Haahr, Elizabeth Tully, Amelia Sheldon and Elizabeth Leiknes, who've also served as dedicated critics of my writing. To Lora French, Sidney Thomas, and Gabriel "The Dorito Book's OG Fan" Cohen, I am so glad that when I think of my friends from college, I'll be thinking of you. Many high fives to my BFA cohort-mates, Cesar Piedra and Robert Ibarra. Your work continues to inspire and inform my creative research, and our "Mexhibitions" remain some of the proudest moments of my life. To my longtime brothers and partners in writing crime, Chris Woody and James Miller, thank you for hoping, scheming, and dreaming with me. I hope the spirit of our bromance shines in these pages.

Big hugs to all the incredible writers I worked with for the better part of a decade in Lone Mountain Writers, with especially long squeezes for Wilma Counts, Angela Laverghetta, and Kevin Burns. When I showed up at your doorstep as a baby writer with big dreams and disturbing scenes, you could easily have sent me packing. Instead you embraced me and became my first teachers. I am so grateful to you.

To all in the Cult of Marilee, much gratitude for your investment in me and for believing that one day, when I was ready, I'd end up here with a real published book in my hands. I'd like to send special shout-outs to Michael Richardson, Carol Kalleres, Cathy Vairo, Kathy Walters, Amy Roby, Vicki Carmack, Doug Deacy, Joy Phillips, Teresa Breeden, Lorie Schaefer, and Ginger Starrett. You're gems, one and all.

To my family—Kathy, Jamy, Whitney, McKinze, and Vance. Thank you for being my first and still most-dedicated fans, and for loving me when I've been easy to love and, especially, when I've been hard to love.

Finally, I'd like to extend my deepest adoration to Claire McCully. My life changed profoundly the day you sat me down in your office and told me there was something special in my essays. I will be forever grateful.